# Twixt

**Also by S.E. Diemer**

*The Dark Wife*
*Love Devours: Tales of Monstrous Adoration*

**Writing with Jennifer Diemer**

*Sappho's Fables, Volume 1*
*The Dark Woods*
*The Monstrous Sea*
*Uncharted Sky*
*Artificial Hearts*
*Myth, Magic and Glitter*
*Project Unicorn, Volume 1*

# TWIXT

S.E. DIEMER

Twixt

Second edition, March 2016



ISBN-10: 1484085973
ISBN-13: 978-1484085974
Cover image by Laura Diemer| Cover design by S.E. Diemer

*For Jenn, always.*

*And for Maddie*
*who loved and believed in it from the very first moment.*
*You are a cherished, ink-stained pillar of my life.*

# Chapter One: Asleep

I open my eyes.

The sky is dirty red, like drying blood. I sit up fast, heart pounding, fingers curling into the brittle leaves beneath my palms, the mud sucking me under a little more. I'm dripping, shaking. The whisper of the stream beside me, water rushing under the hole in the ice, sounds like voices.

I lift up my hands, stare down at them. For a moment, I marvel: are *these* my hands? They're bloody, my fingers. And blue. My dress is black, with more holes than fabric. The laces on my boots are frozen solid, and as I struggle to get up, turn over, kneel on the bank of the stream, blood drips from my face, plunking hollowly upon the snowy mud beneath me.

A shadow—to my right. I turn, but I'm not fast enough. Something filthy and covered in furs is scrabbling away, leaving wet footprints upon the stone of the escarpment that huddles over this little valley and spit of stream. Its dripping bulk is familiar to me, but it crawls too quickly over the edge and is lost, hidden amongst the skeletal trees beyond, branches scraping together.

I'm shaking so hard my hands blur.

I reach up, brush a knuckle over my lips, smearing my mouth with blood. I creep forward and dunk my hands beneath the hole in the ice, let the freezing water sweep over my skin, dragging at my fingers like it wants to take me down and in, devour me.

"Hello?"

I scramble back from the edge of the stream, turn so fast that the world spins, and there, behind me, is a girl, a young woman. Pale and thin and stark, she stares down at me. Her dirty blonde hair is hacked short, feathering around her ears like bird down. She's wearing a shabby brown coat, two sizes too big, tied around her middle with sawn rope. Her face is grubby, but her brown eyes flash as she squats beside me, and though fear runs through me like blood, I'm not afraid of *her*.

"What are you doing here?" she whispers, looking me over, reaching out a hand toward me. I flinch away, and she frowns, leans back. "What are you doing here?" she repeats then, voice soft, gentle, curving toward me like a beckoning finger. "It's almost sunset."

"I don't…" I gasp, start. That voice. That was my voice? I stare down at my hands, white and blue with streaks of red, still trembling.

"What's your name?" she whispers.

I close my eyes, feel the press of mud beneath me, the pulsing ache in my hands, the blood running over my face, dripping off my chin in a heated rhythm.

"I don't know." My voice—not my voice—quivers in the air between us. I stare down at my hands again, desperate, turning them over and over, scratching at my skirt, the sleeves of my blouse, my boots with their frozen knots. "I don't *know*," I say again, desperate. My words echo back to me from the trees as if they shattered against their roots.

"It's all right. I promise, it's all right." Her voice is soft, smooth-edged, as she reaches out to me, her hands against my arms. There are holes in my sleeves, and her palms press against my bare skin, warm. It's the warmth that makes me pause, makes my thundering heart quiet for a moment.

She looks in my eyes, looks hard, staring deeper and deeper. "I'll explain everything," she murmurs after a moment, and then she's standing, helping me to my feet. The mud squelches in protest, and I find that I can hardly rise. Everything seems to be spinning. Blood falls onto the sleeves of the girl's coat from my chin as I totter. My eyes fixate on the blood, dark and ugly spots that stain.

"We have to get inside before sunset," she whispers, glancing up at the sky. "They come at sunset."

Her words are so breathy, so quiet, they almost don't exist.

"They," I whisper, and something moves through me, a shudder, a shake, and I stare at her, open-mouthed, as she tilts back her head, watches me.

"Come on," is all she says, putting her arm around mine, all but dragging me over the half-frozen ground, away from the whispering stream. I glance over my shoulder at the bright-red blood surrounding the hole in the ice.

"We've gotta be fast." She leans toward me, shaking her head. "I know you must be stiff, but—"

"What's wrong?" I ask, breathless, as we mount the escarpment and enter the forest. I trip on a frozen gouge in the earth, but she catches my elbow, helps me up. "What's happening?"

The light seems to lengthen between the trees, drawing toward us like thin, red bones.

"We'll talk about it when we're inside." Her voice is still warm, but sharper now. Urgent. And then, as she glances up at the fading light, her eyes widen. "Do you think you can run?"

I can barely *move*, boots clumping down at odd, awkward angles. It's as if I've never walked before, though I know I have. I grit my teeth, take a running step and sprawl on the ground, chin banging against another frozen rut of earth. My teeth clatter together, and I shove myself upward as she grabs at my elbow again, hoisting me to my feet gently, steering me between the trees.

"What comes at sunset?" I ask as she glances at the branches overhead again, cursing under her breath.

She rakes a hand through her hair, eyes flashing. Her words are heavy with regret: "I guess you'll see."

My heart is beating so hard, it's all I can hear. The trees sigh around us, shifting, as if they're waiting. We move faster, faster, and even though I have to watch my feet, I keep taking in little glimpses of what's in front of us—and far ahead, through the huddled trunks, I think I see a long, dark shadow rising along the ground.

A wall?

It's as sudden as a cut-off breath, the change from the deep, dripping red of sunset to the absoluteness of gray. The color is gone—one blink to the next. I trip again, falter, as I whirl about me, staring at the absence of red, at the heaviness of monochrome that seems to steal up the trunks of the trees like wrinkled hands.

The girl drags at my arm. "Run," she says, and then again, voice cracking, "*Run.*"

We move between the trees, two shadows, breath coming out in jagged scratches as she helps me up again and again. My limbs move looser now, as if they're slowly thawing, but the ground is rough and ragged, and the darkness is crawling toward us like the gray now. I can't move fast enough, but the girl's patience is absolute, even as she glances over her shoulder, panting, her brown eyes wide and anxious.

All I can hear is my heartbeat, is our breathing,

is the breaking twigs and the *oof* of my gasp when I go down again.

But then I hear *them*.

A wail—long, thin, piercing, like a flashing silver hook that arcs through the air and into me, cutting bone deep. I jerk around, as if dragged, and I see it in the air between the trees…descending toward us.

It's a human skeleton, but it isn't—the skull has a thin, wicked beak in place of a mouth, and wide, black-feathered wings heave up and down upon the thing's back.

The creature is huge, three times the size of a person. The sharpness of its beak flashes in the dying light as it unhinges its jaws again and screams. The sound is the world, is *everything*, as the creature pumps its black wings, reaching toward us with bone hands that curve into claws. The sockets where its eyes should be are as hollow as heartbeats, and it comes after me, after us, faster than sound, dragging its wailing behind it.

The girl yanks my arm, and then somehow, impossibly, we're running again, the screaming behind us growing louder, larger, with more wails of thin, piercing sharpness. I glance back and feel my heart stop within me: there are four of them now. No, five.

Fear burns through me, searing my bones and muscles, as ice moves beneath my skin like a wet, crawling thing. They are so close, I can feel the chill of their wings, the gusts of air rushing forward, stealing my balance.

A whistle, a tear in the air, as one of the things drags its claws down and toward me. It is going to catch me, hook its sharpness through me, and I am all animal, all fear, as I cry out something wordless, moving through the dark, hunted.

The long shadow rises ahead, near enough now to make out silhouettes of stones. It is a wall, and we're aiming for it; we're going to run *into* it, collide with it as it arcs higher and higher, huge and solid. We can't stop. We're running too fast to stop, and the things are too close. If we stop… I hear the slice in the air behind me as one of the creatures extends its claws, nearly grazing our heads, and I close my eyes as the wall looms before us, as we run, never slowing, because we can't—

Darkness.

My arm jerks as I'm halted, skidding to a stop, the girl gripping my elbow so hard that it hurts. I can hear her panting beside me, feel the aching surge of my own breath, and there's only darkness, darkness everywhere. No trees, no sky, nothing.

I gulp, cry out—

A flare of light, thin and yellow, in the deep black space.

The girl lets go of me, and I watch her move her hands through her hair as she leans forward, staring at the light with narrowed eyes.

We're in a small room, I see now, with walls towering around us on three sides. On the fourth side, there's a door. A door that's open, cracked, an eye and wrinkled nose peering through, along with the light.

"*Charlie*," sighs the old woman, pulling the door open fully. She's layered in sweaters and shawls and skirts, her gray hair sticking up at odd angles. She peers at us, squinting as she looks at me, raising the lantern higher. Inside of the lantern, three golden orbs bump lazily against the glass.

I stare, swallow.

"Charlie, what have we here?" The old woman moves closer, shoving the lantern beneath my nose. "Who's this?"

The girl—Charlie—slumps against a wall, sliding down as she runs her hands through her hair again, knuckles white. "It's complicated, Abigail. This is a new Sleeper."

The woman takes a step back, draws the lantern away, clutching it to her chest as she stares me up and down, shaking her head slowly.

"I found her by the stream before sunset. But she has no memories. She must be a Sleeper."

"That's…not possible." The woman turns from me to glare at the girl, but Charlie shakes her head, too, and lifts an eyebrow. "*Before* sunset, Charlie?" She sniffs, stares down at my boots, at the tattered edge of my skirt, and then rakes her shrewd gaze over the rest of me—as if I'm a thing, an unusual object whose worth might be guessed at by a glance.

I raise my chin, and she sighs then, and softens a little, though she's still frowning, thin lips angling down over jagged, brown teeth. "It gets stranger every day, don't it, Charlie, my girl? Why *not* before sunset?" She steps toward me, head to the side, cocked like a bird, as I crush back against the wall, flinching as she reaches a hand up, as if to touch me. She stops, fingers poised in midair, and glances to Charlie, who shrugs.

Then the old woman backs away, and I let out a shaky breath.

"My name is Abigail," she tells me, lowering the lantern and pressing a palm against her chest. Her eyes are wide and wild in the circling light. "Welcome to Mad House."

"*Don't*, Abigail," Charlie hisses, rising, rubbing at her shoulder. "Not yet. She was nearly *Snatched*—"

"Rubbish." Abigail sniffs, stares up at me with one eye closed, one eye narrowed. "She's gotta know where she's found herself—"

"She'll know soon enough." Charlie sighs, glances at me, shaking her head. "Come on," she says, holding out her hand. "It's all right. You're safe here."

"Safe?" I whisper. I'm shaking, and the word

shivers into the little room.

"Yes," says Charlie, nodding, smiling softly, encouraging. "I promise, you're safe."

"For *now*." Abigail grins toothily up at me, drawing out the word.

Charlie rolls her eyes, takes my arm gently, tugs me out of the little room, a closet—how did we get into a *closet?*—into a high-ceilinged hallway with peeling wallpaper. The thick, red carpet swallows my boots to the ankles. Glittering chandeliers loom above our heads, though no light sparkles within them. The windows are covered with draping curtains, concealing the outdoors, but I still shy away from them as we three pad down the hallway, the lantern in Abigail's fist casting a trembling bubble of light around us. Here, the light is close and warm, but it does little to comfort me.

"What were those *things*? The…monsters?" My voice is a panicked whisper. I grit my teeth together to stop them from chattering.

Charlie sighs, bows her head. "We call them Snatchers. They come out at night, take new Sleepers, old Sleepers… Whoever they can catch. But don't worry, because you're safe now—"

"Safe?" I say the word again: it tastes desperate, sour. "Where do they take the people they…Snatch…*to?*"

Charlie glances sidelong at me, eyes narrowed. "We don't… We don't really know. But it doesn't matter. They didn't Snatch you. We were faster. Fast enough." I stare at her until she breaks the gaze, biting her lip. "You're a new Sleeper, and Twixt is very confusing in the beginning, but I promise that—"

"No promises, Charlie," says Abigail, waving her arm at me. "You know how I'm always telling you—'Charlie,' I says, 'you waste your time on the new ones, trying to make 'em more comfortable,' and you know it's a sweet thing, but you could be saving your energy for them that *needs* it, not them that wants coddling."

Charlie closes her eyes, rubs at her nose. "And you know how I'm always telling you that you purposefully *terrify* the new Sleepers with too much information?"

Abigail laughs, a thin, piercing cackle that makes me shudder. "Coddled Sleepers are Snatched Sleepers. They gotta know what they're facing, or it's over. I just tell 'em the truth."

"And what's that?" I ask, breathing out the words. "What's the truth?"

Abigail stares at me, eyes narrowed. "The *truth*, girl? The *truth* is that you're in Twixt," she says, holding up one, sharp finger. "And that you're a Sleeper. And that Snatchers like Sleepers mightily. That daylight is safe, and nighttime is not. That you'll probably get Snatched long before you Fade, and most of what you have to look forward to is *fear*." She's grinning as she growls out the last word, eyes wide in the skittering half-light of the lantern. "So you best not need *coddling*, girl, because you'll last *five minutes* here if you don't toughen up, and fast."

Charlie grips my arm a little tighter, shakes her head. "That's not all true, Abigail..."

The old woman sniffs, turns back, continues hobbling down the hall. "Yes, it is, and you know it, Charlie, my girl. And soon enough, she will, too."

With a heavy sigh, Charlie leans toward me, eyes lowered, mouth close to my ear. "Ignore her. It's all right. Tomorrow, you'll decide if you want to stay in Mad House. You get to choose. You won't have to put up with her if you don't want to."

"Twixt," I murmur, swallowing. My mouth forms the word easily. "Twixt," I say again, and shake my head. "What's Twixt?"

"Well," says Charlie, clearing her throat, "it's where you are. You're in Mad House. In Abeo City. In Twixt." She shrugs her shoulders. "It's where Sleepers go," she finishes, as if that explains everything.

"Sleepers." I bite my lip, walking faster to catch up to the spheres of light Abigail carries in her lantern.

"You're Asleep right now," says Charlie, lengthening her stride, too. She lets go of my arm, and I stumble a little, surprised. But I do seem to be walking better now, more smoothly.

"I'm Asleep, too," Charlie says. "We all are. We're waiting to wake up."

"This is a dream?" I ask, glancing at the walls that look so solid (but weren't when we somehow passed through them, moving from outdoors to in, through the wall, into the closet), at the carpet that swallows my boots, at the frozen knots of laces scratching my chapped knees, at the dark clothes that shift against my body, the dried blood caked on my hands.

Charlie regards me strangely, biting her lower lip. "Not exactly a dream…" she begins, but Abigail stops in a doorway, stops so abruptly that I have to trip a little in order to avoid colliding with her small, sneering bulk.

"In there," she says, jutting her chin toward the room before us. Inside, there are lanterns and glass jars containing orbs on every available surface, washing the furnishings and the faces of the people with a trembling yellow glow.

And the people… There must be twenty, at least. They stand around the empty fireplace, sit stiffly on plush couches and chairs, lie sprawled upon the floor. Young and old, men and women, boys and girls, wearing ragged clothes, their heads tufted with ruffled hair. Their expressions are wary, their eyes glassy and wide.

They speak in whispers amongst themselves, but the room falls silent as they notice us, turn toward us in the doorway.

"A new one," announces Abigail—loudly and without explanation.

Charlie ushers me in, hand at the small of my back. I make a conscious effort not to stumble, feeling all of those eyes, hardly blinking, trailing my every move.

A young woman rises to her feet. Her hair is black and short and thin, curving upon her head softly. She's pretty as she shoves her hands into her hoodie's pockets, as she cocks her head to the side and smiles shyly at me. Others gather in small, tight bunches, staring, but none steps forward or speaks except for this girl, who glances from me to Charlie and back again.

"Charlie, a new one?" she's asking, and Charlie shrugs, shakes her head.

"Yes."

"But it just got dark—"

"Don't ask me, Vi. I don't know how or why."

"Things are getting worse," moans a woman then. She has tangled red hair that shifts over her shoulder as she looks toward us, her skin pale as milk. "New Sleepers in the *day*time? What *else* will change? Will walls grow solid, or fail to keep out the Snatchers?"

"New Sleepers in the daytime is *good*, Ella," says Charlie with a tired sigh, rocking back on her heels. "That would make Fetchers' work easier, and Twixt safer."

"But what *else* will change, Charlie?" asks an older man, sucking on the ends of his mustache. He brings his cane, a ragged stick, down upon the floor with a loud thump. "That's the thing: what *else?* What will change *not* for the better?"

"Listen, we'll worry about all of this later. This

girl was almost Snatched. Try to make her feel comfortable." Charlie falls onto an unoccupied couch, leaving me standing alone in the center of the room. I clasp my hands before me, uncertain.

"I'm Violet," says the girl in the hoodie, angling her chin up to grin at me again. "Have you got a name yet?"

"I…don't know my name," I whisper, panic threatening to eat me up, but the girl shakes her head, still smiling.

"Oh, no, it's all right. None of us had names when we first got here. Charlie, have you thought of one for her yet?"

"No," she says, opening one eye to look at me. "We'll think up a name for her tomorrow. I'm sorry. I'm fried, and I still have to go Fetching tonight. I was just out for a walk before night fell and—"

"Who knows if there'll even be new Sleepers tonight," says the older man, throwing up his arms. "This is serious. We need to hold someone accountable, is what we need to do. I've said it before, but—"

"Robert, ease up," commands Abigail, setting her lantern down upon the dusty piano. She hobbles over to Charlie's couch and perches primly on its arm. "Ain't nothin' happening that we can stop, anyway, and you know it."

Silence descends, hazy as a shroud, and I shiver, rubbing at my arms. Everyone watches me, the new Sleeper, the oddity. My eyes flit over the pale gathering of people with their wide, sunken eyes. Beneath their many gazes, I'm strung as tight as a violin. To shut them out, I close my eyes, but then I see the shadows—white and black and winged—descending from the trees.

My eyes spring open, wider than before.

I don't want to be here, amongst these people with their probing, accusatory stares. I don't know them. I don't know any of them.

I want to feel safe.

How can I feel safe?

I don't know if I'll ever feel safe again.

Suddenly, the hairs on the back of my neck prick up. I stand a little straighter and notice Violet straightening, too, peering behind me with her large, bright eyes.

I turn, following the line of her gaze.

There's a shadow in the doorway—small, slight, only a girl, not a monster, I realize, as she rocks on her bare feet, swaying back and forth. *Not a monster*. Just a girl. She's nearly bald, with scraps of hair tufted on her head, small, ragged knots of lanky blonde, and when she looks up at me, still swaying, I see by the sharpness of her face that she's thinner than any creature ever should be, and bones poke out at odd angles beneath her formless brown dress.

"Oh," she whispers, then, staring at me with wide, bloodshot eyes. Animal eyes. "*Oh…*" she says again, stepping forward, faltering, a skeletal hand stretched out toward me.

She hasn't glanced away, hasn't even blinked. She's staring so intensely at me that I cringe and step back as she moves forward. Her smile isn't right… It's too wide, that smile, as she pauses, trembling, before the doorway. "Oh, she has such *pretty* hair."

And then I notice something silver in her palm. It flashes in the half-light as she runs across the floor toward me, hands curled like claws, mouth open, teeth bared: everything else but her too slow, tilting.

"She's got shears!" Violet wails from somewhere far away.

I move as if through water. I try to deflect the girl, but she's on me too quickly, too ferociously, and I tumble to the ground as she straddles my waist, my shoulders, pinning me with her knees to the floor. She holds up a great fistful of my black curls—I hadn't noticed my hair before this moment—and, in her other hand, she brandishes a small pair of gleaming scissors, sharply glittering as she unhinges them, still smiling. Tears stream over her face, falling warm upon my cheeks, as she closes the pointed jaws around her handful of my hair.

I wince.

And then, just as suddenly, I can breathe again, and I sit up, gasping, because Charlie knocked the girl off of me. Together they tumble across the floor, the shears skidding, clattering toward the empty fireplace. Violet snatches them up as Charlie pins the girl down, hands at her wrists, sitting upon her waist as the girl sat upon mine.

"Violet, *help*," Charlie hisses when the girl begins to scream. The sound is slight at first, almost pathetic, but after a moment it rages, piercing, like the monsters' shrieks.

"Florence," Charlie murmurs, over and over. "Florence, it's all *right*. Florence, *look* at me."

The girl spasms beneath her, shaking violently, back arching, snapping. Violet falls to her knees, smoothes her palms over the girl's cheeks and her bare, tufted head.

"Florence, breathe. Breathe, baby girl," Violet whispers, voice catching. A single tear falls from her eye, splashing against the girl's nose, and then, suddenly, with a wracking sigh, the girl just…stops. Her eyes close, and she shudders once and slumps, like a boneless thing, and all is still.

Charlie curves forward, crawling off of the motionless body and falling to her back on the floor, beside Florence, breathing out and then shutting her eyes, too.

“Well,” says Abigail, with a quiver in her tone, “that might have gone much better. Or much worse.” Her sharp eyes pierce through me.

I sit up carefully and then stand, bending away from the lot of them and folding my arms across my middle. I’m ready to run if I need to, to flee into the hallway and just go. I don’t know where I'll go. But I’ll leave. I'll find someplace else, someplace…safe.

The hair that the girl snipped off with her shears lies limp upon the floor, curled in upon itself.

“I thought it was Nancy’s turn to watch her,” says Charlie, rubbing at her eyes. "Where'd she get those scissors?" She sits up, leaning back on her hands as she stares down at the unmoving girl. Face falling, she rubs her eyes again, and I see tears on her fingers. She stands, sniffing. “Violet, will you help me?”

Violet, pale and wide-eyed, rises to her feet, nodding, as Charlie reaches down to lift up the broken girl as if she were only a doll, cradling her length in her arms.

“Are you all right?” asks Violet quietly, reaching out and touching my elbow. Startled, I flinch away, and Violet stands beside me awkwardly, biting her lip, before she straightens, tucking her hands into her hoodie pockets. “If you…if you come with me, I’ll show you a room where you can stay tonight.”

Florence is out cold, lying limp against Charlie's chest, and Charlie stays very still, watching me, her eyes red-rimmed and shining. “Sorry,” she mutters, noticing my gaze, and then ducking her head to stare down at the girl. “She’s been getting worse, but I didn’t… I thought she was being taken care of. I’m just…so sorry.” The words catch in her throat, and I flush, suddenly ashamed for flinching away from Violet. But I don’t know what to do or say. I shift from heel to heel as the people staring at us all around the room maintain their heavy silence.

“Let’s take her upstairs,” Violet whispers, and I don’t know if she means the girl or me, but I follow Charlie and Violet out of the room, away from the heat of those probing eyes. There’s movement behind me as I leave, and I glance back over my shoulder to watch a small woman steal quietly toward the lock of hair coiled on the floor and snatch it up, her thin hands curling around it greedily before pocketing it in one jerky movement.

I look away and shiver.

Violet takes up one of the lanterns from the floor outside of the entryway, holding it in shaking fingers, angling it overhead so that it casts flickering light on the dark red carpet.

I notice Charlie watching me carefully as she shifts Florence's weight in her arms.

“Upstairs, Violet,” she says gently after a long moment, and Violet starts, nodding, leading the way down the corridor with the lantern aloft in her hand. Within the confines of the glass, the golden orbs swing about in lazy circles, resting for a heartbeat on the bottom only to rise and try to move through the glass again, bobbing in place.

“What are those?” I gesture toward the lantern.

“Oh, Wisps,” Violet murmurs distractedly, glancing over her shoulder at Charlie, who isn’t paying any attention to either of us, only staring down at Florence with a grave downturn of her mouth.

“I’m really sorry about…you know.” Violet regards me with too-bright eyes, her voice pitched low, as if to prevent Charlie from hearing her. “I hope that doesn’t mean that we’ll lose you to another Safe House. I hope you won't be afraid to stay. It was only a fluke, I promise.”

“But why did she—”

Violet shakes her head, puts a finger to her lips, leans closer.

“She wanted your hair," she whispers. "Florence has been desperate for…" She frowns, her words trailing off. Her teeth worry at her lip. "Anyway, I guess seeing so much of it—hair, I mean—triggered her, flipped the switch. She usually has better self-control. Lately, at least.” Violet studies the lantern in her hand for a long moment.

I glance at her own short black hair, sticking up like the points of arrows around her ears. “I don't understand. Why would she want my *hair*?”

Violet swallows, her eyes downcast. “I'm not the one to tell you this stuff. Charlie’s the Fetcher. She has to talk to the new Sleepers, because you have to be told things the right way. Gently.” Her eyes are wide as she turns toward me. Wide and frightened. “I could tell you something the *wrong* way, and then you’d…" She swallows again and shakes her head. "It wouldn’t be good.”

I stare at her, but she faces forward again and begins to ascend a broad staircase; the wood groans in protest beneath her feet. I follow, but Charlie brushes past me, bumping against my hip.

“Sorry,” she mutters, as she shifts Florence in her arms.

Two steps up the stairs, and the darkness seems to swallow the lantern light. It’s sudden and intense, how the panic consumes me in the half-darkness. I lift my ruined skirts and take the steps two at a time until I stand beside Charlie upon the landing.

“We’ll come for you in the morning,” says Violet, and then looks to Charlie, who nods once. “You can stay here, in this room.” She rests a palm on the door to her right. Inclining her chin toward me, she turns the knob and steps inside, the lantern illuminating a small, shabby room with sheets covering three large pieces of furniture, turning them into dingy, hulking beasts. Whisper-thin curtains blow over the single—and broken—window.

Violet crosses to the window quickly, pulling the curtains closed and shoving one of the sheet-covered pieces—a desk, I think—against them to hold them in place.

"Always keep the windows covered," she says, "just in case," and she glances past the curtains, toward the sky. My blood stills as I follow her gaze, as I remember what flies and claws beyond these walls.

*Snatchers.*

"They…" I swallow. "They can't get in, can they?"

Violet glances to Charlie again before she shakes her head slowly. "No," she says, but hesitantly—as if she isn't certain. "You're safe here," she whispers, holding the lantern to her chest. "And I'm just next door. If you need anything, come right in, all right?"

"I…" I shift from one foot to the other, look to the window again. "All right."

"Morning will come soon," Violet promises, smiling softly at me. "Morning is safe."

*And night is not.*

"I'm two doors down." Charlie clears her throat and removes her gaze from Florence, catches my eye. "Come see me, too, if you need to. But the Snatchers aren't coming in. Don't worry about that." Her voice is clear, soft. She angles her head toward me and says, so quietly that I almost can't hear it, "Again…I'm so sorry about what Florence did to you."

I open my mouth but don't know how to respond, so I just nod and look away. Then Violet holds out the lantern to me. I take it, peering at the orbs inside before hugging it against my stomach.

"Good night, then," Charlie says, her brown eyes still sad, regretful, as she backs away, through the doorway, with Florence still in her arms. Violet follows close behind, shutting the door without a sound.

I'm alone with countless shadows.

I sit stiffly on the edge of the bed, the lantern on my lap, and watch the curtain waft in and out, as if Mad House itself is breathing.

# Chapter Two: Wanting

When a dusting of light appears at the edge of the curtains, brightening the wall, I blink at it, shivering. It's so cold in this room that I can see my breath, even though I'm huddled beneath the covers with my strange lantern.

I feel as if I've sat here for hours, forever.

The knock at the door is so loud that it shatters the stillness into jagged shards. I cough, sit up in bed, still clutching the lantern close.

"Come in?" I whisper, teeth chattering.

The door gapes, and Violet peeks her head around the frame, then slips in, with Charlie behind her.

I stare at them both from the mattress, trying hard not to shake.

Charlie glances at me, eyebrows up, but goes to the window, pushing the desk aside and peeling back the curtains. Cold air gusts in past the broken, grimy glass, but there's daylight, too—enough daylight to see by.

I set the lantern down on the floor and slide my boots out from beneath the covers.

"You need good clothes," says Charlie, angling her mouth sideways, glancing at my tattered skirts. "We'll take you to the Wanting Market, get some for you."

Violet glances at her quickly. "But Charlie, how will she pay—"

"She has to know what everything means before she starts making decisions. And it won't cost much."

Violet's mouth is drawn in a thin, disapproving line. She looks away from Charlie, and she shoves her hands into her hoodie pockets.

I glance between the two of them, and frustration begins to bubble up within me, scratching at my insides, replacing the fear. "I need to know what everything means *now*. Please."

Charlie bites her lip and puts her hands on her hips. "It's better if we show you," she says, catching my gaze and holding it.

"But how can we show her the Nox—" Charlie gives Violet a warning glance, brow raised, and the girl falls silent.

"Nox?" I ask weakly.

Charlie shakes her head, offers me a hand, and I slide off the bed, helped up. I'm so stiff, I feel like a piece of clockwork that needs to be wound.

"All right." Charlie sighs, her hand still in mine. "Let's start at the beginning again. It's best to start there. Like I told you last night, you're in Twixt." She waves her free hand toward the open window. I let go of her and cross the room slowly, limping, dragging one of my booted feet behind me, and place my fingers upon the splintered sill.

Beyond the window, buildings and streets stretch toward a long, low wall that hugs the whole city. The buildings are just as shabby as our clothes, the roofs falling in, the walls discolored and crumbling. Most of the windows have no glass, and bricks lie in piles along the cavity-filled streets.

I can see children climbing on small hills of rubble, scrabbling toward tiny pinpoints of light—yellow orbs like the ones in the lanterns, but these orbs are unconfined and dancing in the air, floating above the rocks and moving away from the kids.

There's no color, really, besides those bits of

light and the red sash on the dress of a little girl who shrieks with delight as she catches one of the orbs in her hand. It glows upon her palm like a tiny captured sun.

I see, beyond the wall, that tall trees curve toward the city, with branches sharp and thorn-like, piercing the gray fold of clouds overhead that hangs close enough to touch.

"You're in Abeo City," Charlie says, coming up behind me and gazing over my shoulder, her hand resting against the wall. I feel her warmth against my back. "In Twixt. Abeo City is full of Sleepers who live in Safe Houses, of which Mad House is only one."

I look back at her, and she gives me a little smile.

"I know it's a lot to take in. Come on. We'll talk as we walk along."

"Safe Houses," I say, turning away from the window, moving after Charlie and Violet as they leave the room.

"Safe Houses keep you safe from Snatchers." Charlie glances back at me as we descend the stairs. "There are six Safe Houses here in Abeo, and each Safe House is run by a different person with different…" She pauses. "Well, *beliefs* is a good word for it, I guess. Abigail, the woman you met last night, runs Mad House."

"And what are Abigail's beliefs?" I ask, as we reach the first floor and my boots sink into the thick carpet.

Charlie shakes her head, huffs out. "You'll see." She pauses at the door, fingers lightly touching the knob. "Are you ready?"

I close my hands into fists. "For what?"

Charlie laughs a little, but it's a humorless sound, even though her mouth is curved up at one side. "The wonder that is Abeo."

She opens the door.

I take in a cool breath, and then, moving over the porch, down the steps and onto the uneven street behind Charlie and Violet, I twirl and take in the city. The buildings, all leaning, are caving in: landslides of stone sculpting dangerous geography. Again, I see the children, moving in a little pack now, away from us, their eyes wide and wild. One stooped man, wrinkled and grey, scuttles out of the mountain of rubble like a beetle, takes one glance at us, and then scuttles back in again.

Mad House, behind us, is perhaps the least dilapidated house on the street, though that says little: none of the windows in Mad House, I see now, has unbroken glass, and, tilting my head back, I notice a great gouge out of the roof, as if something large and heavy crashed against it.

*Something large and heavy...*

Charlie breathes out, begins to walk down the street quickly. "Come on. Time's kind of funny here. We need to get to the Wanting Market and the Need Shop and back home before darkness falls."

"The Need Shop, Charlie?" asks Violet, scampering after her.

I try to keep pace with them but don't quite manage it, settling for a jerky stride that makes my boots clomp loudly against the uneven stone beneath my feet.

"I want to take her to see Edgar," says Charlie, glancing over her shoulder at me. She lowers her voice: "I didn't find her at midnight at a crossroads, Violet, and...that's obviously unusual. I want to find out if he's Fetched anyone like her recently, anyone during the daylight, or in a strange place."

"I know, and I'd like to see Edgar, but it's just...the *Need* Shop." Violet's tone is nervous. She throws a glance back toward Mad House and then steps forward, hooks a hand on Charlie's arm. "What if *she* finds out?"

Charlie shakes her head. "She won't. Don't *worry*, Vi, seriously. We need to figure out if the new Sleeper patterns are shifting, and that's much more important than whether Abigail *disapproves* or not."

"Still, she's a terrifying woman," Violet mutters. Then she grins at me, but it's half-meant, the curve of her lips quivering. "I mean, she *can* be terrifying. She's…mighty, is all."

Charlie laughs a little, mouth in a wry twist. "Aren't we all at Mad House?"

"I like to think so," Violet ventures, raising her chin in mock haughtiness before giggling behind her hand.

We reach a crossroads in the street. Until this moment, we've seen few other people, save for the old man and the skulking children, who follow after us, scampering in and out of buildings and alleyways, as if trying to stay out of sight. The slide of rock against rock is sudden in the stillness as it shifts out from beneath one of their feet, but when the stones *clink* together with finality, another sound overtakes them.

Voices.

Charlie jerks her chin ahead. "The Wanting Market," she says, and we move out from a narrow road between two buildings into a large city square.

It takes me a heartbeat to realize that it *is* a city square, for it's filled with little shacks and tents, colorless pieces of cloth propped up on sticks and metal rods, and piles of garbage that stretch away to the buildings on the far side of the square. There are people here, people in the tents and people outside of them, digging through the piles of trash, climbing over garbage on hands and knees.

The pack of children trailing us wanders toward

the outside edge of the square, drawn to the mounds of stone rubble as if they are their natural habitat. Only adults, I notice, move amongst the tents.

A woman is striding slowly between two mountains of ruined things, a stuffed animal under one arm, her robe trailing behind her, falling off of one bare shoulder. A few grubby young people—around Charlie's and Violet's ages, I think, and…maybe mine?—sit together on a sloping hill of dirty clothes, bending their faces toward one another, and I can't tell if they're boys or girls or both. Every person here is so filthy, their hair short or matted, their faces smeared with grime. And their clothing is worn, though, I must admit, more intact than the black strips of lace dangling from my waist in a poor imitation of a skirt.

"Come on," says Charlie with an indulgent smile, as I turn and gawk at the scenes surrounding us. She hooks her arm through mine, tugging me along a row of towering scraps. "Let's get you some clothes."

The closest mound of junk is heaped up under a drooping awning made out of hole-ridden cloth. A young woman peers up at Charlie, narrowing her eyes shrewdly beneath her greasy hair as we duck under and into her tent of grubby wares.

"Charlie, darlin', good to see ya," says the woman, pointing toward a heap beneath the awning. "Some new stuff there. Anything in particular you're lookin' for?"

"A dress or pants and sweater or something for our new friend here, Sandy." Charlie drops to her knees and begins shoving junk aside: rusted bits of metal, chunks of stone, eyeless stuffed animals… Finally, she begins to pull out tangled bundles that resemble clothing.

"Your new young friend got a name?" asks the woman, Sandy, watching me with one wickedly blue eye, while her other eye squints tightly. She rubs her dirt-stained hands on the sides of her blue jeans before chewing at a ragged nail.

I stand very still before I shake my head, angle my chin up.

"No," says Charlie distractedly, tugging at something under a corroded sheet of metal. "Not yet."

"You ain't got a name, you got nothin' around here," says Sandy, winking at me. "But you sure got a lovely head of hair, darlin'—"

"*Leave it,* Sandy,' Charlie snarls, standing abruptly. In her arms, she cradles a bundle of cloth, and after staring Sandy down, making the other woman shrug and look away, she turns to me, sizing me up. "All right, let's see what we have…" She shakes out the twisted fabric in her hands. It's a dress. Perhaps it was once cream colored, but it's now rusty and brown. Still, it isn't tattered; there are only two holes in the bottom of the skirt, small and sad, like frowning mouths or half moons.

"I think it'll fit you, if you like it," says Charlie, holding it out to me. "Or I could try to find you pants or—"

"This'll do," I say quickly.

Sandy is standing too close to me, fingering my knotted black curls in her dirty, long-nailed hand.

"Sandy, leave her alone." Charlie steps between us, breathing hard through her nose. "Back off."

Sandy smirks but shrinks away, still staring at me. No, not at me. At my hair…

"You gotta pay for that," she says, scowling and rocking back on her heels. "Ha! I'll take a *curl* from that pretty head of hair. I haven't had a curl in ages!"

"No," Charlie says. "I'm paying." She tugs out a thin, grubby chain from beneath her shirt, drawing up a tiny pair of scissors. They're smaller than the ones

Florence threatened me with last night, but I take an involuntary step backwards as Charlie brings the shears up to her own head of hair. A single *snip*, and a curving lock of blonde falls into her outstretched palm.

"Take it, Sandy. The dress isn't even worth this."

Sandy *harrumphs* but snatches the strands out of Charlie's hand.

I clutch the dress against me, wondering what sort of place this is, where people buy old, dirty clothes with cut-off hair.

"Let's go," says Charlie, steering Violet and me away from the tent.

"Well, come back soon, Charlie!" Sandy laughs. I watch over my shoulder as she pushes the lock of hair into a leather purse at her belt.

"She's despicable. She'd sell her best friend's scalp for Nox," Violet mutters, her hands drawn into fists at her sides.

Charlie glances at her with a weak smile, her hand poised lightly at the small of my back.

"Here, who wouldn't, Vi?" she whispers. "We're no better, and you know it."

"I wasn't..." Violet colors, and then her fists tighten. "Actually, yes, we *are* better. *You* know it."

"We aren't," says Charlie with finality. "We're all Sleepers. We're all in this—whatever it is—together. None better, none worse."

She pauses in an alley, glancing back and forth. No one stands nearby. The narrow space is dark, angled away from the Wanting Market.

"You can try the dress on here, if you'd like," Charlie says, turning her back on me. Violet turns away, too, still huffing, crossing her arms over her chest.

"You can't let Abigail's stupidity get to you. You can't," mutters Charlie tiredly, rubbing at her face as I stare at her back, Violet's back, for a moment, holding out the stiff dress before me.

"I'm not. It's just...*Nox*, Charlie. It isn't—"

"Not now, Vi."

Gingerly, awkwardly, I peel off my tattered dress, tearing the thin fabric at the shoulders, and let it settle into a pile of gauzy black at my feet. It takes my warmth along with it, so I shiver and quickly pull the new dress over my head. It slides over my skin easily, the fabric soft and cool. Reaching behind me, I zip up the back and tug the sleeves down to cover the chilled skin of my arms. The dress is long and whole, but I'm shaking from the cold now.

I clear my throat, and Charlie and Violet glance over their shoulders, then turn around.

"Good. Better," Violet nods, and without a second glance, she begins walking back down the alley, toward the Wanting Market. But Charlie watches me for a long moment, arms folded, her brown eyes dark.

"Is it...is it all right?" I ask her, tugging at the sleeves again. I have no idea how I look, and Charlie's stare is unreadable, shadowed.

But she nods—once, twice—glances at my face again, right corner of her mouth angling up.

"Very pretty," she says, her voice light and low.

I laugh a little. I'm wearing a dirty dress Charlie found in a garbage pile. *Pretty*? But I feel soft, somehow, as her words sink deeper into me, filling me with warmth.

*Pretty.*

I blink at her in the dark alleyway, wondering what she sees, truly, when she looks at me.

She waits for me to move past her, then slips her arm through mine again. I thought she was staying close by before because of my stiffness, my uncooperative joints, and...I think she was. But I'm not stiff anymore, not hobbling at all. I'm moving just as well as Charlie and Violet, as anyone. And still she holds my arm.

In all this strangeness, it's comforting to feel her beside me.

"Why…why did you give that woman a piece of your hair?" I ask, when we're back amongst the noise and bustle of the Wanting Market. "Why did she *want* it?"

I watch a woman curl her dirty hand toward a man wearing a bright yellow raincoat. He draws out a small pair of scissors on a chain from beneath his slicker and raggedly hacks off a bit of hair from his scrappy beard. He drops the wiry lock into her palm, and she grins toothily.

Charlie pats her own chest, fingers moving against the blades beneath her shirt.

"Hair is currency here," she says simply. "Hair buys you what you need. But you don't need much. So, mostly, hair buys you Nox." She glances sidelong at me. "That's why Florence came after you last night." Her brown eyes fall, and she clears her throat. "I'm very sorry about that."

"Nox…" I prompt, shying closer to Charlie as a fierce-looking man watches me from beneath his tent flap. His eyes flash wide under his black baseball cap: he's staring at my hair, like Sandy was, with starvation in his eyes.

"For many Sleepers, Nox is the most important part of Twixt." Charlie closes her eyes and pinches the bridge of her nose. "If you take Nox, it makes you Mem. When you're Memming, you get a memory, something you've forgotten. From your waking life."

Memming.

A *memory…*

Violet pauses ahead of us, turning back and watching me closely.

I have no memories. None. I'm hollow, full of nothing, of emptiness. I tried so hard all night long to remember, but my earliest memory is of Charlie finding me at the edge of the stream, of red blood upon the ice, of the Snatchers' claws gleaming in the darkness, of the golden light bobbing in Abigail's lantern.

Before that, there's only a dark wall, impossible to climb over or break down.

There is such a hunger in me, then, such a burning *need,* that I'm struck breathless by its ferocity.

I break away from Charlie, stumble a little, turn around to look at both Charlie and Violet with my hands curled into fists.

"I could... I could *remember* something?" I whisper, unable to contain my excitement, but Violet folds her arms, her gaze hard, and Charlie...

Charlie won't look at me.

"Well...yeah." She sighs. "But there's a cost to everything." Another sigh, and then her gaze lifts, intense, and claims my eyes. "Nox isn't as lovely as it sounds. Think of Florence."

Despite myself, I shudder.

"Nox is addictive. Highly addictive. You trade bits of yourself away for a handful of memories, and then, when you've sold all of your hair, you become..." She bites her lip. "You become nothing. You Fade."

"Fade," I repeat, voice dropped down to a whisper.

Charlie nods, watching me. "You Fade away when you've sold all of your hair for Nox. You...go. Vanish." Her shoulders rise and fall with a heavy breath. "You become nothing," she says again.

"But you can't become *nothing*—"

"You *can,*" Violet says urgently, her eyes full of fear, stepping forward to place her hand on my arm. "It's happened so many times that...that some people, like Charlie and me and Abigail, started to think that maybe you *shouldn't* take Nox. Maybe Nox is…bad."

Charlie moves toward us, resting a hand on Violet's shoulder. "But there weren't many people who thought that way," she says, "because nearly everyone was addicted. So Mad House, our house, was formed by the people who took a stand against Nox."

Violet shakes her head and laughs. "The reason it's called *Mad* House is a joke, you know? People say we're mad for refusing Nox. But we think *they're* the mad ones—"

"Violet," Charlie sighs.

"Well, *I* think they're mad. Anyway, Nox isn't allowed past Abigail's doors."

Charlie breathes out. "So that's the thing," she says, turning to face me and again pin me beneath her deep, soft gaze. "If you decide that you want to stay with us at Mad House, you can't take Nox, not while you're there."

I blink, uncertain as to how I should respond. We hold our silence for a long moment, and I feel Charlie's eyes on me, even as I stare down at my boots.

A *memory…* I could have a *memory…*

Finally, Charlie clears her throat and slides her arm gently through mine. "But you don't have to make any of those decisions right now. I know it's a lot to take in. And a lot to give up. The need for memories, for something to hold onto here… It's powerful. Believe me, I understand that."

"I just… I don't know who I *am…*" I begin, but Charlie smiles at me, and my words fall away.

"None of us knows who we are," she whispers, voice soft. "And that's the hardest part of everything here, I think. Beyond the Snatchers, beyond the fear of night. Beyond the Sixers, even."

My lips part, and I stand very still. The ground

seems to stretch away from me, elongating, as the word—*that word*—cuts against my insides, rends apart my thoughts, like shears snipping recklessly inside of head.

Slowly, slowly, everything in me breaks apart into tiny, frozen shards, even as, outwardly, I remain motionless. My heart pounds against the cage of my ribs.

The ground seems to move beneath me, then, or bend, or rock, because I trip on nothing at all. Charlie catches me neatly, steadying me with her strong hands, but I struggle away from her, lower myself to the ground and kneel there, panting, because I know my legs can no longer hold me up.

"What's the matter? What is it?" asks Violet, dropping to her knees beside me. "Are you okay?"

"My head…" I whisper, brushing fingers over my pulsing temples.

Charlie squats at my side, her forehead creased.

"What…what is that?" I ask her, grabbing at her shirt, knuckles white.

Startled, she places her hands over mine and whispers, "What is—"

"*Sixers*." The word slices my mouth as it razors past my lips. I drag cold air into my lungs to chase the dizziness away. "*What*," I breathe, "is *that*?"

"Oh." Charlie smoothes her fingers over the backs of my hands. "The Sixers… They're in charge here," she offers quietly, glancing to Violet, who nods, urging her on. Charlie's voice drops to a whisper: "They control…everything in Twixt. Nox is Snatcher feathers, and only the Sixers are strong enough, brave enough to pluck Snatcher feathers. So they control Nox, and because of that—and maybe other reasons—they control Abeo City. That's how it's always been. The Sixers rule us all."

When she says the word again, *Sixers*, my chest heaves. I'm so sick, so cold, but my skin is slick with sweat. I rock back and forth, feel the grit of broken stone beneath my knees. But it's good, this pain. It brings me back to myself, makes this moment feel real, or at least more real than everything else about Twixt.

"I don't like that word," I hiss through clenched teeth.

Violet frowns, her eyebrows drawn low. "Most people don't," she murmurs soothingly. "It's okay."

Charlie helps me to my feet, holding me up when my legs wobble beneath me. No one here in the Wanting Market seems to have noticed my collapse, or maybe no one cared. But I'm still self-conscious as I brush the dirt from the seat of my dress and tremble in Charlie's arms.

"The Need Shop is owned by the Sixers," says Charlie softly, leaning close.

I shudder as the word incises my ear, but my knees remain locked; I don't want to fall again.

"All right?" Charlie asks, her eyes dark with worry.

"Yes. Sorry. I don't know why..." *Why I'm falling apart at the seams.* "I'm fine, just... Everything's so strange."

Violet rests a cool hand against my cheek. "We all go through it," she smiles. "The strangeness wears away, in time. For the most part." Her eyes glaze over as she stares past me, toward the people shuffling all around.

The three of us begin to move through the market, Charlie guiding me along with her arm around my waist.

"Edgar works at the Need Shop during the day," she tells me. "Fetchers—like Edgar and me—are usually the ones who sell Nox to the Sleepers in the Safe

Houses, and we get the Nox from the Need Shop. Because Mad House doesn't allow Nox, I don't have that duty, so I don't have to deal with the Six—um, *them* on a regular basis."

"What…what *are* they?" I grip her arm tightly, my fingertips pressing hard into her skin.

Charlie breathes out, stares down at her feet. "They're just women…"

But Violet shakes her head, almost too softly to notice, her eyes round and wide. "They're *more* than that," she tells me.

"What do you mean?"

"They're monsters," Violet whispers, coming up behind Charlie and me and planting her head between our shoulders. "Just because they don't Snatch us up into the sky doesn't mean they're not monsters, too."

"*Violet*," Charlie says. "Keep your voice down. And don't spread rumors. You have no proof—"

"It's not a rumor." Her eyes are as large as bowls, as blue as water.

Charlie rakes a hand through her pale hair, then tightens her grip on my waist, urging me forward.

"She's going to learn all of this soon enough, anyway, Charlie." Petulant, Violet follows after us.

"The thing about Twixt," says Charlie over her shoulder, with finality, "is that there are as many stories as truths. And you have to figure out which is which. We'll do our best to help you, but even we don't know everything, and even *we*—" she adds pointedly, glaring at Violet, "—can get it wrong."

Violet shrugs her shoulders and points her gaze toward one of the tents as we pass by.

In the middle of the square is a dried-up fountain. The statue at its center is that of a man, headless and armless, torso and legs blackened by dead moss. A real man stands beside the statue, perched on the lip of the fountain's bowl, watching us as we move past him. He's older, with a tangled beard and little hair remaining on his head. He exhales loudly as we walk by, stands up straighter, and then he shouts so loudly that I start: "The Snatchers are coming to get you! They'll get us all!"

"Shut up, Carl," Charlie mutters, but he shakes his head at her, bellows, "Snatchers!" and "All of us!" at the top of his lungs. A small crowd of thin, hairless people gathers at his feet, hands clasped together, eyes closed, bodies shaking.

I remember Abigail's words, then: *Most of what you have to look forward to is fear.*

Everything here, *everything,* is so drab and gray and dirty and tattered and shabby and broken and falling apart and fearful and terrible, and I stop for a moment, press my fingers to my eyes, press so hard that purple circles spiral out, warping my vision. All I can see is spheres in darkness...spheres that eat each other, devouring. Devouring...

I feel a hand on my shoulder, and I open my eyes, turn back, look at Charlie and Violet. They watch me, both of them, with drawn, sympathetic expressions.

"It's hard in the beginning," says Violet, voice soft. "It gets better if you try."

"Try?" I ask, the word breaking. "Try what?"

She shrugs, bows her head, looking very sad and very small. "This. Us."

I rub my cold arms, stare across the Wanting Market, at the piles of refuse, at the dirty, scrounging people, scavenging after garbage. It turns my stomach, how filthy and little and desperate it is.

"What's beyond Abeo City?" I ask, surprising myself. "What's in the woods out there, where I came from?"

"Where you came from..." Charlie breathes out,

and her eyes flit over my face. "Just the woods, the stream. And the Red Line. It's a spot out in the woods to mark time... If you started toward the Red Line at the earliest point in the morning, and you don't turn back when you reach it, you won't make it back to Abeo City and the Safe Houses before dark. And the Snatchers will get you."

"You can't *leave* here?" I hate how my voice cracks, how anxious it sounds, betraying me.

"No." Charlie looks away.

Violet stares down at the ground, at her dusty sneakers on the broken street.

The enormity of this revelation presses down upon me until I feel so trapped, so weighed down that I can't breathe, but instead of fear...anger rises within me, white and hot and potent.

"Has anyone ever tried to get past the Red Line?" I ask. My words are sharp. Violet's eyes—already wide as moons—widen further, and Charlie studies me for a long moment before she answers.

"Yes," she says finally, evenly. "And they've never come back."

I look at the trees that tower over the wall edging the city. They're almost twice the size of the wall, taller than all of the buildings. It feels as if we're in a bowl, a valley surrounded by woods, with gray clouds crouching over everything, enclosing us, too close, reflecting Abeo City's colorless hues.

Charlie reaches forward, takes my arm.

"Let's go see Edgar," she says gently. "Like I said, time is hard to keep track of here, and darkness comes before you expect it." Her eyes stare before us, hollow. "We can't be out after dark."

I stumble alongside her, eyes scarcely seeing.

But I glance up, curious, at the edge of the Wanting Market's city square, because ahead is a house that looks solid, low-roofed and built of dull-colored bricks. It's not as dilapidated as the buildings surrounding it, and a scrawled sign hung over the front door reads *The Need Shop: Purveyors of Nox*. The *x* in *Nox* has more lines through it than necessary, giving it the appearance of a rough black star.

Charlie ascends the four crumbling stone steps to the door and pushes it open with her shoulder, glancing back at us. I follow with Violet behind me, her hands stuffed in her hoodie pockets, a frown pinching her pretty face.

The interior of the shop is so dark that, even though it is an oppressively gray day outside, it takes a few long moments for my eyes to adjust to the dimness. There are lanterns full of Wisps lining the walls, but their light seems to be swallowed up into the cubbyholed walls. Tall, rickety shelves sway from floor to ceiling, their surfaces covered with small, lidded boxes and baskets full of shadows.

Charlie moves down one of the aisles, ducking into a small back room and speaking with someone there in an eager tone. I begin to follow her, but Violet rests a hand on my arm, pausing and removing the lid from one of the boxes on the shelves.

"This is Nox," she says quietly, drawing out a long, thin bit of darkness. She holds it up to me, and we both watch as the translucent black feather moves in the gust of her shallow breath, arching away from her, toward me. I stare at it, transfixed. It's small, dainty, and lovely, really, as it shines—a deep, dulled shine, like stars in water—against her fingers.

"Vi," Charlie calls, and Violet drops the feather to the floor, stooping to pick it up hastily, her eyes brimming with guilt as she places it back in its box.

We walk the cramped hall lined with shelves until we enter the little room in the back. It holds a single wooden desk and chair, along with crates piled on top of crates, all filled, I can see, with Nox. The darkness is absolute in those crates, like ink, like a mass of captured night. It's as if tatters of night sky have been gathered and stuffed into boxes far too small to contain them. I can't make out individual feathers; the black is too much, too deep.

In the center of the room, a young man stands with his thumbs in his pockets. He wears a stained waistcoat and a pair of grubby pants, but his white collared shirt is spotless and stiff looking, as if it's been starched. He sports a wickedly sharp, thin black mustache over a mouth angling up, and his green eyes flash brightly in the yellow glow from the lantern on his desk.

Charlie stands beside him, her hands on her hips. They look so different, the pair of them, but comfortable together, like a brother and sister, I imagine, might appear.

"This is Edgar," Charlie tells me, smiling a little and gesturing me further inside. "Don't worry. He's a friend." And then to him, in a lowered tone, she says, "Edgar, this is the Sleeper I was telling you about." She points her chin toward me. "Have you *ever* found a Sleeper outside of Abeo? And before midnight?"

Edgar clasps his hands behind his back and circles me, shaking his head. "No. But I'm not surprised. Stranger things have happened."

Violet snorts, folding her arms and leaning against the wall.

"Once," Edgar tells me, his eyes aglow, "while I was Fetching, a Snatcher swooped down and stole a Sleeper from my arms, and I *swear* it was trying to *talk* to me. I'd never heard a Snatcher make sounds like that before, almost like…words."

I take a step back from him, bending away.

"Lovely to meet you," Edgar says, then, performing a sweeping bow. I swallow, working my jaw, then nod to him stiffly. He laughs a little at that, at me, running his slender fingers through his hair.

"It was likely a hiccup, her showing up when and where she did," he tells Charlie, turning to face her and shrugging. "Don't worry your pretty yellow head."

Charlie sighs, rolling her dark eyes to the ceiling. "Don't worry, he says. Right."

"Listen. The *important* thing is that this lovely lady wasn't Snatched right from your grasp." Edgar winks at me. "But of course she wasn't. Has Charlie told you that she's the best Fetcher? She's *terribly* humble and hasn't brought it up, I'm sure, but if you'd been Fetched by *me*, you wouldn't be here right now, I can promise you that. I don't keep a good head under abnormal circumstances." He hooks the chair out from the desk and perches on it backwards, shrugging his shoulders in an exaggerated way.

Charlie smiles down at him, folding her arms and shaking her head a little, laughing to herself.

"So have you given the pretty thing a name, Charlie?" he asks, steepling his fingers in front of him and examining me.

Charlie sighs. "Stop flirting," she admonishes, though she's still grinning. "You'd warm up to a stump if you thought it might present a challenge."

"I'm an equal opportunity master of smoothness." Edgar winks at me again. I venture a small smile, glancing uncertainly to Charlie.

Then Violet rolls her eyes, says, "Oh, Edgar," and the three of them laugh together—freely, without restraint. My smile widens, though I can't force out a laugh, not yet.

"To tell you the truth, I haven't been able to think of any name that seems right for her." Charlie's eyes find mine and linger upon them for a long heartbeat. My lips part, and I feel stilled, calmed, wrapped in the warmth of her clear, brown gaze.

Then, with a furtive glance at Edgar, she turns her eyes to the floor.

Edgar raises a single eyebrow, watching Charlie for a moment before looking to me again.

"Ah," he says simply, cocking his head to the side. "I see." This earns him a toe-poke from Charlie, who, I realize, is blushing. I watch her, brows furrowed, as warmth begins to creep over my own face.

"Charlie, Charlie…" murmurs Edgar, tapping his fingers on the back of the chair. "I've always told you that the prettiest of names is wasted on you. Charlotte is lovely, and you chose the boyish part of it, the common nickname."

"It suits me," says Charlie, brow up.

"Definitely. You're no Charlotte." He grins at her, then glances to me. "But what if *she*…is?"

"Charlotte," I whisper, tasting the word. It's light, airy, like dust in my mouth.

Charlie gazes at me for a little while, then clears her throat, tilting her head toward me. "What about Lottie? We'll share the name, if you like. You take half, and I'll have the other." She's smiling softly at me, hopefully.

"Lottie." My tongue trips over the syllables. The word is sharp and soft at the same time, and I think… I think that describes me well enough. I stare down at my hands, at the healing wounds there. "Lottie. Yes. Lottie."

"Good!" Violet hooks an arm through mine and squeezes tightly, grinning. "I love it. It fits you."

I smile at Violet and then glance at Charlie, and I feel warm again, all over. She rakes a hand through her hair, pushing it away from her eyes, and she watches the ground, mouth curving up.

"It's a lovely name," she says softly, nodding. "For a lovely girl."

Edgar snorts, rolling his eyes. "And *now* who's flirting?"

They laugh again, and it's such a happy sound, and for a moment, I think I hear a sound like it come from my own mouth. Small and soft, but still…a start.

I realize something, then. Something important that opens up within me, unfurling, like a leaf or a wing:

There's no fear here, now.

Edgar cranks back one of the small shutters over his desk, and daylight spills into the dark little room. "Well," he declares, drawing out the word. "I'm almost done for today. Walk you back to that Maddest of Houses?"

"Yes," Charlie agrees, and as Edgar pats his pockets and tidies the pile of papers on the desk, she asks him, "Edgar?"

"Hmm?"

"Has anything…strange happened to you in the past day or night?" She bites her lip. "You haven't found any Sleepers in odd places. I know that. But has there been anything else that seemed unusual?"

He pauses for a moment, fingers lingering above the desktop before he shakes his head. "No. Matilda is her usual… Well." He chuckles. "She's a fright. High-and-mightiness all around. Thank the *Snatchers* she's not here today." He winks at me. "She's a horror, truly. She runs the Need Shop for the Sixers."

Again, that word…

I quell my revulsion, curling my hands into fists.

"Don't get on *her* bad side." Edgar whistles, shaking his head. "Well, Charlie, there weren't any new Sleepers at the crossroads last night. But that's nothing to remark about. Things have been slowing down in my part of Abeo, it seems. And yours?"

"None last night, either," says Charlie, frowning. "But what if, like Lottie, they're appearing in odd places and at odd times? Maybe they don't show up at midnight now. Maybe they're arriving during some other part of the night, or even the day?" Charlie's eyes meet mine, and there's a desperate gleam in her gaze. "What if they're not appearing in Abeo anymore? What if they're showing up out in the woods?"

"Well, now, I think we need to wait awhile before we start worrying about all of *that.*" Edgar shrugs into a long black coat. He picks up a top hat from a peg on the wall and plunks it atop his crown. "Now to escort the most charming of ladies—"

Charlie laughs, brow raised. "You know, *I* should really be escorting *you.*"

"Too true. You're the only one I'd trust with my life around the Snatchers." He tips his hat at her, winks at me, and shuts the door to the little room as the four of us walk down the hallway. We move together through the darkness until Violet opens the outer door and we step into the square of the Wanting Market.

Edgar locks the Need Shop door with a long, spiraled key and drops it into his waistcoat pocket.

"You locked it." I glance back over my shoulder toward the brick walls of the Need Shop, and then stare at Edgar, confused. "But couldn't anyone go through the walls? Couldn't they glide through the door, even if it's locked, and steal some Nox, if they truly wanted it?" I turn to Charlie, confused. "Didn't we go *through* the walls last night, when the Snatchers were chasing us?"

"We did." Charlie nods, eyeing me softly. "And it's true. We can pass through walls, all of us, just as easily as if they were made of fog. But..." She tilts her head, lowering her voice, "No one would dare steal from the Sixers."

"No, indeed. That would be a mistake," Edgar states a bit too brightly, tapping the top of his hat and tossing me an unconvincing wink.

"Oh," I say, falling into step as Violet leads us out into the street.

We walk along the edge of the Wanting Market, and my eyes are drawn to its hulking piles of trash, to the tents crowded with haggling Sleepers.

"Why would anyone want all of that…garbage?" I watch a man, nearly bald, exchange a lock of hair with a tent owner for a misshapen lump of teddy bear. He turns quickly, holding the bear in front of him like a shield, then crushing it to his chest.

"Comfort," Edgar replies simply, softly, following my gaze. "We've very little of that here in Abeo, Lottie. Nox—that's comfort. Good company. That's comfort. Safe Houses. And…" He gestures widely with his hands. "That's it."

"Try a *little* harder, Edgar," Charlie groans, casting her brown eyes skyward. "I swear, I'm surrounded by pessimists—"

"Reality is not pessimism, Charlie. And I prefer to be *real* with our dear new Sleepers." Edgar tips his hat to me. "Present company not excluded. It's difficult here, Charlie. And if you tell them otherwise, if you lull them to complacency, they won't last long."

"You sound like Abigail," Charlie grumbles, eyes flashing stubbornly, shoving her hands deeper into her pockets. "Okay, I don't deny it: it *can* be awful here."

"Worse than awful," Violet whispers, bowing her head.

"But it's not *all* awful." Sighing, Charlie takes up Violet's hand, squeezes it. "We have each other, after all."

Edgar watches Charlie with a curl to his lips. "Okay. So there's that. You see, she's an optimist," he whispers to me, elbowing my ribs gently. "There are few of them here, so they're quite precious, really."

"I'm so precious," Charlie laughs—a bright, joyous sound that makes me feel bright, too, light. Like something different than I am, than how I feel...

A movement, just past Charlie's shoulder, catches my eye. A bulky shape, covered in dark furs, bounds in the direction opposite to the Wanting Market, toward the dilapidated houses down the street. There are still children climbing all over the mounds of rubble, but this person wasn't a child. It looked…familiar. But nothing looks familiar here. How could it…

My skin pricks, and as I turn the corner with Edgar, Violet and Charlie, whoever it was has vanished, having leapt down an alley and into the shadows there.

I feel strange, suddenly, like my knees no longer want to obey me. I put out my hand against a brick wall to steady myself, but my fingers pass *through* the wall, and I nearly stumble but catch myself, shaking my head.

"How did I do that?" I ask weakly, leaning against the now-solid bricks.

With a little smile, Charlie removes her hands from her pockets, holding them out in front of her as she walks toward the wall—and right through it, disappearing.

"You just have to think about it," she tells me then, popping her head back out.

"But…*how* is that possible?"

Charlie reemerges fully and shrugs, and Edgar shifts his gaze to the sky, looking ill at ease.

"Well, Lottie, like most things in Twixt, we don't really know *how* it works," he tells me finally, after clearing his throat. He breathes out. "We can just do it."

I blink at him, pushing hair out of my eyes.

We walk on, but my questions torment me. There must be a reason for everything—even in Twixt. I slow, swallowing, because something gnaws at my heart just then, and I try to listen to it, try to *hear*, but it escapes me as another sound draws my attention, a near sound. A slithering sound.

Something *slithers* down an alley just behind us, in the direction of the Wanting Market, and a heavy hush presses down against the conversations there, stifling them to whispers, and then silence.

Charlie pales, turns, gripping Edgar's arm. "It's them," she hisses, as they exchange a charged glance.

"Oh, no…" Violet whimpers, clutching Charlie's sleeve.

A wave of dread crests through my body. "Who—"

Darkness pools at our feet, swirls in the air all around us. Despite my fear, I want to see, need to see, so I step forward, toward the mouth of the alleyway, even as Charlie comes after me, pressing me, face to face, against the wall, out of sight, though I still catch glimpses of the Wanting Market over her shoulder.

"What—" I whisper, but she shakes her head, breathing hard, eyes gazing deeply into mine. I can feel her heartbeat all around me, the warmth of her palms against my bare arms.

*Safe*, I think. Charlie makes me feel safe.

But I'm *not* safe. I sense it, as surely as I feel Charlie's breath against my face.

I watch, peering past Charlie's shoulder, as the shadow widens and lengthens until it eats up the square.

And through the square walks a darkness.

Two tall shadows prowl down the main drag of the Wanting Market. They're cloaked and hooded, the black fabric streaming away from them like wings, the way they flow over the ground, moving like breath, like feathers, like night itself. Dragging behind them, beneath the weightlessness of their cloaks, is hair. Long black hair that extends behind them, spread out over the rubble and refuse of the street, towing within it bits of twigs, trash and debris, though the strands still shine, as only black hair can.

When I see them, when my eyes rest upon their cloaked faces, all other thoughts fade away to nothingness. I am nothingness. I am *feeling* alone, and all I feel is fear.

The two of them move in small, unnatural jerks, animal-like, for there's a feral kind of rhythm as their feet prowl, as they draw closer to us, their hoods drooping like too-wide, grinning mouths.

"Sixers," Charlie whispers against my ear, her breath fluttering my hair, though I already know what they are, knew the moment I first glimpsed them.

I don't know how I knew.

I gaze into Charlie's eyes, basking in her warmth, her *safeness*, as my heart pounds a different rhythm, merging with hers.

"But there are only two," I whisper back.

Charlie's gaze widens, and then I feel her watching me as I watch *them*.

"How did you—" she starts, but the pair of Sixers moves to the mouth of our alleyway now, and she gasps, holds her breath.

I'm hidden. They can't see me, not here in the shadows, not with Charlie's body pressed flat against mine. Still, the cloaked figure nearest to us pauses for a heartbeat, pauses as if suspended into stillness. The hood turns, and I suffer a terrifying moment of wonder. Maybe there's nothing behind that hood, nothing but a void of darkness.

I'm mesmerized, but my eyes tear away, because

there's a sudden movement beyond the two dark shapes beside us.

A Sleeper detaches herself from the crowd that has gathered to watch the procession of the Sixers. She's a young woman, almost hairless, as smooth-headed as the old men who watch her. With a pained whimper, she collapses to her knees and crawls across the rubble, toward the Sixers. They turn to her, as one, waiting.

When she reaches them, tugging at the edge of one black cloak, she pets the night-dark hair that's snagged over the rocks and rubble with a thin, trembling hand.

"Please…" I hear her whisper, her wide eyes blue and sad. "I've sold all of my hair, and I need Nox. I *need* it. Please…"

The Sixer turns its hood—her hood. I remember now that Charlie called the Sixers women. She turns her hood and stares down at the girl who, within the Sixers' line of sight, sags against the ground, trembling.

"Poor child." It's a harsh whisper, low enough that it seems to skip over the ground. I shudder, and the girl beneath the Sixers' gaze shudders, too. The Sixer leans forward, and I watch, speechless, astonished, as I see claw-like hands extend out of the sleeves of the cloak, toward the girl.

The second Sixer turns now, as the first drags the girl to her feet. Whining, the girl angles away from the Sixer, and she's crying, tears tracing down her pale cheeks in thin double lines.

"She needs our *help*, sister," says the first Sixer to the second, drawing out the word *sister* with a sibilant hiss.

The second Sixer tilts her head, gazing down at the girl. She's larger than the other cloaked figure, and there's something more imposing about her bulk, the way she remains silent, even as she and her sister continue along their way, dragging the girl by her arm.

"No, please... I just wanted Nox!" The girl is babbling, kicking her legs, and the first Sixer tightens her claws around the girl's arm. "No, please..."

"Hush. Poor child. We'll help you, won't we, sister?"

Without another word, as the girl's wails echo through the square, the Sixers pass by, and the blackness of their hair recedes, and then they are past the alley Charlie and I occupy and, a moment later, gone.

I'm shaking so hard that I squeeze my eyes shut, trying to still myself. My palms are slick with sweat.

When I breathe out, leaning fully against Charlie, I see Violet and Edgar crouched beside the wall across from us. Were they there all along? I was so frightened, so *consumed* by fear and curiosity all at once, that I hadn't noticed them, hadn't, honestly, given them a thought.

Violet trembles worse than me, drawing in short breaths, nearly doubled over at her middle. Edgar, frowning, has his arm wrapped about her shoulders, but after a moment, she shrugs him off, leaning alone against the wall, head back, her face as pale as milk.

"What are they going to *do* with her...*to* her?" Violet whispers, near hysterics, but no one ventures an answer to her question.

After a tense moment, I clear my throat. "Where was the third?" I look to Charlie, who watches me, eyes narrowed. She hasn't moved away from me yet, though the Sixers have gone, and her warmth against me, around me, is a comfort I'm loathe to lose. I go on, holding her gaze: "And why are they called *Sixers* if there are only three..." I stop, breathe out. "There *are* three, aren't they?"

"How did you know that?" She rests her hand upon my shoulder, her face still, revealing nothing.

"I don't know how I know. Is it true?"

"It's true."

Something seizes within me. I *knew* there were three, knew it like I know how to walk, how to breathe. But *why*? *How*? My skin crawls. "I just…know," I tell her, voice small. "I don't know how…" I trail off, watching her as she turns back and glances to Edgar, one eyebrow raised.

"Why did you hide me?" I ask, pushing off from the wall. She leans back, looks away, straightening her coat collar.

"Because…" she falters, looking down at the dirty snow beneath our feet, but Violet steps forward, mouth drawn in a quivering line.

"Because they're *bad*," she breathes out. "I *told* you."

She did tell me, and then Charlie told her not to make statements without proof. This time, though, Charlie says nothing. I gaze down at her head of soft blonde hair.

Beyond the alley, in the Wanting Market, the people are, once again, moving about, speaking to one another, but in softer, hushed tones, and pausing to glance over their shoulders in the direction the Sixers disappeared. Maybe they're afraid they'll return.

I'm afraid they'll return.

No.

I'm just afraid.

Abigail is on the porch of Mad House, waiting for us as the shadows lengthen, as the sky begins to bleed red. She sits on a rickety wooden chair, front two legs off the ground with her boots propped up against the railing. As we climb the steps, she *thumps* the chair down, her thin mouth twisted into a scowl.

"Edgar, you get off this porch, and you get off it this instant." With surprising quickness, she rises to her feet, hobbles over to Edgar and starts jabbing him in the chest with a bony knuckle. "Get *off* the porch, Edgar!"

"Now, Abigail…" he begins, tipping his hat and smiling beneath his mustache.

"Don't *now, Abigail* me! Charlie, get him off the porch." She turns on her heel, moving to stand before the front door, arms crossed, eyes squinting in an aggressive glare.

"All right. I guess we've got to part ways," Charlie says, her voice placating, even as she grins at Edgar with an apologetic gleam in her eyes. "Well, thanks for walking us back."

Edgar lifts off his top hat, bowing first to Abigail, then to Charlie, Violet and me in turn, before giving us all a rogueish grin and leaping over the railing, to the ground below. "Farewell, lovelies!"

I stare in astonishment as he races down the street at breakneck speed, finally hurling himself out of sight, around a corner.

"Fetcher," says Charlie to me, by way of explanation, her thumbs hooked into her coat belt loops. "We've gotta be fast."

I nod, lifting my gaze to the darkening sky.

"Charlie, you know what I've told you about bringing Edgar by our place," Abigail admonishes as she steps back from the door, allowing us to pass through it. She follows close behind, brandishing a skinny finger at Charlie's back. "'Charlie,' I tells ya, over and over, 'don't be bringing that no-good, Nox-taking bastard back into this house,' and what do you do? That no-good, Nox-taking bastard ends up back at Mad House time and time again!"

"And yet he never gets through the front door," says Charlie soothingly, sliding her coat off her shoulders and hanging it on an empty peg. "How's Florence today?"

"Don't you go changing the subject with me, missy!" Abigail huffs, drawing the topmost shawl closer around her shoulders. Her mouth is set in a firm grimace. "And Florence is *fine*, been watched all day by Ella."

"Good," sighs Charlie, glancing up the staircase. "I'm just going to go say hello to her..." She pauses, hand on the banister, foot on the first step. Her eyes seek mine and soften. I feel myself soften, too, the tension of the day loosening within me.

"We named the new one today," Charlie says, smiling gently. "Her name is Lottie."

Abigail glances at me, sniffing. "Respectable. Good. I like it."

"I'm glad." Charlie's mouth twitches up at the corners. "Vi, Lottie...you want to come see Florence with me? You don't have to," she adds quickly, looking to me, then ducking her head. "I know she gave you a fright yesterday. But I really want to show you...she's not like that."

I consider for a long moment, remembering the silver gleam of the shears so near to my face. But I trust Charlie.

She's watching me, waiting, and I nod once, only a small nod, and we ascend the stairs together, with Violet behind us, leaving Abigail to *harrumph* in the entryway before she scuttles back down the hallway, skirts swishing, grumbling beneath her breath.

"Every time she sees Edgar, same reaction." Charlie shakes her head. "He's such a good sport about it. He's the Fetcher for Black House, another Safe House," she tells me, glancing sidelong, "and Black House and Mad House have a habit of…not liking each other very much."

"That's an understatement," Violet mutters, rolling her eyes as we reach the landing.

"But why?" I ask.

"Well," says Charlie, hand on the door to Florence's room. "Like I said, we don't take Nox here. And Black House lives for Nox." She pauses, lowering her voice, smile slipping off her lips. "We used to live in Black House—Florence, Vi and me. Before Florence got so addicted. It wasn't good for her. It hurt her. Changed her." She turns away, opens the door.

Florence sits in the middle of the floor, facing away from us, as if she's watching the window. She looks so small in the dregs of daylight seeping through the curtains, past the broken windowpanes. Her almost-bald head nods back and forth as she rocks and rocks, her thin arms clasped around her knees.

A woman, sitting nervously on the edge of the bed, stands bolt upright when we enter, twisting her fingers together nervously.

"Thanks, Ella," says Charlie, nodding to her, and the woman bows her head, with a furtive glance at me, before crossing in front of us and exiting through the doorway.

Charlie looks after her, sighs, and then steps forward.

"Hi, Florence," she whispers, squatting down beside the girl. "Florence, it's Charlie…" Her voice is warm, inviting, and Florence stops rocking, turning her face slowly to take Charlie in.

I gaze down at the two of them from a safe distance, positioned near the door, standing beside Violet.

Florence has been crying, or maybe has been angry, because her face is flushed a blotchy crimson. She gulps down air like an animal drinking water, and then she flings her arms around Charlie's shoulders.

"She wouldn't let me out, Charlie. I wanted to go outside so bad," she whispers into Charlie's ear, but it's a stage whisper, loud enough for us to hear it. "Why wouldn't she let me go outside?"

"It's all right, baby girl," says Charlie quietly, wrapping her arms around Florence's frail shoulders, helping her up to her feet. "We'll go outside tomorrow. It's not good to go outside without me, because sometimes bad things happen…"

Violet sniffs, exchanging a pained glance with me before she sits down on the edge of the bed, head sagging.

"Now, Florence, honey," says Charlie, helping her turn around so that she can see me. But she doesn't look at me, looks everywhere *but* at me. Finally, her darting gaze stills upon the floor, and her hands begin to pick at one of the holes in her skirt, nervous fingers shaking as she teases at the ends of the threads, twirling them around and around and around her tiny fingers until they turn pink.

"Florence," Charlie says, "this is Lottie. She's a new Sleeper here. I'd love for you to meet her, say hello."

Florence glances up at me, but only for a heartbeat, moving her gaze down again, quickly, to the floor. There was no rage, no feral *wanting*, when she looked at me, but I sag a little with relief when her eyes are no longer pointed in my direction. Her glassy eyes, dull eyes, doll's eyes.

I realize, watching her, that she's younger than the rest of us, a child, really. Florence is a slight little girl with almost no hair, so flimsy, so breakable that if she takes one misstep, I'm afraid she might shatter.

Charlie holds her as if the cage of her arms can protect her from every wrong in this place, and I think that if it were entirely up to Charlie's strength and resolve alone, she could. She gazes down at Florence's red face with a mixture of deep pain and relief.

Florence is still here, after all. And she's not trying to cut my hair off of my head.

"She just has these…these *episodes,*" Charlie murmurs distractedly, picking Florence up as if she truly were a doll. She carries the girl to the little bed, sets her down upon it, and draws the covers up to her chin, then gazes upon her with misty eyes.

"One day," Charlie whispers, "she's like this—docile. Listless. And the next, she's desperate. The way she was when she first saw you."

Charlie watches me with a downturn to her mouth. Then she looks away, sighing. "I want to take her outside, but I don't know if that'll be the day that she runs after people with scissors, trying to snip off their hair." She rubs her fingers over her face, setting her hands on her hips, staring down at Florence, who blinks slowly before closing her eyes. Her features smooth, and her breathing grows slow, even—in and out, in and out.

"I do the best I can by her," says Charlie. "But I don't think it's ever enough."

Violet rises from the mattress and puts a hand on Charlie's arm, shaking her head emphatically. "You know that's not true. We came here because of her. We promised her we'd take care of her—"

"That was before she got like this, back when she was still Florence. She doesn't feel like Florence anymore." Charlie's eyes are bright, and she blinks a few times, coughs a little, leaning away from the bed, against the wall. "Every day, bit by bit, what was

*Florence* slips away. That's how it always happens here." Her eyes find mine. "They just slip away, become less and less like themselves until there's nothing left of them at all. And then they just…disappear."

I swallow.

Charlie rubs at her face again, stares up toward the ceiling. "Anyway… Lottie, I'm sorry. I just… I just hate this."

I stare at her, wide-eyed, heart panging for her. I clear my throat, take a step forward. "*I'm* sorry," I whisper to her, and she glances at me in surprise. "It must be very hard…to see your friend…" I sigh, watching Florence, lying so still upon the bed. Her eyes are open now, but her gaze is faraway, unseeing. I look to Charlie. "It seems like you care for her a great deal."

"A great deal," Charlie repeats, staring at the sad little girl in the bed.

Florence looks barely there, as if she might sink into the dirty mattress, into the floor.

As if she might just disappear.

Everyone in the room is quiet, still, when we three enter. Abigail sits propped up on the edge of a couch, beady eyes staring toward the cold fireplace, flickering not with fire but with a collection of Wisp jars, glowing golden. The old woman breaks her gaze when Charlie walks up to her, folds her arms, and kneels down beside her.

"It's nearly twelve. I'm going Fetching," she says, voice low, running a hand through her pale hair.

Abigail glances down at Charlie, then raises her eyes to observe Violet and me standing just behind her.

"You should take someone with you tonight," says Abigail, cocking her head in one quick turn. She watches the fireplace again, the orbs bobbing against the glass of the jars. Her voice is flat, devoid of spirit, as she says, "I got a bad feeling in my bones."

"Abigail." Charlie spreads her hands, sighing. "I'm *hampered* by another person, not helped, and you know that. We've been through this a thousand times. I'm the fastest. That's why I'm the Fetcher."

"Violet, go with Charlie," says Abigail, ignoring Charlie's words, never removing her eyes from the jars.

Violet shrinks back from the staring Sleepers, from Abigail, shaking her head so that it blurs. "I can't, I can't, I can't," she says, breathing in and out so quickly, her chest rises and falls in a too-fast rhythm. "They'll catch me. They'll—"

"All right, all right, *hush*," groans Abigail, rolling her eyes. "So help me, those new Sleepers out there are done for if Charlie's ever Snatched. Not a one of you brave enough to go out and—"

"I'll go."

They turn and look at me, all of them, hollow eyes wide, and it's then that I realize that the voice was mine, those two words—mine.

My heart is beating so quickly, I feel it carving a tunnel beneath my ribs, but I don't back down, don't *want* to take back what I said. I nod, clench my hands. "I'll go," I repeat, eyes locking first with Abigail's, who scans me up and down, and then with Charlie's, who watches me, her brown gaze glittering in the half-dark. I can't tell what she's thinking, whether she wants me or not.

"Well, well," Abigail murmurs. "Why not? We've all got to start somewhere. And it'll put hair on your chest," she smirks, pushing off from the couch and stretching overhead, yawning so hugely that I can see how many teeth are missing in her mouth.

Abigail shuffles past the still-staring, wordless people, hooking a bony arm through mine and pulling me out of the room and down the hall. "Now, Charlie," she says over her shoulder, as Charlie rises to follow us out, "you know the drill. If anything happens, *you* come back first. Leave the others. Leave *this* one behind if you must. What's your name again, girl?"

"Lottie." I swallow, tasting the name, my half of the name Charlie and I share.

I glance over my shoulder at Charlie, whose jaw is set, her mouth a thin line as she takes in a few deep breaths.

We reach the front door, shut tight. Outside… Outside, I know, is the blackness, the night…

And the Snatchers.

The terror of last night rears up, and I cower reflexively. What am I doing? Why did I offer to do this? I barely survived the race through the woods, and now I'm *willingly* going back out into that blackness, with its shrieking and its claws?

But if I'm honest, beneath the fear, there's a thrill racing through me, just under my skin, untouchable, electric.

We were *fast* last night. Together, Charlie and I—we were fast. Together we escaped the groping, screeching creatures. We could do it again, couldn't we? I glance at Charlie, but she's not looking at me. She's gazing back down the hall at Violet, who follows about ten steps behind us, hugging herself.

"Vi, watch Florence, all right?" Charlie murmurs, taking her coat from the peg. Violet nods twice and then climbs the stairs, mounting them two at a time.

With a sigh, Charlie fingers the other coats on the wall until she settles on a long black one. She takes it down, offers it to me, and that's when she finally looks into my eyes. Her gaze is hesitant, but also hopeful. It warms me, and I take the coat from her, shrugging into it. It fits, won't impede my running, I don't think.

"Good luck!" cackles Abigail, patting me roughly on the back. Charlie puts her hand on the doorknob, turns back to me again.

"You don't have to do this, you know," she whispers, brown eyes sparking, and I nod, bite my lip, breathe in and out, curling my hands into fists.

"I know," I say. "But I choose to."

Charlie walks through the door.

# Chapter Three: Faster

The air is cold as ice water, drowning and sucking at our breath as we pause on the porch, as Charlie jams her hands into her pockets, scanning the dark street spread before Mad House. My eyes skim over the wall that crouches around Abeo City, the wall Charlie and I moved through when we evaded the Snatchers last night.

"The Sleepers always appear at crossroads at midnight," Charlie tells me, her shoulder brushing against mine. "First one's over there, to the left." She juts her chin toward the place where two roads join, and draws a sawed rope from her pocket. She ties the rope around her waist tightly, bringing her buttonless coat closed. "We wait here until I think I see something at the corner, and even if I don't think I see something, we'll run out there and see what we can find."

I nod, my throat too tight to speak.

Charlie watches me in the darkness and exhales through her nose. "We run all the way there, and we grab any Sleepers that appear, and whether they appear or not, we run all the way back. You don't stop running. Okay?" She leans nearer to me, and I swallow, nod.

She steps forward, putting her fingers upon my arm. "You don't have to come, Lottie. Abigail always tries to bully someone into..." She rakes a hand through her hair. "I don't know why you volunteered to come."

"To help you," I breathe, trying to keep my teeth from chattering—from the cold or from fear, I can't tell. "You've been kind to me, and…" I trail off, mouth dry, bowing my head. Despite the dark, the fear, the promise of *Snatchers*, my face flushes, warmed by Charlie's nearness. Whenever I'm near her, even now, things feel less bleak. Less dangerous. And, perhaps, a little more lovely.

I blush, glancing past her, looking over the railing and toward the street.

"Well," she says, her voice husky and low, "what I said back there, about hampering… I didn't mean it. You won't hamper me. I know that."

She's watching me with shining eyes, and when they lock with my own eyes, my heart skips a beat.

She seems…*different* when she looks at me. Am I imagining it? Do I just *want* her to look at me differently than she looks at everyone else?

Maybe I do.

I know I do.

I swallow, turning that awareness over and over in my heart.

I'm daring monsters for her, aren't I? But if I fall, if I get Snatched, if the monsters fly me away to… Wherever. Just away. Then what? Then I'll never see Charlie again.

I wring my palms, breathing in and out, putting forth my best impression of calmness, confidence. Really, I'm just trying to avoid hyperventilating.

"Are you ready?" Charlie asks, crossing to the end of the porch, her toes edging out over the first step. "We've got to be *fast*, okay, Lottie?"

"Yeah." My voice is a gravelly whisper, dry and breaking apart. I steel myself, moving to stand beside Charlie on the edge of the night.

After one heartbeat, two, she reaches across the space between us, takes my hand in hers. It's a balm, her sudden warmth against my cold fingers, how she curls and threads her own fingers, smoothly, through mine.

"Charlie…" I gasp out, but she's already off the porch, already down the steps, and my hand is cold again because she's gone. I gulp down air, and I leap off the porch, hitting the ground running, following her.

I feel everything: my beating heart because she took my hand; my wonder if it meant what I hoped it might mean; and the slow creeping fear that seems to run beneath the ground like lightning, beneath my boots, following me no matter where I step. I run into the night, behind Charlie, catching up to Charlie, the two of us bolting quicksilver-fast down the street, avoiding the ruts and rubble as if we've done this a thousand times together, as if our feet know the steps by heart.

Suddenly, my feeling is replaced by reflex: breathing in and out, the movement of my arms at my sides, my boots thumping against the ground. All I am is quickness, is motion, as Charlie and I draw nearer to the crossroads.

I hear a scream behind us, a sound that pierces the night. The downdraft of wind—from wings, black wings wide enough to smother Charlie and me both in one bone-and-feather embrace—causes me to falter, to nearly trip, but I catch myself, even though the sky is tearing apart, even though *monsters* fall from above in a rain of black, screaming hail.

"C'mon," says Charlie, putting on a burst of speed, and I surge forward alongside her, transforming my fear into stumbling action.

We reach the crossroads, our feet skidding over the broken stone of the street, because there, in the center of the junction, lays a girl. She's still upon the rubble, unnaturally still, thin arms straight against her sides, eyes closed as if she's sleeping.

I stare at her, fingers trembling at my mouth, thinking, *This is how Sleepers arrive. This is how the Fetchers find them. Not in the woods, beside the stream... Not bleeding beneath an angry red sky.*

Moving fast, Charlie falls to her knees beside the girl, begins to shake her shoulders in her gentle, yet urgent, way.

Swallowing, knees shaking, I dare a glance behind us. There is a darker shadow against the sky, bearing down, and for a moment, I watch it in wonder: the wings widespread and brilliant against the duller black sky. But it's the white bones, white as warm breath against ice, that shatter the brittle lull in my terror.

Claws extend toward us, sharp beak open as the Snatcher dives down.

Charlie picks up the girl—who won't move, won't open her eyes—with a grunt, and hisses at me, "*Run.*" We turn, the two of us, racing back to Mad House. I gulp down air, cough as the coolness of it fills my throat. Despite the extra weight of the girl in her arms, Charlie's right beside me, her hip grazing mine as we run.

We're running toward the Snatcher.

There's this tiny slice of time, a slowed-down moment, where I'm *certain* it's going to grab us, sink down and rake its claws against our backs, enfold us in its wings. It's going to Snatch us. The Snatcher seems certain of this conclusion, too, because it folds its wings behind its bony body, diving toward us fast, too fast, like a stone flung from the sky.

But then Charlie and I, together, in the same heartbeat, arch ahead, step faster, arrows aiming for the same target, my breath burning through me like fire, and the Snatcher dives and misses us, and we're racing through the night as the monster hits the ground with a crunch and a scream, rolling end over end before hunching its shoulders and righting itself. Over my shoulder, my panting loud in my ears, I see the Snatcher crouched upon the ground, a heap of feathers and bones. It watches us for only a moment before it pushes off, heaves its body up into the air, unhinging its jaw and crying out.

It's *angry*.

"C'mon, c'mon," huffs Charlie, and we run together, so close to Mad House I can make out the folds in the curtains past the broken windows. But I hear another cry, then, and I skid, startled, because the girl's woken up in Charlie's arms, and she's screaming, yelling, beating at Charlie's chest, kicking her legs up and down, begging to be let go, even as she stares at the beast above, bearing down on us again.

"No, no, please—we have to get inside, we'll be safe inside, it can't get to us inside," says Charlie, the words spilling out of her mouth in a thin, trembling string. She's panicked; she's not watching her feet, and there's a rut—

"Charlie!"

Charlie and the girl go down, tumbling until they settle, groaning. Without a thought—there's no *time* for thinking—I drop to my knees beside Charlie, help her up, her face white, pained, eyes wide as she stares past me, at the Snatcher flying toward us.

"Please..." Charlie grits her teeth, standing, limping, offering a hand to the girl who crawls backwards, whose eyes focus on nothing but the Snatcher angling down, down, almost near enough to pet, to kiss...

It lunges at the girl, sweeping past us, one of its wings knocking against Charlie's head and my shoulder, sending us both in a twisted heap to the ground. We scramble to rise, but we're not fast enough, because then it spreads its great wings and pumps upward as the girl, Snatcher claws wrapped around her belly, reaches out her hands to us now, screaming the scream of a horror beyond description. I feel dizzy from the might of her terror; it becomes my terror, too. But Charlie surges upward, leaps into the air, almost seems to, for a moment, fly. And when she extends her arm, her hand, the girl's fingertips touch hers—a graze of skin…and then a grappling of thin air.

Charlie falls down to earth, because she is wingless, after all, and the Snatcher rises with the girl into the dark.

They rise and rise. I watch them draw away from us until the girl's scream is cut off, as if a blade sliced the sound from her throat.

The Snatcher and the girl are gone.

More wingbeats, more white-and-black monsters with widespread wings, claws bared, beaks unhinged as they scream toward us, veering down. Charlie grabs my hand, yanking me from the ground, dragging me along until my feet find their balance, catch up, and we run the last few steps up to the porch, tumbling together straight through the door.

Charlie leans against the wall, still clutching my hand, her knuckles white, her face whiter as she slumps down, down, thunking against the floor. I kneel beside her, and she presses her other hand to her eyes, breathing in and out too quickly, panting.

Abigail comes down the corridor with a jar of Wisps, carrying it in front of her like something sacred. She takes a single look at us, sniffing, nose up.

"I take it that things went *well*," she says dryly. Charlie stares up at her, her mouth twisting, but Abigail raises a finger. "At least this new one didn't get Snatched. Count your blessings, girl."

Charlie doesn't speak. She closes her eyes, presses her forehead to her drawn-up knees, breathes out.

She still has not let go of my hand.

Another day in Abeo City. Another day in Twixt. I watch the light edge my curtains, and I leave the room this morning of my own accord.

I walk down the stairs, hand trailing lightly along the banister, letting my feet sink into the deep carpet.

Below, in what I'm beginning to think of as the Great Room, several of the Sleepers have gathered. One of the older gentlemen glances up, twitching his mustache into a semblance of a smile when he sees me. "New girl!" he calls, crooking his cane in my direction. "Good morning! Charlie and Violet went outside to catch some more Wisps. These ones have been looking a mite poorly," he says, tapping one of the glass jars with his cane. "They'll be out front. Told me to let you know."

"Thank you." I return the smile, and traveling the hallway to the front door, I concentrate a little, though I couldn't really say what it is I'm concentrating *on*, only *concentrating*, and then my hand is through the wood, and so am I, standing on the porch. It feels natural to me, somehow, to pass through doors and walls as if they were made of air.

I inhale a deep, chilly breath.

From the street, I hear laughter.

"To the right! To the right! Oh, *Vi*..."

"You're the one who let it slip right out of the open jar!"

More laughter.

Charlie and Violet are scrabbling over the rubble pile down the street from Mad House. They both hold jars, pressing down on the lids with their flat palms, and inside the jars glow yellow orbs, bouncing against the glass. Wisps. There's one Wisp in Charlie's jar, two in Violet's.

I cross the street, standing at the foot of the pile, peering up.

"Don't move!" Charlie calls out, sliding down. She runs past me and dives a little, and then she holds up her jar triumphantly, lid replaced. Two Wisps now float within the glass container.

Above the broken stones and bricks and rusty metal and dust and dirt, the Wisps dance, glowing softly in the daylight, but glowing all the same. The worry lines that normally mar Violet's face are gone, replaced by smiling mouth and eyes. She looks so different when she smiles, as if all of her fears have gone. She's running now after a Wisp that zips and darts—unlike the rest of the orbs, turning lazy circles, light and slow.

"You wanna try?" Charlie asks, grinning, holding out her jar to me. I shake my head but tap the glass gently; the Wisps swarm to my side, bumping up against the jar, as if to get a good look at me.

"Another!" Violet shrieks, clutching her jar tightly. She slides down the pile, skidding stones, and screws on the jar's lid. "I think that's enough, Charlie. Do you think so?"

"We'll see what Abigail says." Charlie groans, casting her eyes skyward. "You know how she is. There's no pleasing her. Don't say *anything* about going to visit Edgar later on, because she'll ask us to go out and catch more Wisps, just to sabotage us."

“We’re visiting Edgar?” Violet's blue eyes shine, and Charlie glances at her, her mouth turned up at one corner.

“Thought you’d like that,” she says, raking her fingers through her hair, grinning at me knowingly.

Violet flicks her eyes to the ground, but she’s smiling, too, and her cheeks are pink.

“It’s just…the Need Shop,” she says, after a long moment, and Charlie sighs. The three of us walk back together toward Mad House, Charlie's arm brushing against mine.

“It’s all right, Vi. We don’t take Nox. That’s the only rule in Mad House. Abigail can’t—”

“Abigail can’t what?” Perched on the edge of the porch, Abigail peers down at us with narrowed eyes. “Are you planning an insurrection, Charlie, my girl?”

“It would be a dull day without one, wouldn’t it?” Charlie counters, brow raised. She places her jar of Wisps upon the porch step, and Violet does the same.

Abigail watches the two of them, blue-veined hand pressed over her mouth. It’s when she turns that I realize she’s positioned herself to hide the indulgent smile teasing her lips, even as she shakes her head and huffs out a longsuffering sigh.

“Watch Florence, all right?” Charlie says, as she ascends two steps, taking one of Abigail’s hands and squeezing it.

Dropping the stern façade, Abigail squeezes Charlie's hand back and, stooping over a little, winks. “Don’t you worry your pretty head. Florence will be fine. Now go have fun with the bastard.”

“That’s not even nice.” Charlie's tone is admonishing, but she’s grinning, too. Abigail shuffles back into the house, muttering to herself, like always, as we turn around to walk again down the street.

Though I’ve only been to the Wanting Market

and the Need Shop once, I remember the way this time. Walk down the one main street, make those two turns, and then there it is, crumbling before us, the center of Abeo City, with the Wanting Market and its piles of junk, its shuffling and trading Sleepers. And there, on the edge of it all, is the Need Shop.

"Edgar told me that Matilda wouldn't be in again today," says Charlie, glancing to Violet, "so we won't have to deal with her."

"Thank goodness." Violet shudders, and says in a loud voice, "She's as bad as the Sixers—"

Charlie presses a finger to her lips, shaking her head, turning to glance toward the Wanting Market. "Vi, you can't go on like that. No one can hear you talk like that. You don't want..." She swallows, words trailing away.

Violet seems to shrink into herself, nervously scanning the crowd, her Wisp-catching smile gone.

You don't want...

I think about the girl who was dragged away by the Sixers.

I think about the girl who was dragged away by the *Snatchers*.

I wring my hands together, breathe out.

It's an impossible situation. We're supposed to live, carry on with daily activities, and yet there's so much that's unknown, and so much that might go wildly wrong at any moment...

Charlie, noticing my mood, turns toward me, resting a hand against the small of my back.

"No dark thoughts," she whispers in my ear, her mouth a little upturned, a little hopeful. "It'll be a good day, Lottie."

I look up at her; my doubts melt as I gaze into her warm brown eyes. And then, surprising myself, I reach behind my back, take Charlie's hand. Her eyes widen, and her lips part, but then she ducks her head, smiling as the three of us travel the narrow lane between piles of garbage, aiming for the Need Shop.

Edgar's sitting outside on the front steps, arms folded, watching the people in the Wanting Market with his top hat tilted down over his eyes. Charlie toes his leg with her shoe, and he startles, blinking, gazing up at us.

"I thought you'd never get here," he says, grinning broadly, and then he's standing, taking off his hat, running a hand over his carefully styled hair and smoothing nonexistent wrinkles from his too-clean shirt. "Charlie, Lottie, lovely to see you." He nods at us, and then his eyes linger on Violet. "Sweet Violet, you're looking particularly *fetching* this morning."

She blushes, looks down at the ground, says nothing, and a long, silent moment passes by. Edgar deflates a little, clutching his hat, glancing away.

Someone snickers.

Ahead, down the narrow lane, four people stride toward us. Three teenage girls and a boy. The young woman at the front of the group wears a blue dress, as immaculate as Edgar's shirt: no holes, no loose threads. It's made of clean, shiny cloth that bells around her hips, the lace-edged skirt grazing against her calves. Her hair isn't tangled, either, but curled into brown ringlets that sweep over her shoulders as she turns her head.

I feel gray and dingy in comparison.

But the pretty picture is marred by the ugly sneer on the girl's face, directed, very obviously, at Charlie.

"Edgar, you mustn't be seen with..." Her mouth curls, as if in disgust. "*People* from Mad House." Stepping forward, she crooks one long-nailed finger toward him. "There might be *talk*."

"As ever, Isabel," Edgar says, curving into a stiff bow, "I couldn't give a shit less."

Charlie laughs and rolls her eyes.

"Careful, Edgar." Isabel's mouth downturns into a pout, and she folds her arms in front of her, raises her voice: "When *I* am in charge of Black House, I won't *allow* you to consort with riffraff from Mad House—"

"You and what flouncy army?" Edgar regards her coolly, one brow raised. "Careful, Isabel. You're making an unfortunate impression." He gestures toward me. "We wouldn't want our newest Sleeper here to get the wrong idea about you."

She laughs as her gaze rakes over me, lips drawn above her teeth, exposing their sharp tips. "She *looks* like she belongs in Mad House."

I narrow my eyes, and beside me, Charlie says nothing, but she stiffens, and her hands ball into loose fists.

"Charlie," Isabel says, stepping forward like a dancer, all grace, her feet clad in black slippers with white bows. "*Charlie*," she whispers, drawing out the word, hooking her arm through Charlie's as if they're friends, familiar. "Let's declare a truce. Come by tonight, Charlie. Come to our Memming party. I'm giving you a special invitation. You know how Edgar would love to see you there, and I would, too, and..." She squints at me, her mouth drawn tight. "You can bring your drab little friend, if you'd like—"

Charlie shrugs out of her grasp. "Isabel..." There's warning in her voice, a sharp tone I've never heard Charlie use before.

Isabel glowers at me, stepping nearer. "Has she even Memmed yet?" she snorts, looking me over again, head to toe.

My own hands are curling into fists as she tosses her glossy curls over her shoulder. "Why don't you give her a choice, instead of shoving your *mad* shit down her throat?" Her eyes flash at Charlie. "Who knows? She might choose Black House over Mad House. Who *wouldn't*?"

With a wave of her hand, she turns on her heel, the others—spitting at Charlie's feet—following close behind her, like shadows.

"Open invitation!" Isabel calls, arcing her arm over her head, and then she's moving toward the Wanting Market, the blue of her dress lost in the grime-colored crowd.

Edgar steps behind Charlie and begins to rub her shoulders, shaking his head gently, his eyes unfocused, staring toward the ground. After a moment, Charlie blinks, softens, though her fists are still clenched.

"That—" He shrugs. "Forget that. She enjoys irritating you. She likes to get under your skin." Edgar, leaning close to Charlie's ear, lowers his voice. "You've got to ignore her. Don't give her what she wants—"

"But she's right, Edgar, and you know it." Charlie moves away from him and seeks out my gaze, exhaling a heavy sigh. "Lottie *should* get the choice. Didn't we all? If she wants to stay in Mad House, she needs to understand why we do what we do. Why we don't take Nox."

"But why Black House? There are Memming parties at all of the Safe Houses." Edgar sighs. "Don't misunderstand—I'd love to have you come tonight, but *you* wouldn't love another run-in with Isabel."

"She doesn't bother me," Charlie whispers, voice hoarse. A lie. She turns to me. "I want to give you choices, Lottie. It's only fair. Do you think that you want to try to Mem?"

*Mem.* The word births a shiver, a delight, a fear. "I don't know," I tell her honestly. "I think I'd like to try. But after all you've said…I don't know."

"*I* don't want to go," Violet whispers, then, her eyes dark with fear. "Charlie, she's probably going to do something terrible, like last time. You know you're not her favorite person anymore, and what if…" Charlie looks at her with hooded eyes, and Violet trails off, swallowing, fidgeting with the edge of her hoodie.

There's such sadness in Charlie's gaze that my breath catches in my throat.

"What happened?" I ask, placing my fingers on Charlie's wrist. She stares at my hand for a moment, biting her lip.

Then she jams her own hands into her pockets, leans against the wall of the Need Shop. "Isabel and I were together," she begins, her tone begrudging. "For a little while. When I was the Fetcher—with Edgar—for Black House."

Edgar doesn't glance up at this, his gaze pointed down the lane, toward the Wanting Market.

"She was only with me because I was the best Fetcher." Charlie shakes her head. "You heard her. She aims to own Black House when Miss Black Fades or is Snatched. So she was only with me because she thought it might—I don't know—raise her status, because I was the best, and don't the best always own the houses? When I began helping Florence…" She breathes out. "Isabel got angry. She wanted me to forget about Florence, said she was a lost cause."

When Charlie looks at me, her eyes are shining. "She never really cared about me. It was very shallow, all of it." She bites her lip, and Violet comes to her side, hugs Charlie's arm and rests her head on Charlie's shoulder.

"You loved her," says Edgar then, plainly, quietly. "And she ripped up your heart into neat little shreds, tidy monster that she is. And she can't seem to stop picking at the scabs she left behind." He casts a mournful glance at me. "Isabel is a dedicated asshole, and has always been, and shall continue to be, an asshole."

"She wasn't always," says Charlie, voice soft. "Things happen to us here in Twixt. This place changes us. You know that, Edgar."

He raises one brow and slowly shakes his head. "You've always been more forgiving than me."

"I'm sorry," I breathe, because I'm desperate to ease Charlie's grief but feel helpless, unequipped. All I have are words, and they're not enough.

Charlie shakes her head, rubs under her nose, sniffing. "It's long past," she tells me, straightening. She laughs a little, though it's a weak sound, halfhearted, and she glances to the sky. "Soon this daylight will be past, too. We've got to get inside. We should probably start going—"

"Going where?" asks Edgar, then, watching her closely. "Mad House? Or..." He quirks a brow. "Black House?"

"Once we *get* where we're going, we'll have to stay there for the night. Because of the Snatchers," Violet explains to me, crossing her arms, shivering. "Charlie, I think—"

"Let's leave this one up to Lottie," Charlie says, casting me a sidelong glance. "Abigail promised to watch over Florence, so we don't *have* to go back." Her eyes search mine, and I feel my cheeks warm, even though I'm cold and shivering. "Do you want to go to the Memming party, Lottie? Do you want to try Nox?"

That word—*Nox*—so short and sharp, *does* something to me, licks up my spine, sets my whole body trembling. I don't know what to compare taking Nox to; I've never tried it. I know there are consequences, but I don't know what they are, exactly. I know so little, really, hardly anything at all.

But...

What if I truly could have a *memory*? What if Nox could help me make sense of who I am, where I am? I'm so hungry for *knowing* in that moment that it's an ache in my belly. I feel starved for it.

I examine Charlie's face, but her expression betrays nothing. She wants me to try Nox, doesn't she? Does she? A war wages within me, and I surrender, say the words that come naturally, unthinking, to my tongue: "Yes. I'd like to try it."

It.

Nox.

"You're sure," says Charlie, not a question, and I'm nodding. Edgar takes off his top hat, runs his hands through his hair, mussing it. And Violet carefully avoids my gaze.

"Then let's go," says Edgar, words soft.

"I'll go with you," Violet pipes up, her voice too high, her brows arched with surprise. "I don't..." She clasps her hands before her. "I don't want to be alone in Mad House."

She wouldn't be alone, and I can see that Charlie is going to say something, make that point, but she stops herself, nods firmly, and pats Violet's arm. "It'll be all right, Vi. One night. And Edgar will be there with us. And Lottie can decide for herself. It's the right thing, Vi. We can't make this decision for her."

Violet searches my eyes, looking lost and frightened. She's shaking a little.

"Come on," says Edgar, drawing the key to the Need Shop out of his pocket. "It's almost sunset."

A chill shivers over my skin.

With a click, Edgar locks the shop's door, and the four of us run down the alleyway as the light fades, seeping away.

Darkness oozes out of the sky, thick as blood, coating Abeo City slick with shadows. I watch this transformation from the open doorway, until Edgar shuts the door with finality, shrugging out of his coat and balancing his top hat on the wrought iron hook affixed to the wall.

"Welcome to Black House," he says, mouth sideways, gesturing toward the high-ceilinged hallway that seems to hold us within a cage of smooth marble pillars. He adjusts his collar, smoothes his hair. "You're sure about this, Lottie?"

"Yes," I whisper, breathless, feeling the certainty move through me. Violet is staring very hard at the floor, and Charlie is watching me but not really watching me—she's looking through me, hands lost in her pockets.

"We'll go Fetching together tonight, Charlie," says Edgar, moving forward. "It'll be like old times, won't it?"

She stares up at him, mouth twitching, before settling on a feeble half-grin.

"Sure," she whispers, coughing, clearing her throat. "Like old times."

The front hall of Black House is wider and cleaner than the one at Mad House: there is no dust upon the banister bordering the spiral staircase, and the front windows have unbroken glass, with heavy drapes drawn back. We walk over the gold carpeting toward a sprawling curve in the corridor, toward an archway and glimmering lights and eager voices.

*A ballroom*, I think, when we stand—Charlie, Violet, Edgar and me—beneath the arch. The space glows with warmth: the chandeliers dangling overhead are alive with Wisps, and there are stoppered jars of

Wisps lining the walls, set upon shelves carved with spirals.

Charlie takes my arm gently, walks beside me as we step into the room, beneath the sparkling light. Motionless beneath a chandelier, yellow stars dance over Charlie's face, and her eyes seem to change color: from brown to copper to shimmery gold. I gaze at her, smile at her, and, surprised, she blinks, smiles back.

"All right, Lottie?" she asks.

I nod, speechless, and move further across the floor.

The people—some standing, some seated—seem strange to me, and it takes me a moment to realize that it's because they are all dressed well, cleanly and neatly, like Edgar, like Isabel.

Isabel…who sits on an overstuffed chair by the fire, laughing behind her hand at something a slim, dark-haired boy just whispered into her ear.

I remove my eyes from her, feeling Charlie's comforting warmth at my side.

Unlike the many bald or nearly bald people I glimpsed wandering the Wanting Market, the people here tonight all have hair on their heads, though some have far less than others. Still, it isn't hacked or sawed off but evenly cut. Neat.

Everything here is neat.

And I dislike it, though I can't say why.

Violet and Edgar are talking quietly behind us, and I hear snatches of conversation from the rest of the room, but the only sound that begs my attention is Charlie's voice, speaking softly to me, only me: "I should've asked you yesterday if you wanted to Mem, if you wanted to try Nox. I should've given you the choice from the start. I just… Well, I'm sorry I didn't—"

"Just stay with me," I whisper back to her, squeezing her arm and smiling weakly. "Stay with me until it's over, the memory, the…Mem—please?"

"I'll stay." Her eyes gleam. "I'll be there, and after, too."

A group of Sleepers brushes past us rudely.

"Sorry," laughs a woman, who bumps particularly hard against my shoulder—intentionally—then glares back at me.

"Who—"

"They know we're from Mad House," Charlie groans, rolling her eyes. "The Sleepers from Black House tend to dislike the Sleepers from Mad House, like I told you. It's…stupid." She shrugs, clearing her throat. "They think they're better than us. But we think we're better than them—or some of us do. So we're both to blame."

The woman, wearing a long black dress that looks tailored to her figure and freshly pressed, is leaning close to one of the men she strolled in with. "Do you think Alice will make it back from the Harming Tree?" she whispers, tapping her fingers nervously against her throat. "She should have been back by now. It's after dark, and if—"

"You know Brown House is closer to the forest than Black House. She likely made it there and back and is just waiting until morning to return here, because she's a *sensible* woman. Don't worry," he mutters, caressing the small of her back.

The woman twirls a lock of her hair over her shoulder and around her finger. They move away from us, and I lean toward Charlie, one eyebrow up, questioning. She shakes her head once, quickly.

"The Harming Tree is just a superstition. They say that if you tie a lock of someone's hair to the tree, nothing terrible can ever happen to them. They can't get Snatched, or Fade… But it's not true, only a myth. Still, people go out into the woods, try to find the tree and make it to the Red Line. And most of the time, they don't make it back."

*The Harming Tree.*

I tuck the thought away in my heart.

Isabel rises, then, grinning smugly, striding toward us across the cold marble floor. Charlie stands her ground, feet hip-width apart, chin jutting out toward the approaching girl, eyes slitted: a warning.

"So glad you came." Isabel's grin grows smugger the nearer she draws to Charlie. "Will you *all* be Memming tonight?"

"I'll show her how," says Charlie, voice gruff, stepping closer to me, putting her arm around my waist.

Isabel's eyes lock onto Charlie's hand upon my hip. She stares for a silent moment, breathes out.

"Suit yourself." She lifts her gaze, lingering on Charlie's face, and Charlie doesn't look away, doesn't even blink, until Isabel, at last, breaks her stare. She steps back and away from us as a piercing voice makes us all start.

"*Chaaaaarlie!*"

Charlie's arm falls back to her side as she spins around.

The woman who dances across the room to meet us has dark hair piled atop her head, her shoulders bared and her chest *almost* bared, the V of her black dress's neckline plunging halfway down her ribcage. Her smile is wide and natural, though her eyes are shrewd, missing nothing.

"Charlie, *darling*, I've *missed* you!" she squeals, throwing her gloved hands around Charlie's neck and squeezing so tightly that Charlie is forced to plant her face along the woman's shoulder.

"Miss Black," she says, grinning when the woman eases back, and Charlie takes another *whoosh* of breath, staggering a few steps away from the woman, toward me.

"Charlie, we miss you *so* much here. Not that Edgar isn't a *good* Fetcher, because of *course*, everyone knows he's a *good* Fetcher." She pulls a black lace fan from the crevice of her bosom and begins to fan herself, shaking her head and frowning. "But I've said to myself all this good long while that we need our *best* back, and if we had our *best* back, we'd save more new Sleepers than all the other Safe Houses combined, and you know what I always say, *more is more*, so—"

"So glad you think so highly of me, Miss Black," Edgar smirks, sidling up, single brow raised, with Violet standing stiffly by his side. Miss Black snaps her fan shut and smacks Edgar on the shoulder with it.

"Edgar, you *know* that I love you truly, but Charlie's the *best*, and Black House should *always* have the best." She turns to Charlie, placing her hands on her hips, eyes narrowed. "Promise me that you'll think about coming back, Charlie."

"You know I can't do that, Miss Black, but thank you for the invitation." Charlie is visibly uncomfortable, shifting from one foot to the other, leaning back when Miss Black darts forward, placing her arms around Charlie's neck again and forcing her into another tight squeeze.

"You'll always have a place here, darling," she promises, kissing Charlie's left cheek and then her right, before dancing off, snapping her fan open with a resounding *clack*. Charlie breathes out, rubbing at her shoulders stiffly, shaking her head as she watches Miss Black's retreating form.

"She always did love you best," says Edgar, teasing, until Isabel, pushed aside by Miss Black, regains her ground and advances on him. Edgar crosses his arms, sighs, cocks his head.

"You owe me three," says Isabel sharply. "*Give* them to me."

"Always a pleasure," mutters Edgar, drawing a small pouch from his waistcoat pocket and pulling out three quivering black feathers. They seem to dance in his hand, bending toward Isabel.

Nox.

Isabel snatches them from him, crumpling their fragile forms into her palm before she flounces back across the room, away from us—though she tosses a glare back over her shoulder.

Charlie sighs, leans toward Edgar. "Two for us, I guess." She tugs her little scissors up on their chain, nudging them out from beneath her shirt.

"Wait." My heart is pounding so fiercely, it's difficult to breathe. "You don't have to Mem, Charlie. Not for me. And I…I want to pay for mine. Let me pay with—"

"No," Charlie and Violet say at the same time.

But Edgar watches me, frowning. "Everything comes at a price, Charlie. You always say that. And it's true." His words are sympathetic, but fast. "Let her buy her own Nox."

Charlie grimaces, raking her hand through her hair, but she takes the chain with the shears over her head and coils it upon my palm. The metal is still warm from her skin, but the scissor blades are sharp.

"What should I—"

"A curl," Edgar says, eyes downcast, avoiding Charlie's gaze. "A piece of Nox will cost you one curl."

I pull my tangled mane over my left shoulder, staring down at it, trying to separate it with my fingers. I draw out a black coil, glancing to Edgar. He nods, and I swing Charlie's shears open with a gentle creak. One snip, and the bit of black falls into my hand. Something inside of me sinks, then shrivels, as I hold my hair out, palm up. Edgar plucks it and, in its place, drops a small black feather.

"Here," says Charlie, taking my other hand gently. She draws me toward the far edge of the room, sitting down with her back to the wall, below a collection of Wisps in faceted glass decanters. She pats the floor beside her, and I sit down, too, clumsy as I try to fold my legs, tucking my skirts and my boots beneath me.

I'm so nervous… I feel clunky and graceless on the floor of Black House's ballroom, next to Charlie, who looks edgy but comfortable enough leaning there, one knee up, the other drawn beneath her. Violet lowers herself then, crouching beside me. I raise my eyes, scanning for Edgar, and find him striding amongst the gathered people, making small talk and trading feather after feather, their dark translucence ethereal in the softly lit room, for snips of hair.

"Okay. All right." Charlie holds up the small scissors in one hand; they tremble a little. "I'm going to help you, okay?"

"Yeah," I whisper, leaning close. Charlie takes my hand in hers, long fingers curling around my wrist.

"It's going to hurt a little," she whispers, and opens her own hand, showing me a thin, arcing line of black that runs across her palm, curving to follow her hand's natural line. "That's how you can tell I've taken Nox. Once you take it, your lifeline blackens, like this."

I stare down at my own palm. No blackness traces it yet.

"I'm going to cut now, okay?" Charlie whispers, and I grit my teeth, close my eyes as she places the edge of one of the shears against the beginning of my lifeline. The cut is quick, expert, following the line. I swallow as I open my eyes, staring down at the wound, red bubbling up where the skin was gashed.

Charlie takes a feather and sets it against the line of red, black covering the red, absorbing it, until there's nothing left *but* blackness. I watched, transfixed, as the feather seems to melt, merging into my skin, and I close my eyes tightly, ready…

Everything is focused on the pain in my palm, the strange coolness of the feather as it shrinks, vanishing.

I wait.

After a long moment, Violet beside me breathes out, shifts, leans closer.

"Charlie…" she whispers.

I open my eyes.

Charlie's staring down at my palm curled into hers. My skin now bears a single black line, and the wound is gone, healed, with no blood remaining.

Charlie glances up into my eyes, her own wide, her brow furrowed.

Across the room, there's a gasp, and my head turns toward the source of the sound. I watch a girl collapse upon the floor, body shaking as her hands, black lined, lay open and flat beside her. Her back arches, mouth distended and eyes wide, unseeing. She holds that posture for a long time—too long—and then relaxes, lays perfectly still, chest rising and falling in short breaths, head tilted back and mouth curving, as if she's in ecstasies.

"*That's* Memming," murmurs Charlie, voice husky, fingers grazing the new black line upon my hand. "I don't—"

"What's the matter?" asks Edgar, moving through the crowd to stand beside us. "What was Lottie's memory like?" Behind him, more people drop to the floor, drop at random, all around the room, and my eyes dart from one to the next, my heart skipping, because that—none of that—happened to me when

Charlie put the feather on my hand. I feel a pang of disappointment, but deeper, colder, there's only fear.

"She didn't..." Charlie's staring up at Edgar, mouth open. She breathes out. "Edgar, it didn't *work*."

He blinks, then stares down at me, at the black line on my open palm. "That's impossible." Edgar kneels, removing a pair of shears from his pocket with practiced ease. The scissors, delicately engraved, dangle from a long, thin chain buttoned to his breast lapel.

"May I?" he asks, and I nod. He takes my other hand, the one not yet lined with black. His shears are wickedly sharp and slice along my palm so smoothly, I feel no pain for a heartbeat—but then I gasp, suffering the burning sting of the wound.

Edgar has drawn a single feather from his pouch, and he presses it now upon my sliced palm. The feather, as before, seems to melt into my skin, blackening the lifeline. And the wound seals, like a mouth closing, and then—

I should gasp and flail and fall backwards, arching, moaning...

Nothing.

I feel nothing, not even the pain of the cut inflicted by Edgar's shears.

I stare up at him, heart beating fast. "Is it supposed to happen now?" I ask him, wetting my lips. He watches me closely, carefully, then sits back on his heels, hands on his knees.

"That's...not possible." He turns from me, glancing to Charlie. "I've *never*—"

"Me, either. What does it mean?" she whispers.

Edgar flops down onto the floor, hands behind him, propping him up. "I, lovely ladies, have no idea."

Violet, Edgar and Charlie's heads all turn toward me, as one, watching me so closely that I blink at their wide eyes, staring right back. "What's happening? Why isn't it working?" I ask them, examining my hands, palms up, upon my legs. They both boast thin black lines now, curving away from each other in opposite directions.

"Nox always works, Lottie," Edgar states finally, heavily. "And it didn't work on you. You haven't got a memory, have you?"

"No." The anticlimax is bitter. I try to swallow it, but my throat is too dry. "Maybe... What if we—"

"We've tried *twice*. It's *never* not worked, and *twice* it hasn't worked." Edgar's mustache twitches sideways, bewildered. "I doubt it'll work if we try again."

The room feels too loud all of the sudden, and warm, stuffy. I watch the convulsing forms upon the floor—bodies arching at unnatural angles and falling still, arms spread out wide, as if they're waiting, as if they're prepared to embrace an old acquaintance.

Isabel sits on the edge of a plush chair, watching us above the writhing, shut-eyed mass. Two of her friends from earlier, a boy and a girl, stare toward us, too, standing on either side of the fire. I don't know why, but with their narrowed eyes, the way that they lean toward us, sighting us, singling us out, I feel...hunted.

Isabel stands, then, begins to weave between the prostrate forms of Memming Sleepers. Beside me, Charlie sits up straighter, and I rise, too, pressing my back against the wall.

"Well?" Isabel asks, hands on her hips. "How was it?" She's talking to me, I know, but she's staring at Charlie, can't seem to remove her eyes from Charlie.

I open my mouth, but Charlie gives me a warning glance, and I stare down at the floor, heart racing.

"Fine. Don't tell me," Isabel mutters, cutting the

words short. I look at her, then, at the sharp lines of her face, wondering why she bothered to ask at all.

Charlie glances at the tall grandfather clock beside the fireplace, at the hands moving too quickly over its face.

"Almost midnight," she says, frowning. "Isabel, do you have a room that Violet and Lottie can stay in while Edgar and I go out Fetching? I don't think that Memming is something Lottie's much interested in now. And Violet, as you know, doesn't enjoy it."

"Oh, but the party is *such* fun." The brown-haired girl's eyes flash as she folds her hands prettily in front of her. "If you insist, though, of *course.* Why, they can stay in *my* room!"

Edgar and Charlie exchange a glance. "Surely you have plenty of spare rooms for new Sleepers..." Charlie begins, but Isabel's smile stretches across her face, curving up wickedly. It's not a real smile. There's a bite behind it.

"I'll find them a room. Don't worry." She looks to the clock. "Now, you two hurry along. You don't want to be late. The new Sleepers count on you, Charlie."

The clock strikes midnight with a harsh gong that startles me.

I narrow my eyes. Wasn't it only just sunset?

*Time's kind of funny here.*

"Come," says Edgar, tugging on Charlie's sleeve. "We *are* late already, and the Snatchers might beat us to the crossroads."

Charlie bites her lip, eying Isabel.

"Miss Black won't let Isabel do anything foolish, Charlie." Edgar pins Isabel down with a piercing glare. "You know that, and so does she."

Isabel's jaw tightens, and Charlie's helpless gaze holds mine for a long moment after she rises. I nod at her, urging her to go, remembering the girl we lost to the Snatchers only last night.

With a sigh, Charlie turns and follows Edgar through the archway, down the hall. The distant creak of the front door opening and closing reverberates throughout the tall-ceilinged space.

They're gone.

I feel cold on the side that Charlie had filled beside me. I bring my knees up, wrapping my arms around them to stop my shivering, and half-listen to the strange, shuffling sound of the Sleepers Memming, Miss Black among them, eyes closed as her back arches upon the floor, curving a question out of her spine.

"So, Lottie, let me guess. Charlie couldn't be bothered to come up with a name for you, so she just gave you the leftovers of hers." Isabel's head is cocked to the side, and her fingers remain on her hips, splayed and pointy. "Is that how it happened, Violet?"

"Shut up," Violet whispers beside me, shoulders up, face white.

"You know, Lottie?" Isabel leans forward, bending at her beribboned waist. "I think Charlie *likes* you."

I stare up at her, eyes wide.

"But Charlie's a strong girl. She only *likes* strong girls." Straightening, looming, she taps her chin, as if a thought just occurred to her. "You know what I thought we could do to pass the time, a fun little game? Let's *prove* to Charlie how strong you are," Isabel says, shifting her weight forward. "We do it every night here at Black House. Do you remember, Violet? I'm sure you do."

I hadn't thought it possible, but Violet blanches, paling further, shrinking back as Isabel snatches at her arm, pinching her fingers around the fleece.

Violet winces. "No, I don't—"

"Hush, baby." Tightening her grasp, Isabel tugs, pulling Violet to her feet. "She used to live with us at Black House, you see," Isabel tells me. "And you *do* remember, Vi. You were very good at the game, as I recall."

"Leave her alone," I growl, standing up, balling my hands into fists.

Isabel ignores me, so I step forward, shoving hard against her shoulders. With an arched brow, she drops Violet's arm, staring at me with her perfect lips parted. Then her eyes begin to flash, wild.

"You *touched* me." Her teeth are bared, sharp as shears. "No one from *Mad* House is allowed to *touch* me," she snarls, then blinks, smoothing her features, as if she just remembered her manners. "I think you'll be adept at our little game, Lottie. *I'm* very good at it. That's what impressed Charlie…in the beginning." Her eyes darken, dangerous.

"Isabel, just leave us alone until Charlie gets back. We'll just stay here," says Violet, but Isabel ignores her, is still staring at me with bright, sparking eyes.

"What kind of game?" I ask, curiosity—and a streak of competitiveness I hadn't known I possessed—getting the better of me. Violet shakes her head emphatically, but Isabel's mouth curls up into a smile, and she folds her arms in one smooth gesture.

"It's called Faster," she whispers.

"No, no, *no*," Violet wails, tugging at my sleeve. "Lottie, *please…*"

I watch Isabel carefully, my anger cooling into a rigid, unbending stubbornness that frosts my limbs, making them stiff.

"Aren't you curious?" asks Isabel.

I shake my head, lying.

"Ah," she whispers, rolling her eyes. "You're

*afraid.*"

I am. It's the truth, and we both know it. But fear doesn't rest easy with me, the holding of it in my bones, in my stomach. I want to get rid of it, throw it away, push it off from me, and I feel so *strange*, staring down at the palms of my hands that now bear black lines from Nox. Nox, that should have given me memories... That didn't.

I stare down at my hands, then back up at Isabel. The blood rushes through me, and as Violet pinches my skin, I say, clearly, "Tell me about the game."

"No...no..." Violet whispers so softly as Isabel crooks her finger toward the boy and girl lounging by the fireplace, urging them forward.

"This is Anthony and Gerda," she tells us. "And these are Lottie and Violet," she tells them, her eyes slitted toward us, mouth smirking. "They've just agreed to play *Faster*!"

Anthony stares us up and down. He has wavy brown hair that's perfectly curled around his ears, is wearing jeans and a very tight black jacket. The girl, Gerda, has on a slinky red dress, her blonde hair swept in one soft wave down her back. She smiles at me, teeth flashing in the half-light.

"Violet, I'm sure, remembers the rules," says Isabel as we move out of the ballroom, into the hallway, and down another corridor. "Tell Lottie how to play, Violet."

My heart is pounding so loudly, it's hard to hear anything else.

"You just have to be faster," Violet breathes, her teeth chattering together as she pants beside me. "Isabel, when Charlie finds out that you've goaded us into this—"

"Charlie loved this game and would be *disgusted* by your sniveling." Isabel tosses a sneer over her shoulder. The hallway is narrow; her wide blue skirt brushes against the walls as she walks quickly along. "Did you forget that Charlie *invented* Faster?"

Violet falls silent, hugging herself and falling a little behind me.

My heart stills for a moment. *Charlie* invented this game? Then maybe it won't be as bad as Violet makes it out to be. I think of Charlie's warm brown eyes, her gentle manner and her soft voice. I think of the way she holds my hand, and places her hand against my back, always letting me know she's there, beside me. I think of how fast she was, how steady, when we ran from the Snatchers that first night…

*You just have to be faster*, Violet said.

Faster than what?

Surely not…

A sinking feeling drowns my ribs in a wave of fear as we come to the end of the long, low hall, dark save for the handful of Wisps knocking against glass bulbs affixed to the walls. Isabel's hand is on the doorknob as she turns back to look at us, her grin chilling in the yellow-hued light.

"We have a courtyard at Black House, Lottie," she whispers. "That's where we play." She nods toward the door beside her. "You run across the courtyard toward the other door, on the opposite side, and pass through it. You win when you get inside."

"And you lose if you don't," Anthony snickers.

"This is so stupid. This is *so stupid*," says Violet through clenched teeth. "We don't have to do this, Lottie!"

Gerda sneers at Violet, then reaches behind her own back, undoing the buttons of her dress. She steps out of the smooth red garment, leaving it upon the floor like a shed skin, and straightens the thin white slip clinging to her body.

"I'll go first," she says, smiling widely. Anthony opens the door, and Gerda steps forward. We all do, peering behind her out of the door into the blackness. After a moment, my eyes adjust: I can see, across the small courtyard, the door Isabel was talking about, rounded at the top and built of dark wood, and clearly visible, even in the night.

We all seem to glance up at the same time, heads tilting back on our necks, eyes wide. My heart, knocking against my bones, doubles its efforts, hammering hard enough to hurt.

There, perched upon the roof, silhouetted against the absoluteness of night sky, is a Snatcher. That's the only thing it *could* be, with that wicked curve of beak, its hooded wings hunched around its skeletal form, the white bones practically glowing in the darkness, like a contorted grin of moon.

Violet's breath puffs out in quivering wheezes. "Don't—" she begins, but Gerda yells out something unintelligible, something loud—perhaps a scream, or a battle cry—and then she darts out the door, bare feet thrusting her across the courtyard.

She's starkly visible in her white shift, like a moving beacon of light, and instantly, the sharp shadow detaches itself from the Black House roof, wings arching as it dives toward her.

Until now, I've only glimpsed the Snatchers in fits of panic, tearing over earth and pavement to escape them, but here and now, sheltered by the doorway, I watch this creature, several times the size of Gerda, drop like a stone toward her, impossibly fast, certain to reach her before she flings herself through the opposite door. Its individual claws are jagged and longer than my hands, curving toward Gerda, poised to grasp. The wings are massive, feathered night, absorbing the feeble light, but it's the skull that stills my roving eyes, that stops my heart's hammer.

There is nothingness where the Snatcher's eyes should be, and I wonder if it's to that sort of nothingness that they carry Sleepers, a place of nonexistence, of oblivion.

The beak unhinges like scissors snapping open, and the scream that arches out of the maw toward Gerda is a sick, sickle thing, caught upon the air, hanging there.

But Gerda is fast—faster than I thought—and, as the Snatcher lunges, she hurls herself through the closed door on the other side of the courtyard, gone.

She made it.

She won.

The Snatcher pulls up, pumping its wings so quickly that they churn up the thin dusting of snow, twigs, and dead leaves. It turns its head toward us, empty eyes seeking us out, as if it might try to pluck us out of the alcove, but before it changes course, Anthony slams the door shut.

There's another scream, a terrible scream that saws through the wood of the door, and then all we can hear is a rush of wings buffeting the sky, rising, moving away.

"Oh, it's angry tonight!" Isabel squeals, bouncing in place. Her eyes flash at me. "Who's next?"

"I'm not going to do it." Violet's voice is shaking, but the words themselves stand firm in the air. Isabel turns toward her, mouth curved as she advances on the smaller, trembling girl.

I take a single step and stand between them, my hands fisted at my sides.

"She doesn't have to take a turn. But I will," I say, staring Isabel down. A strange, cool peace descends upon me, then, draping over my shoulders like a cloak. I uncurl my fingers, look down at my palms. Nothing has changed; the two black lines are there as before.

But something's different… Clearer, sharper.

"I'll go next," says Anthony, shoving me aside, and then he's wrenching the door open, tearing across the courtyard without a moment's pause.

Violet grips my arm, breathing fast, and she drags me down to her ear as Anthony bellows something I can't quite make out, as the Snatcher takes off from its perch again, arcing toward him.

"Why are you doing this? You don't *have* to do this," Violet says, her voice rising up to a thin whine.

I shake my head once as Anthony reaches the opposite door. He has the nerve to yank it open, rather than just passing through. But he made it, escaped the Snatcher. He was fast enough.

Again, Isabel slams our door shut as the Snatcher turns, watching us with intention, and without eyes.

Violet's right.

I don't have to do this.

Fear races across my skin, morphing and changing as Isabel begins to undo the zipper of her own dress, letting the blue, luminous thing puff down from her shoulders, revealing the pale blue slip beneath. I tug at the edges of my dress's sleeves, my thin dress that clings to me, that I can still be fast in.

I'm afraid.

Of course I'm afraid.

But there's something else stirring within me, too.

Isabel wrenches the door open.

Outside, the Snatcher wheels over the courtyard, pumping its wings and screaming with poisonous sharpness into the Nox-black night.

"Are you coming?" asks Isabel, turning, eyes wide and goading in the darkness.

Violet lets my arm go, steps back, holding

herself, and I move forward, my legs stiff beneath me, everything pounding—my blood, my breath—as I stand beside Isabel in the open doorway.

The Snatcher is curving overhead now, its maw open, the sound firing from its throat a cross between anger and pain. I notice something as it circles, as I stare: the top part of its right wing is crooked, like the structure beneath it was broken once, and healed.

I swallow, still staring. Somehow the imperfection makes the monster seem more real.

"Ready?" Isabel whispers, and all that I am intensifies, pinpointing and shifting until I hear her shriek, "Go!"

And I go. We go.

The light disappears as the darkness swallows me, gulping me down into the pitch-black night, my feet stumbling over the earth and rubble beneath. The sky tears overhead as a punch of wind pummels me, the thunderous *whoosh* of gigantic wings turning toward me, so loud in the stillness, loud like my heartbeat, like my breathing, like my boots connecting with little stones.

I run, moving through the thick blackness, pushing it away, refusing it—the dark and the fear—and a great joy moves through me: I'm fast. I'm going to be through the door in two breaths. I'm fast, faster than Isabel, faster than Anthony was, or Gerda, and I'm evading the Snatcher, the stupid, slow Snatcher, that could never dream of catching me, if Snatchers ever dream.

And I trip.

And I fall, sprawling, my chin banging against the ground in a great explosion of color and searing pain as I tumble end over end until I land on my back, staring up at the absoluteness of black and the slash of white that moves through the darkness toward me.

I've lost.

Isabel's already passed through the door, has opened it from the other side, is peeking out at me.

It's going to get me. I recognize that distantly, as if from a place outside of myself. I can't move, pushed flat to the ground by the force of the wings. I hear, far away, Violet screaming: "Lottie! Lottie, get *up*!" But I can't get up, so I simply *stare* up and up and up at the Snatcher, at the holes in its skull, its eyeless gaze pinning me. I want to shut out its searing whiteness, its crushing blackness, but I *can't…* I can only watch, breathing in and out, as it spreads its wings and alights upon the tattered awning that arches above the door in the courtyard, causing Isabel to gasp and close the door further, so it's only open a crack, her large eye peering out.

I sit up, panting.

The Snatcher…*landed.*

It spreads its wings, stretching them overhead, shaking them out. Black feathers glisten in the halfhearted light filtering out from the hallway where Violet stands, gaping.

The Snatcher stares down at me, still, claws gripping the awning ribs.

It stays there, unmoving. It does nothing.

It doesn't come for me.

I hear footsteps pounding against the ground as I rise to my feet, keeping the Snatcher in front of me. Violet collides with my shoulder, gripping my arm so tightly that the pain jolts me awake, out of my trance. She tugs on me with a strangled sob, and I back away slowly, dragged every step by Violet. The Snatcher watches me, head and beak tilted to the side, the hollows of its eyes empty and black and pure *nothingness*, but watching me all the same, until it turns its head toward Violet, and it rises on its haunches, as if it's about to leap, to dive again.

Violet heaves me back through the door I ran out of, banging its solid weight shut behind us, making it rattle on its loose hinges.

She presses her head to my shoulder, squeezing me tight, sobbing.

Three forms move down the hallway toward us, and even in the blur of silent hysteria, I recognize them: Gerda, Anthony and Isabel, having come around Black House from the other side of the courtyard.

I stand, waiting for them, strangely still, as Violet weeps against me.

Isabel, looking thin but fierce in her short blue slip, marches up to me, whispers, "What *are* you?"

Fear brightens her eyes as she watches me carefully, back against the wall, her friends gaping beside her.

I don't speak, look away, patting Violet's shoulder gingerly.

Outside in the night, beyond the door, the Snatcher screams, and I listen to it, my body and my heart numb.

# Chapter Four: Harming

Isabel won't even look at me.

I huddle in a corner of the ballroom in Black House, arms clasped around my knees. I watch the Sleepers mingle, hands on shoulders, lips on cheeks, on lips, touching one another, laughing as they bring out small pairs of shears that gleam in the light of the Wisps. I watch as they cut their hands, as they press delicate black feathers against the oozing wounds, as—instantly—the Sleepers become writhing creatures, bizarre creatures, arching upon the floor until they still, slumped and unconscious, their mouths fixed with eerie smiles.

Then, after a few moments, they shake themselves, come back into themselves, get up, eyes tear-filled, murmuring about how beautiful, how altering, how *important* it was, that Mem.

How *worth* it.

And how they must have another.

Isabel is on the other side of the room, speaking with Miss Black, whose mouth cuts a small, still line across her face. Her dark eyes narrow as they settle upon me, measuring me up.

Beside me, in a quivering heap, Violet pillows her head in her arms. She's staying near me, her hip pressed against mine. But she won't look at me, either.

I wish Charlie were here.

How long will it take her and Edgar to Fetch for two houses? Have they been gone too long? Should we be worried about them? Should someone go search for them?

I start to ask Violet, but the words catch in my throat at the sight of tears slipping from the corners of her eyes.

My insides turn and twist; it's sickening, uncomfortable, and I can't find any comfort, anything good to think about, anything *else* to think about besides the fact that the Snatcher *refused* me.

It refused me.

That's what I heard Isabel say when she went running back into the ballroom, straight to Miss Black.

I was refused. By a *monster*.

My thoughts spin in tight, dull circles, rehashing every detail I remember, from the beginning, from the stream and the woods. And Charlie.

She found me in an odd time and place.

Nox doesn't work on me, doesn't do *anything* for me.

I can't Mem.

And the Snatcher didn't even *want* me, though I lay defenseless and immobile, the perfect prey.

What does that make me? What *am* I?

Isn't that what Isabel asked me, back to the wall, her eyes—normally slitted, scornful—wide with fear?

*What are you?*

I don't know. I don't know, I don't know, I don't know…

My forehead against my sleeve, eyes tightly closed, I'm so lost in my downward spiraling thoughts that I don't hear the front door creak open, don't feel her, Charlie, come back into Black House, back into the sanctuary of Snatcher-proof walls and doors.

But the Sleepers in the ballroom—those who

aren't Memming, anyway—welcome the returning Fetchers with a congratulatory shout.

I open my eyes.

Edgar and Charlie stand together beneath the archway, a frightened man held between them, his eyes wider and darker than the hollows in a Snatcher's skull. He struggles in their grasp, and Charlie drops his arm, moving into the room to lean against the wall, panting. But Edgar grins, letting the man go, too, and whispering something near Charlie's ear, patting her on the shoulder. She returns his smile, though hers is tired, fleeting.

I gaze at the man, the new Sleeper, as he staggers on stiff legs, taking in the sights before him with haunted eyes. I wonder if he'll ever stop shaking.

I have stopped shaking, though I feel so numb inside, I can't feel much of anything, besides a cold, deep-lodged dread. Still, I'm glad for Charlie, relieved that she's back safe and that the Fetching, this time, was a success.

Violet is on her feet in a heartbeat, practically vibrating in place as she reaches down, taking me by my hands and dragging me up to my feet, too.

"We've got to get out of here," she murmurs, dropping my hands, crossing over to Charlie, leaving me behind, leaning against the wall. I'm too tired to argue with her, though I know Charlie will tell her no. We can't leave, not now.

Charlie and Violet...they're *normal* Sleepers, and normal Sleepers have to fear the Snatchers. Normal Sleepers don't go out at night, ever, except to Fetch.

Because that's just how things work in Twixt.

For everyone, it seems, except me.

That first Snatcher, when I woke up beside the stream... Was it after Charlie, then, never me? And last night, the Snatcher only took the new Sleeper, only her.

Too many questions scrape at the edges of my

heart. I want to test it. I want to walk out the front door right now, challenge the Snatchers that must circle above Black House in the darkness, waiting, watching. Patient. Hungry for Sleepers.

Violet whispers something in Charlie's ear, whispering fast and forcefully, and Charlie's brown eyes, hooded with exhaustion, go wide. She straightens her back, her wondering gaze finding me across the room, and I can't bear it, the way her forehead is wrinkling now, the way her mouth opens, though no words pass her lips.

I need to tell her myself, need to talk to her myself. So I push off from the wall, move across the floor, taking small steps, biting my lip, twisting my fingers together, trying to hide the black lines in my palms from my—and her—sight.

"You played Faster?" Charlie asks, her gaze skipping over me as she runs a hand through her hair when I step closer, as if she's nervous. "Lottie, you could have been—What were you *thinking*?"

It comes out, all in a rush, before I can stop or second-guess myself. "I tripped, and the Snatcher came after me. It didn't want me, Charlie, didn't *take* me," I whisper as Violet grips Charlie's arm, nodding her head, insistent.

Charlie *stares*. At me. She's surprised, at first, but then it's unmistakable. What was written so plainly on Isabel's face is spelled out on Charlie's features now. Except Charlie tries to hide it, to spare my feelings.

But I see it. It's there.

Fear.

For a split second, Charlie is afraid of me.

"Don't—" Charlie whispers, grasping at my wrist as I push past her and Violet and Edgar, angling for the front door. "Lottie, *listen* to me."

I do listen, pausing as she tightens her fingers on

my wrist. My heart pounds.

"It's all right," she tells me, though she doesn't sound as if she believes *anything's* all right, and it's not. I know it's not. I breathe out, clenching my jaw, staring down at the ground. The single tear that escapes my right eye traces down my cheek, and in that heartbeat, Charlie steps forward, drawing me to her, squeezing tightly.

I choke back a sob.

Maybe I'm afraid, too.

"What's wrong with me?" I whisper, so that only she can hear. "What's *wrong*?"

She shakes her head, holds me tighter. "I promise, we'll get to the bottom of this. We'll figure it out together."

I close my eyes, bury my nose in her shoulder. She smells of metal, of cold night air. I inhale, sigh.

"Trouble..." Edgar mutters, and I straighten, stepping back from Charlie, wiping the tear from my chin as Miss Black and Isabel approach. Miss Black's jaw is set, but Isabel's eyes still betray her fear, and she curves away from me, leaning toward the wall.

"Charlie," says Miss Black, clipping the word, "what *is* she?" Right to the point. I stare at the black lace fan angled toward me, now shut tightly, as if it might be used as a weapon.

"She's a Sleeper, Miss Black," says Charlie, slipping her hand into mine.

"The Snatcher *refused* her. That does not happen. You know that does *not* happen." The words are spoken with finality, as Miss Black shakes her head. "She cannot stay in my Safe House. Whenever anything...changes in Twixt, terrible, *terrible* things follow behind. You know that as well as I do, my dear. She must leave. Presently."

Charlie squeezes my hand, her fingers warm

against my cold ones. "You can't send a Sleeper out into the night," she tells Miss Black calmly. "It's against the code of a Safe House."

"Well..." Miss Black shuts her mouth, tapping her fan against the palm of her black-lined hand. Her shrewd eyes narrow. "If she is not out of my house at first light, I will send for the Sixers."

Charlie pales but nods, mouth drawn into a thin, downward curve. "She'll be gone by morning. We'll all be gone, back to Mad House."

"See that you are." She turns without another word, black skirts whirling, and weaves into the silent crowd of Sleepers watching us—staring, listening.

"A Snatcher refused her?" I hear the whisper. And then there are more whispers, as Sleepers speak behind cupped hands, pointing to me, *staring*, eyes wide and fear-filled, mimicking Isabel's eyes. Isabel still watches me, though she's moved across the room with Miss Black and taken up her chair by the fireplace.

"Come on," says Edgar, breathing out, stepping back. "I'll take you all up to my room. It's more...private."

"Great," mutters Charlie, putting her arm around my waist and steering me away from the gaping, gossiping mass. Violet follows behind us, her eyes on the floor.

"This just keeps getting more and more interesting," Edgar grins, wolfish, as we ascend the staircase. There are little faces carved into the railing, baby faces with sharp teeth and wide, wooden eyes. I look away from them, shudder.

"Hey," says Charlie, pressing her fingers against my side, drawing me back to the here and now of the wide, plush staircase and her warmth beside me. We're at the top of the steps, and Edgar is leading us down the many-doored hall, eventually opening a nondescript door on the right and tilting his head to usher us inside.

In the center of the room, there's a large, soft-looking bed covered in rumpled covers and a simple washing table holding a slouching, cracked bowl. Edgar sits down on the edge of the bed, patting either side of himself with a wide smile.

"So many pretty ladies... I'm a lucky guy today," he says, but he quickly sobers when Charlie gives him a hard glance. He leans back on his hands, almost pouting. "So the Snatcher didn't want her." He glances at me. "That doesn't...*necessarily* mean that—"

"Don't, Edgar," sighs Charlie, sitting next to him, rubbing her face and looking up at me with her brows furrowed. She takes my hands in hers and squeezes, half-smiling. "It'll be all right," she tells me in her soothing, husky voice. "I promise you, Lottie. We're going to get to the bottom of all of this, and then..."

"Then?" Violet sinks down to the floor, rubs her face. "What if we *can't* figure it out? Things have gone strange here before—but never like this. Not with a Sleeper. What does it *mean*, Charlie?"

Charlie shakes her head, glancing to Edgar. "I don't know. But just because we don't know doesn't mean we can't figure it out. We will."

"You *know* who could figure it out," says Edgar mildly, staring down at his fingernails as if they're a source of sudden fascination.

"No," says Charlie, standing. The word is unyielding, but Edgar's eyes flash when he turns and looks at her.

"*Lottie* should be the one making that decision, shouldn't she?"

"What decision?" I'm so tired, I feel like I'm wilting. I slide down the wall to rest upon the cold, wooden boards, crumple there. My mind tumbles a single thought, over and over and over: *The Snatcher refused me. The Snatcher refused me.*

Edgar crosses his left leg over his right and regards me evenly. "The Sixers know everything about Twixt—or at least more than we lowly Sleepers do."

A chill creeps along my spine, and my head is shaking long before I will it to do so. "No. I mean, I don't know…" I begin, and breathe out. "I'll…have to think about it." I slur the words together so quickly, they sound like one word, like nonsense.

Violet, standing next to the door, is watching me, picking at the edge of her hoodie's sleeves. "The thing about the Sixers," whispers Violet slowly, "is that once you've been seen by them, you can't be unseen. If something intrigues them about you, they'll *keep* you." She pauses, her blue eyes distant, glazed. "The Sixers take what they want. They always have." She slumps against the wall, her head bowed to her chest.

I glance down at my palms again and, scowling, curl my hands into fists, hiding the failed shadows of Nox from my sight.

"It's not so bad," says Charlie gently, leaning forward, lowering herself to the floor beside me. She takes one of my hands in hers and slowly uncurls my fingers. "You get used to the lines. I can't remember a time, really, when I didn't have them on my palms."

I glance up at her. She's not watching me, is still staring down at my hand, unseeing.

"What was one of your Mems like, Charlie?" I ask her, voice soft. She looks up, locks eyes with me and glances away, breathing out.

"Um..." She sits back, filling the space beside me, resting her head against the wall. "Very few of my memories were good ones, to be honest." She glances at me quickly. "It's not like that for most people. Usually, they experience good memories," she says, shrugging slightly.

Edgar draws up his feet, curls up on the bed with his chin in his hand, and Violet crosses her arms over her stomach, watching us.

Charlie clears her throat, turns her head back to stare at the wall above the bed. "My mother and father fought all the time. I got a lot of Mems of their fights." Her mouth twists. "Screaming. Doors slamming. My Waking life… It doesn't have monsters, I guess, but it's not all that much better than here. I don't think I have a lot of friends…" She gazes down at my palm, threading her fingers through mine. "Here I do. So that's different. Nice."

"There's this boy," says Violet so quietly, I wonder if I imagined it. I gaze at her, see her eyes bright with tears. She rubs at her face, sniffles, sighs. "His name's Billy. He was my first kiss. I was fourteen, and he said I was *fucking beautiful*. He said it just like that. He didn't make fun of my worrying like everyone else did. We stayed together for a couple of months. Most of my memories are about him. I think I loved him." Her voice catches. "I…can't be certain. But I think I did."

Edgar watches her quietly, frowning, and then casts his gaze away, to the floor, staring at it as if it might open up, or show him a lost scene from his Waking life. As if it's a door to another time and place.

After a long moment of silence, he takes a deep breath, says, "Mother was a nurse. She used to sing me lullabies. I remembered them, all of them… Most of my Mems were of her singing, rocking me to sleep her in lap. She had a starched cap, kept it very neat. She contracted a coughing sickness from her ward, and she was…gone before I was fifteen."

I sit up straighter. The walls had seemed to stretch around us when he whispered, struggling, the word *gone*. There's another word, a word he wanted to use, a stronger word, but he couldn't think of it. I can't think of it. Edgar seems to concentrate for a moment, eyes closed, but then he looks around the room, claps his hands, and everything's, seemingly, back to normal.

"There were many girls," he laughs, voice catching. "But there was one I loved more than all the others. Lucy. But she didn't love me. Heartbreaking, isn't it?" He snorts, runs his fingers over his moustache, glancing at Violet again. "She said I was one of *those types*. Not certain what that means. I'm still trying, in my Waking life, to win her, I think. That was my last Mem…"

Violet, very pointedly, doesn't look at Edgar, though he seeks her eyes for a long while, finally giving up and contemplating the floor again.

Charlie's fingers are twined around my hands, holding me softly but securely, somehow fiercely. "I loved a girl…" she whispers, her eyes closed, her eyelids trembling.

I gaze at her, swallow. She's so lovely, with her pale lashes grazing her cheeks, with that shock of unruly blonde hair falling over her forehead. But she's lovelier still because of the way she's touching my hands, because…she hasn't abandoned me, the Sleeper that Snatchers won't even touch.

Bowing my head, I squeeze her hands, listening.

"The girl didn't love me," Charlie goes on, her mouth fixed in a straight line. "She was…disgusted by me when I told her how I felt about her. And that was the last Mem I ever had. Her staring at me as if I were a monster. I gave up Nox after that."

She opens her eyes, brimming with tears, and they spill over her cheeks, glistening in the light of the Wisp-filled lanterns.

I breathe out, squeeze her hands again. "Oh, I'm

so sorry…" I whisper. One of her warm tears falls upon the back of my hand, tracing over my skin. "I don't know how anyone could say that to you, how they could *ever*…" I shake my head, dark hair shifting over my shoulders. My heart hurts, and I'm breathing too quickly, as if I've just run too far, or fallen from a great height. I watch the sadness move over Charlie's face, tearing at all of my sharp edges.

"You're wonderful, Charlie," I say quickly, words tumbling out of my mouth, tasting golden and true. "And anyone who doesn't see that isn't worth the pain of knowing. Isn't *worthy* of you."

Charlie looks at me, then, for a long, still moment, and we share the same air, both of us breathing fast, hard, our eyes locked on one another.

Edgar clears his throat, stands smoothly. "Violet, dear…" he murmurs, holding out a hand to her. "Will you come, uh…help me situate the new Sleeper? Bless my garters, but I forgot about the poor man."

"But—" Violet resists, even as Edgar places a hand at the small of her back and more or less pushes her through the door.

Charlie laughs a little, wipes away her tears, sighing. "He's ridiculous."

I watch her in the half-light, breathless.

Even when she cries, she's beautiful. The realization of that is warm as it fills me from the inside out.

"You…you must have a good memory," I murmur, watching her. "At least one?"

She runs her fingers through her hair, sighing, thinking, eyes up to the ceiling, head tilted back against the wall. "I did once." She grins then, a private grin, and glances down at the floor again. "It was a short Mem. It was cruel, how short it was." She shrugs her shoulders, still smiling. "But I'm at a school dance with a girl. And I put my arms around her, because I don't care who sees us—and *everyone* sees us—and I kiss her." Her eyes skip over me. "I felt so happy in that moment. I don't know what happened after… But that moment, short as it was, was good. So…I have that." She pats the pocket over her heart, smiling.

I'm suddenly so hot, I feel flushed, as if I'm sitting before a fire. I lean toward Charlie a little, trembling. "What was it like?" I whisper. "A kiss?"

Charlie's eyes go wide, brows up, wondering. She watches me for a long moment, licks her lips. Then she says, "Lottie…?" The word is weak. It questions everything.

I close my eyes, breathe out, lean forward just a little more…

"Oh!" Violet's voice. I open my eyes, inhaling deeply.

Violet stands in the doorway, hand on the knob, mouth open a little. "I'm sorry! I'm so sorry. I wanted to ask—"

"Don't worry, don't worry," says Charlie, shaking her head. She looks my way for a heartbeat, and I feel that rush of warmth again.

She'd leaned forward, too.

Light streams through the open doorway as we slip out of Black House, into Abeo City.

Morning. Finally.

I don't think I could have endured another heartbeat in Black House—all of those suspicious, fear-filled eyes trained on me, on Charlie's hand in mine, as we came down the staircase. Judging, expelling...

We pause together on the porch outside, and I breathe out the stale, musty air of Black House, breathe in the cool air of Twixt.

"The Bone Feast is coming up in a few days," says Edgar, falling into a chaise lounge on the porch. He stretches his long legs in front of him, his arms drawn up overhead. "So that'll be something different. Matilda's coming into the Need Shop this morning to take inventory on the Nox we have left for it."

"The Bone Feast?" I ask.

Someone twitches a curtain inside the house, peering out at us. I try to ignore that, stand still, though I know all of the residents of Black House want me *gone*, are likely *quivering* with the need to see my back from a safe distance. And I *want* to go, but I wait as Charlie stretches her arms above her head, then places her hands on her hips, while Violet, beside her, is hugging herself, shivering a little, looking uncomfortable and cold.

"Oh, it's great fun," says Edgar dryly, brow up. "The Sixers come out to Abeo City, and they pluck a few Snatchers and hand out free Nox." He rolls his eyes, smoothes his mustache. "And then they parade a Snatcher around in a cage, and everyone feels wonderful for a night, or pretends to—or is too busy writhing under a Mem to notice their surroundings."

"All of the Houses must be represented," says Charlie, folding her arms, breathing out through her nose, "so even though Mad House doesn't allow Nox past its doors, Abigail must go, and I must go, and Abigail complains the entire time about being around so many hooligans. So like Edgar said, it's great fun." She grins a little, sighing, pushing her fingers through her hair. "Speaking of Abigail, we'd better get going. There's going to be hell to pay, and I'll have to explain about..." Her eyes find mine, regard me uncertainly, almost shyly. "About what happened in the courtyard," she finishes, biting her lip.

I take a deep breath, remembering the Snatcher on the awning, the tilt of its bony head as it watched me, only watched…

"I'll see you later," says Edgar, waving at us from his chair. His eyes linger on Violet, I notice—though she doesn't notice—before he rises and slips back into Black House, where he'll likely be bombarded with a thousand questions about me. He shuts the door as we troop down the steps.

We walk close together, quickly, Charlie's hands deep in her pockets, shoulders slouched, Violet's arms swinging loose, though she blows on her fingers to warm them. After awhile, lost in dark thoughts, I slow my steps, follow after them rather than beside them, two paces behind.

"We're going to get to the bottom of all of this," says Charlie over her shoulder, shoving the hair out of her eyes. "We're going to figure it out, Lottie, even if I have to talk to every Fetcher in Abeo. Even if I have to talk to the Sixers." She whispers *Sixers* like it's a forbidden word, a curse.

"You wouldn't," Violet hisses out.

But Charlie shrugs, shakes her head. "What choice do I have? Edgar's right. They would have a better idea than the Fetchers as to what might be going on. It makes the most sense, Violet."

"I just…" Violet turns her head to stare at Charlie, and her eyes are round as she breathes out, slumping a little. "I just think the Sixers should be the last resort."

I shiver, skin crawling, and I peer over my shoulder, back the way we've come, back toward the Wanting Market. My eyes alight on a shadow that moves beneath the overhang of a building's slanted roof, a shape swaddled in furs.

When I blink, the shadow is gone.

"The last resort," Charlie promises, quickening her step. The road blurs around us, and then I recognize the pile of bricks and rubble, the turn of the street, and ahead of us, like a beacon, like a home—*home*, I mouth, recognizing the word with a pang I can't place—lies Mad House.

Abigail is bent in the doorway, drawing her many shawls closer around her, wrinkled fingers paling in the growing light. When she sees us, she waves us toward her. *Hurry, faster.* Charlie breaks into a trot as my heart, already a rock in my chest, grows heavier.

Even from this distance, I can see that Abigail's mouth is puckered, as if she's bitten into a sour fruit.

Something's wrong.

"Florence," she spits out, when we pull even with the porch.

"What's happened?" asks Charlie, her tone frantic, her words crackling into the stillness.

Abigail shakes her head, points back the way we've come. "I couldn't stop her. I tried. At daybreak, she slipped out right past me, pushed past me on the stairs and flew out the door. I think she's gone to the Need Shop, Charlie. You've got to get her before she's Memmed herself away." Abigail works her mouth. "She'll Fade..."

Charlie says nothing as she turns, but I can see the line of her jaw, tightly clenched, and the wild, worried look in her brown eyes. She breaks into a run, long legs eating up the broken road. Violet and I follow after, though we're not nearly as fast. We double our pace, taking in great lungfuls of air, retracing our walk and drawing closer to the Wanting Market.

Charlie slices through the lanes of rubble and garbage, and onlookers watch her move through the rows of stalls in silence. Though it's early, the Wanting Market is filled with people blithely snipping off locks of hair in exchange for stupid, useless junk. The man who stood at the fountain before is there again, yelling something about Snatchers, but I tune him out, pull my gaze away, as we run after Charlie, as we near the steps of the Need Shop.

Edgar walks along the street, top hat cocked on his head, aiming toward the shop, as Charlie climbs the steps two at a time, hurling open the door and moving quickly inside.

"What…?" Edgar turns to Violet, but he makes a guess based on her pale expression—unmasked fear—and bolts up the steps after Charlie. I'm beside him as he opens the door, and we three enter together.

An older woman stands behind the counter, hands folded before her against her impeccable black skirts. Her graying black hair is swept up in an old-fashioned twist, and her features are severe, sharp, like a buzzard. Her eyes narrow as she peers past Charlie to Edgar.

"First off, you're late," she tells him, clipping out the words as she lifts a quill and piece of paper, holding them out to him. "And second, what's the meaning of *this*, barging in here with a gang from Mad House and…" Her eyes find me, then, and her words fall away. She's staring, her jaw hanging open, her gaze still and wide.

It's as if, for a heartbeat, time stands still, because she looks almost like…like she *knows* me, recognizes me. The tension is palpable, the air charged. Her eyes grow too large, then narrow and shrink until she's regarding me distantly, shrewdly, lips clasped together, chin poked high, as if nothing's happened, as if she didn't just greet the sight of my face with open shock.

"Where's Florence?" Charlie demands, sprinting right past the counter toward Edgar's back room. The older woman splutters, chasing after Charlie, though her steps are slow, and then Charlie is throwing open the door, staring down, shoulders shaking.

Violet and I walk together down the hall, with Edgar behind us.

And there's Florence on the floor, stiff and cold, back arched, stilled. A scattering of black feathers litters the boards around her, gleaming like dark snow, and there's a pair of large shears spread out in her hands. Her eyes are rolled back in her head.

She's Memming.

Charlie crouches down beside her, raking her hands through her hair in frustration, tugging, and then she gathers up the feathers, one by one, snatching them and stuffing them into the crates. Florence's breath comes in short, shallow pants, and she shakes as she lays there, arms spread to the world, back flat against the wooden floor. I notice, then, that she's terribly thin, thinner than she was even the day before; it's as if she's shrinking inward, as if her physicality is being stolen away from her with each pained breath.

"*Fuck*," Charlie whispers in a small, broken voice, the word cracking as she breathes out, leaning down gently, scooping Florence up in her arms. She hugs the girl to her chest tightly, bows her head over her. Then, in one turn, she's out of the room, pushing past us all, aiming for the front door, her movements jerky but purposeful, jaw set.

"You can't just *take* a paying customer, one who paid *good hair* for—"

"Matilda." Edgar steps forward, between the old woman and Charlie, shaking his head. He glowers over her, wetting his lips. "*Don't.*"

Undeterred, she snarls in his face. "I'll tell the

Sixers about this. See if I don't," she hisses, but she's not watching him now; she's staring at me. I stare right back, hands balled into fists at my sides as she sneers, scratching her too-long fingernails over her cheeks, raising red welts. It makes me shudder, the way she's staring at me, the way she can't take her eyes off me as she cuts herself with her nails like claws.

I'll tell the Sixers…

I swallow and turn on my heel, and then Violet and I are following after Charlie, running down the steps, through the Wanting Market, over the street, leaving Edgar and Matilda and the Need Shop with its shelves full of Nox behind us.

We return to Mad House, stopping just beside the porch, where Charlie has brought Florence. Charlie's tears course down her cheeks, *plinking* gently against Florence's upturned face. The girl hasn't woken from the Mem yet. Still and panting, she remains tangled in the Mem, cradled in Charlie's arms, eyelids quivering, as if she's searching the depths of her own darkness for something just out of reach, out of sight.

Abigail hobbles back onto the porch, peering out at us beneath a shading hand and grimacing. She totters down the steps toward us and places a hand alongside Florence's sunken cheek as Charlie lifts her gaze toward the old woman.

They say nothing for a long moment, but when Abigail looks up, locking eyes with Charlie, her expression is grim. "Too late," she says, her naturally sharp voice gentle now, soft. "She'll likely Fade today, Charlie."

A strangled sound escapes Charlie's throat, and then she's collapsing down on the porch steps, holding Florence across her lap tightly, eyes squeezed shut. She breathes out raggedly, breathes in again, out again, tears leaking from the corners of her eyes.

“I knew it was coming,” Charlie whispers, as Violet and I and Abigail stand around her, watching her with red faces and trembling chins. “I just didn’t think it’d be so soon. I thought… I thought I could help her. I thought I *was* helping her.” She bites her lip, stares up at the sky, blinking away her tears. “I was so wrong,” she says, and then she repeats the words over and over: “I was *so wrong*.”

Abigail folds her arms in front of her, shakes her head. “Charlie, my girl, you did the best you could by her. That’s all anyone could have ever asked for—”

“It was all *useless*." Charlie chokes on a sob. "You don’t understand.” She stares down at the fragile girl in her arms. “Florence wanted Nox too much, was addicted, and maybe I did her a disservice by trying to keep her from it. If this was always going to happen, if it was inevitable…” She staggers to her feet again, holding Florence before her, a doll with tightly shut eyes, breathing too fast, jagged ribs rising and falling beneath her thin dress.

Charlie looks past us without really seeing, turns on her heel, and walks up the porch steps slowly, carrying Florence with her. Head bowed, she moves into Mad House through the open door.

Violet scrubs at her eyes, stares heavenward as Abigail sighs heavily, shaking her head.

“She cares too much. She’s always cared too much,” Violet’s saying, and then she heaves out a single breath, curling her small hands into fists. “I’ve got to help them.”

“How,” says Abigail, not a question, her mouth drawn flat, an unamused line. “The only way you can *help* Charlie is if you’re there for her when Florence Fades away, which might happen any moment now. I've seen Sleepers like this before… Too many of them." The line of her mouth trembles. "I doubt she’ll last until sundown."

Violet weeps into her cupped hands as Abigail glances up at the sky, squinting. "Charlie loved that poor, troubled girl like a little sister. Always took care of her, she did. You'd have never come to Mad House, Violet, if Charlie hadn't been so worried about Florence taking Nox." She nods, blinking fast. "So no matter what, it was a good thing Charlie did," says Abigail, still nodding, folding her arms and waddling back up the steps toward the door. "You all *needed* to come to Mad House. And now here you are."

She goes in, the door creaking shut behind her, and Violet flops down on the porch steps, running her fingers through her dark hair. "It wasn't supposed to be like this," she whispers, staring up at me, eyes bright. "Charlie brought Florence here so that we could save her. She wasn't supposed to…Fade, not ever."

Violet looks down for a long while at her hands, at the black lines slashed across her palms, and then she stills, and then she's standing, straightening her hoodie, clearing her throat. "Lottie…"

"What is it?" I ask her, resting a hand on her arm.

"I'm going to go to the Harming Tree," she tells me—firmly, clearly, her voice only shaking at the end, and then only a very little. "I could help Florence, save her, if I run there and back."

"The Harming Tree?" I repeat, remembering Charlie's disdain for it. "Charlie said that's just a superstition."

"No," Violet insists. "It's a tree, at the edge of the Red Line." She's breathless, stepping forward, cheeks flushed. "If I run all the way, I'll be able to reach it in time, I think." She slides her hands into her hoodie pocket and brings out a tiny lock of hair. "I stole it from Matilda's counter," she whispers then, swallowing, pocketing the lock of hair once more. "If I can get to the tree and tie the hair on, Florence won't Fade. She'll be fine, good as new. It'll work, Lottie. Everyone says so." She's searching my eyes now with her own, pleading, as if she's begging me to agree, to support her plan.

I glance up at Mad House, black curtains drawn over the windows, and I remember Charlie's hand at my elbow, at my back—strong and firm, safe. I remember the fear in her eyes when she found out about the courtyard game…and I remember how she swallowed that fear, stepped forward and embraced me, anyway, even though the Snatcher refused me. Even though I'm...

I don't know.

I don't know what I am.

I glance down at Violet, small, cowering Violet, who's shaking now as she glances toward the wall that surrounds Abeo, holding back the clawing, bony forest.

Violet, who would risk her life for Florence, dare the night and the Snatchers…

"If you give me the lock of hair," I whisper, swallowing, "I'll go. Let me do it."

Violet jerks her head around, staring at me with wide, unblinking eyes. "You?" she murmurs, and I know before the word is out of her mouth that she's relieved, though it hadn't occurred to her to ask me. She was going to go, she truly was, despite her deep and rational fear.

"Lottie, are you sure? You hardly know Florence—"

"It makes the most sense. You know it does. The Snatcher didn't want me," I grimace, reminding her of something she's surely not forgotten. "I can run all the way. You just have to tell me where to go."

What I don't speak aloud is the compulsive thought that twists in my heart, lodged there like a splinter in skin: *I need to get out of Abeo City. I need to see if there's something* more.

"Ye-yes," says Violet quickly, tripping over the word. "Look…" She points over the wall to the towering trees. "If you keep Abeo at your back—Do you see that tall tree, way out there?"

A single tree scrapes the sky above the others, though it's far away, farther away than I can imagine.

"That's the Harming Tree," Violet whispers, and then she's taking my hand, pressing the warmed lock of hair into my palm. "Lottie, why are you doing this?" she asks, the question I hoped she wouldn't voice.

I stare down at my palm, curled in her small, shaking hands, with the wisp of fair hair nestled against my blackened lifeline.

"For Charlie," I breathe, feeling tears spring to my eyes. "Because Charlie was kind to me, has been kind from the beginning, and even after, when…" I bite my lip, holding back tears, and shake my head. "She deserves kindness in return," I whisper, curling my fingers over the hair. I swallow, blink, breathe out. "And because of Florence," I add, not because it's expected but because it's true. If I can help that poor, suffering girl… If I am the *only* person who might walk through the night unassaulted by Snatchers, it's my duty to try.

Maybe it's why I'm here.

Violet's brow is still furrowed, worried, but she nods, squeezing my hand.

"Please hurry," she whispers, and then I'm tucking the bit of hair into my pocket, leaving Violet by the porch.

*Just concentrate*. I close my eyes as I approach the wall, move forward, holding my breath, holding out my hands.

And then I open my eyes, and I'm on the other

side, Mad House obscured from sight by the stony wall that surrounds Abeo City.

Everyone I know is behind me now. I'm alone in the woods, and I stand there and breathe, my legs shaking. It's all so sharp: the trees, the metal stink of the snow in my nose, the curve of my fingernails against my palms. The branches outlined against the sickly gray of the sky look like jagged bits of broken wood, and snow lies over the fallen branches on the ground like a shroud.

I shiver as I step forward, a twig breaking beneath my boot.

No. I can't walk. I have to *run*. I gulp in a great lungful of air, ball my fists, and then take off, weaving between the trees.

I risk a glance over my shoulder, can hardly make out the shadow of the city behind me now, above the wall, but it's still there. And even though I'm so small, so low in the forest, I can still glimpse the hulking of the largest tree, the Harming Tree, ahead. It's far, but it's there, a lure pulling me forward.

I keep running.

My skin pricks like I'm being watched. I try not to waste energy by glancing up at the trees, where the Snatchers had been perched that first night, when they came for Charlie and me.

Or…maybe just for Charlie. Maybe not for me.

Recklessness tugs at the corners of my heart as I sprint through the woods, the wind blowing my thick mane of black curls behind me, the branches tugging at my boots and my skirts and my arms and my face, but I ignore it all, keeping the towering tree in my line of sight.

The Snatcher did not want me. It only watched me from the awning, wings clasped about it like a great black cloak, watching me with its hollows for eyes but seeing me, I believe, all the same. Its right wing was misshapen, as if something had broken it long ago, and that visual is so crisp within me. Even through the horror of that moment, it surprised me, fascinated me.

The Snatcher was different from the others, and it had not taken me.

Maybe the others won't take me, too.

I run, and I breathe in and out, and I don't grow tired. The trees move and shift around me, slowly, softly, and the snow crunches beneath my boots, and I feel the false heaviness of the slight wisp of hair in my dress pocket. I keep the tree before me, and the shrinking shadow of Abeo behind me, and I dash through the forest, and I don't stop, no matter how my chest and legs begin to ache.

As the gray light around me darkens, as the shadows of the trees reach sharp fingers toward me, as if to grasp me, snatch me up, I reach the tree and stand before it, panting.

It towers, endless, a stark, dark sentinel that points upward to the sky, as if in warning. On the lowest branches, tied with strips of cloth and ribbon and lace, are snips of hair, waving in the wind like leaves. There is red hair and brown hair, black and blonde and gray and white hair, and the locks flutter in the soft, cool exhalations of air that sweep through the surrounding woods.

I pause, breathing out, watching the closest branch to me quiver, the countless scraps of hair and cloth tied to it causing it to bend gently beneath the weight, arching toward the ground as if bowing to begin a dance.

I palm the wisp of hair in my pocket and bring it out, staring down at its smallness, a pale curl against the black line of my palm.

I can't linger, can't delay.

I gulp down air, and I step forward, toward the

trunk of this tree, the trunk that's black, that should not be black but is, like a shadow, and I crouch down, tugging at the edge of my dress's hem, worrying a small tear, pulling. The tearing sound is loud in the stillness as I rip a bit of the fabric free, and then I'm closer to the trunk, staring up at it.

There's so much hair flicking back and forth along the branches, but the majority of the snipped-off strands are tied to the trunk.

How much hair is there? How many Sleepers does this represent? Did the ritual work for any of them? Did it save *any* of them from Fading? I stare up and up, at all of the little flutterings, and I think of the people I've seen in Abeo City. There are always crowds in the Wanting Market, but the people number far fewer than the wisps of hair present here. How many Sleepers have journeyed out to this Harming Tree to keep themselves or someone they loved safe? How many?

*How many failed?*

My heart begins to knock against my ribs with a heavy, pulsing hand as I tie the wisp of hair to a bit of bark that juts out along the trunk, feeling suddenly not as if I'm saving Florence's life but, perhaps, marking a memorial for her. My fingers are shaking, and it takes me two tries to complete the knot. I back away from my handiwork, and three steps back, the wisp of Florence's hair blends into the trunk, as if it's always been there, companion to the nameless others.

A movement beyond the tree catches my attention, then, because it's a band of bright color in this shadowed world, the black of trees and the white of snow. I catch my breath, step past the great trunk.

A red ribbon is tied around a little sapling. It twirls and spins in the breeze as I reach out and touch it. It's as red as blood and as soft as hair. I pull my hand back and watch it twist back to its original shape against the little branch.

Could this be the Red Line?

*If you started toward the Red Line at the earliest point in the morning, and you don't turn back when you reach it, you won't make it back to Abeo City and the Safe Houses before dark. And the Snatchers will get you.*

I can hear Charlie's words as if she's right here beside me, and a shudder moves through me, remembering her soft eyes, our almost-kiss...

I know she wouldn't agree with my coming here alone. She called the Harming Tree a superstition, but if there's a *chance,* if it might work, and the Snatchers don't want me, anyway…

I had to come.

Despite my grim thoughts, why *couldn't* the Harming Tree work? Aren't there stranger things in Twixt every day?

I turn to go. You have to head back when you reach the Red Line, Charlie said, and I didn't even start out at the earliest point in the morning. I breathe in and out, trying to still the hammering of my heart, but I pause in my turning, my back still to the tree, eyes fixed.

My gaze clung to the bright red of the ribbon before; all I could see was the Red Line.

But beyond the Red Line…

I stare, breath frozen in my lungs.

The trees there look…strange.

A line of gray stretches beyond the small sapling decorated with the red ribbon. It's an actual *line*, for the snow beyond it simply…stops. And then, beyond that, the earth is gray, like charcoal, like soot. And the trees look like half-trees, half-imagined, half-real, scribbles in pencil on paper. I rub at my eyes, but the trees don't change, still look *drawn,* one-dimensional, so I step forward, putting a single boot past the sapling, a single boot still on the snow and just touching that gray line.

I'm compelled as if by gravity, a tugging at the center of my ribs—where my heart is, I suppose. Something from within pulls me on, and I take another step. Another.

I'm still half on the snow and half on the gray. I stare down at my boots but stop, gasp, breath coming faster as I stare down, disbelieving, at my hands.

They're not my hands.

I lift them up, heart beating, *beating*, because my hands aren't pale skin and thin, shaking fingers. Not anymore.

I step back so quickly that I fall into the snow, catching myself with hands that are mine again, the nightmare disappearing as quickly as a breath is lost to the air.

I pull my hands into my lap, watch them as if I'm afraid they might change again, right before my eyes.

Because over that gray line, they looked like… They *were…*

*Claws.*

I scrabble to my feet, turn around, and I run. Past the Red Line, past the Harming Tree. I'm afraid, and I don't know why I'm afraid, but there's something deeper and darker coursing through me.

I'm *angry*.

Past that gray line, my hands became claws, became ugly, curving, sharpened things that did not resemble my hands—*anyone's* hands—at all. It makes no sense. None of this makes any *sense*. *Those weren't my hands*. *Why* can't I Mem, and *why* did I appear in the wrong time and place, and *why* didn't the Snatcher *Snatch* me?

Why am I *here*?

A sob catches in my throat, and I swallow it,

gritting my teeth as I run through the trees, glancing over my shoulder at the towering tree that draws farther and farther back behind me, growing smaller as I move faster through the darkening woods.

The *darkening* woods.

My breath catches as I watch the shadows lengthen in front of me—too fast, in a heartbeat; no, less—as the sky turns a brilliant crimson, like blood. Like that first time, when Charlie found me lost by the stream. And I see the stream as I'm running, but I can't stop, can't stop for anything, because the sun is setting, and I'm not going to make it back to Abeo in time.

Which I always knew would be the outcome of this undertaking, deep down.

I knew I wouldn't make it back.

The Snatchers are going to come, and I'm going to find out, once and for all, if they'll take me. Maybe the Snatcher in the courtyard was only tired. Maybe it had grown bored of our game.

But I don't think that was it, and no one else who was there seemed to think it was as simple as that, either.

I need to know the truth.

There's a resolution in that, though terror slips through my belly like a fish, dark and shining and small. A Snatcher didn't want me last night. Here, in the open woods, will the Snatchers want me now?

I breathe in and out steadily as I run, as the shadows stretch to their longest lengths, as the red begins to disappear from the world, replaced with inky black and gray.

And darkness.

Darkness covers the sky and swallows the woods and me in a single gulp. I falter, the steady rhythm of my boots missing a beat, and I trip and tumble to the ground, snow grinding into my palms as I propel myself upward, looking back over my shoulder.

There are white shadows up high, high in the trees. Crouched. Poised. Watching me.

A host of Snatchers.

I gulp down air, blood coursing through me, my whole body a heartbeat, as I run toward the city.

I hear the sound of their wings clicking open, unfurling, beautiful black feathers shielding their monstrous forms. They launch as one. How many are there? Ten, twenty? They open their mouths, and they scream, a thin, hot wail that buries itself beneath my skin, turning and turning like a screw. I cover my ears with my black-lined palms, gritting my teeth as I'm surrounded by that intolerable sound.

I run through the woods as they chase me.

The Snatchers chase me.

They're after me. I don't know what this means. Will they catch me? Will they Snatch me up?

I run, gulping breath, and they fly behind me, shredding the air with their great black wings. After the first chorus of screams, they fall silent. I turn to look behind me and almost trip again.

A Snatcher has pulled up on my right.

I veer to the left.

I run, and they follow, run and they follow. Perhaps I've moved beyond fear to that still, small space inside of it, because the terror that licked through my bones, over my skin, is numbed now. I am running, and they are flying with me. It's a strange sensation, these monsters all around me, above and on either side…

It feels, after a thousand heartbeats, a thousand footsteps, as if my life has always been this way: the running, the chasing…

But then a Snatcher moves, and it's not on my right anymore but on my left, swooping near. I veer right, gasping.

And that's when I begin to realize something.

If they had wanted to Snatch me, they could have done it a hundred times over.

I don't think they want to Snatch me.

I think they're *herding* me, pushing me toward a specific location.

The understanding hits me hard. Maybe I'm wrong, though. How can I guess at the motivations of monsters?

I decide to test it. I dart back to my left, and the Snatcher swoops down, dangerously close to me, and opens its great bird jaws and screams. The sound slices through the air, cutting my inner ears, and I run back to the right.

They are. They're directing me.

But *why*?

In the darkness, I've lost all sense of space. I don't know which way Abeo lies, which way I've come from. I can't see the Harming Tree, can't see the wall surrounding Abeo City. Perhaps I'll run all night with the Snatchers just a hairsbreadth behind me. The fear is waking up again, beginning to prick at my neck, stinging, but then, out of the nothingness of darkness up ahead, there appears between the blackened, dead trunks of the trees…a building.

It's tall, pointing upward like the Harming Tree, with a roof that upholds a small tower ending in narrow sharpness, like a needle's point. Even in the dark, the bright, vivid colors of its high, arching windows are visible, because within the building is *light*.

A word comes to my mind, though I didn't know it, never thought it before this heartbeat.

A church.

That's what the building is. A church.

Suddenly, everything feels strange, like a dream—though I can't dream, can't sleep. Or…Charlie said I'm asleep now, a Sleeper.

Have I ever dreamed?

I grit my teeth, and I make the decision in an instant. I slow down. I stop running. I slow to a trot, and then a walk. And then I stop, completely, abrupt.

The Snatchers land in the trees around me, pumping their wings open, screaming at one another, and then peering down at me with their hollows for eyes.

Silence descends as the trees still, as the Snatchers settle and stare.

Watching me.

It's eerie, how they turn their heads as one. The flashing sharpness of their beaks—all of their beaks, dozens of them—point toward the church.

And then one Snatcher spreads its wings with a snap of finality. And it leaps from the tree, down to the ground. The earth shakes beneath my feet, and I almost fall as the Snatcher begins to crawl over the snow, toward me, its claws crunching against the ice. It's unnatural, how this human-like skeleton moves on all fours, the wings arched overhead, but that's when I notice it…

The right wing is a little crooked.

"I know you," I whisper, frightening myself.

This is the Snatcher from last night.

Though my heart feels as if it will beat out of the cage of my ribs, though my breath comes too fast, though I feel like my legs will buckle at any moment, I stand my ground. I don't know why or how, but I don't run, don't even step back as the Snatcher moves toward me, pausing close enough for me to reach out and touch a finger to a cold, slick bone.

But I don't.

We stare at one another, the monster towering over me, a giant hewn of sharpness, all angles and white and black. The feathers on its wings stand up, at attention, pointing in all different directions, and, this close, I am astonished to see that there's a luminousness to the spaces where the creature's eyes should be. If I stare into those cavities, if it's almost as if, far below, in the void, there's something—*someone*—staring back.

The Snatcher clacks open its beak, and then it unhinges its jaws, and right into my face, it *roars*.

My resolve melts, and I turn, and I walk. I do not run. I walk slowly, stiffly, toward the church, the place the Snatchers want me to go.

But why would they *want* anything? Don't they take people, Sleepers, instinctively? Isn't their purpose for existing terror and nothing more?

I feel the hollows of their eyes against my back, watching me, as the angled church rises ahead, closer, closer.

I trip, sprawling again, but not on a tree root or a branch this time. My foot is stuck in a hole—an oddly shaped one, like a long, thin rectangle. I struggle to my feet, wrenching my boot out of the hole, and I see, then, that there are many holes just like this one, each about a body's length apart. Many of the holes are flanked by urns full of wilted flowers, or only dirt.

I walk on.

Colored glass fills the arching church windows—more color than I have seen anywhere else in Twixt. My heart aches a little at the sight.

And then my hand is on the doorknob of the great entrance, and I take a deep breath, and I turn and look back.

The Snatchers are gone. *Gone.*

And without a sound.

I exhale, close my eyes, listen to my heartbeat pulsing.

And I hear, inside…a voice?

I shove my shoulder against the door, and I push.

# Chapter Five: Bird

"Momma sold my soul for a penny..." comes a singsong voice, a girl's voice, lilting somewhere nearby. "My soul was bought and sold!"

I shut the door behind me, leaning against it, panting, eyes closed.

There's a scrabbling sound, and the pile of debris along the wall, sloping down toward the benches—pews, I remember they're called—slides a little further as the girl trots down the hill of books and splintered wood, crouching at the bottom and considering me.

She has long black hair and is draped in layers of clothes: cloaks and skirts and pants and furs, and her hair is all matted, sticking up around her head in spikes, making her pale skin look whiter, unnaturally white. Her eyes are bottomless, the kind of blue that makes me think of gray, and they're wide and wild as she stares at me and back to the door and then at me again, her mouth drawn into a lopsided frown.

"You've come," she says then, with no introduction. She scurries forward on all fours, and she rises next to me, poking at my shoulder with one dirty finger. "I thought you'd be here before now, *long* before the holiday," she's saying, frown deepening. "You've kept the uglies waiting."

"I'm sorry. I..." I begin, but she's shaking her

head too fast, stamping her foot.

"No, no, no, no, no," she says then, covering her ears with her hands, pressing down and crouching down, rocking back onto her heels as she squats in the rubble.

There's no place for me to go but back out into the woods, back to the Snatchers, so I stare at the girl, breathing in and out as I consider my choices.

I kneel down beside her, biting my lip.

"Are you all right?" I murmur softly.

She shakes her head, staring at me, eyes wide. "It's all wrong," she says miserably, holding her hands out. I stare down at them, at the dirty palms, palms that bear no black lines. She's never taken Nox.

I hold out my own hands, and she snatches them up, turning them over and over as she shakes her head violently again. "It's all wrong," she repeats and huffs out, dropping my hands, almost throwing them down.

"I'm Lottie..." I begin, but she's shaking her head again, tapping her chest, eyes growing wider.

"You're *not*," she tells me, covering her ears with her hands as she breathes out in a whimper. "Oh, it's not working..." she says after a long, tense moment, as I kneel, confused, beside her. She takes a hand tentatively from her ear and then leans close, plucking at my shoulders with her long fingers.

"We're too close to the bad house," she breathes into my face. Around her eyes are red rings, as if she's wept for days. "They can hear us if I talk, so I can't. They'll find us."

"I don't understand," I begin, but she rises quickly, drawing the back of her hand over her mouth.

"You don't," she says shortly, a statement, not a question. And then she points up to the rafters.

I stare up.

Birds. Crows. Perched in the rafters, staring down at us a little too like the Snatchers, shifting their small, slight bodies and ruffling their wings with softly clicking beaks.

I stand, gazing at them, mouth open.

Birds. Animals.

I haven't seen any animals in Twixt, not *any*, until now.

The realization is bright and hot as it burns its way through me. I don't know what it means, what anything means.

I stare at the girl before me, who's sitting back on the pile of garbage, elbows on her knees, watching me, head tilted, just like a bird.

"Who are you?" I ask her, and she shakes her head, pointing up.

"I'm feathered and foul with a blackened heart." She leans back on the garbage, her smile too wide and disjointed to be genuine. "It's from a poem," she continues, bending forward. "The humans write poems. We thought it was one of the most beautiful things about them."

I stare at her as she gets up, begins to pace across the confines of the once lovely floor. It was blue, but now it's dirty and smeared with dust, only the suggestion of blue.

"What's your name?" I ask, considering, for a moment, the closed door behind me. I could leave, take my chances with the Snatchers... But I watch the girl turn quickly, muttering to herself under her breath, and there's something so familiar about her movements... I feel like I've seen her before. But I haven't. I would have remembered her.

I watch her turn again, come back to me, reach out and grip my arms tightly.

"I'm Bird," she says then, as if she's decided to trust me with the word. She searches my eyes. "You don't remember?"

I shake my head slowly. "I don't remember anything."

"It wasn't supposed to be like this," she whispers, voice dropping down to a breathless sort of cry. "They'll know. They know everything. So you've got to find out yourself."

"I don't understand," I repeat, but she shakes her head, puts a finger to her mouth.

"They're so close," she whispers, and the hairs on the back of my neck stand up.

"Who? Who's close?" I whisper back. Her eyes are wide, unblinking as she leans closer, lips to my ear.

"Sixers," she breathes, and shudders against me. I shudder, too, my body, for a heartbeat, not my own as it responds to that word.

"What about them?" I try, but she's shaking her head, dropping her forehead to my shoulder, an intimate gesture but one I don't mind, almost expected. So strange...

"The bad house, their house, is too close to here. I didn't know that when I came here. I wish I'd known. But I knew you'd be coming, so I couldn't leave. I had to stay until you came," she says, locking eyes with me.

"The Sixers…they live near here?" Saying the word makes my mouth hurt; my tongue cuts against it. But I feel a bizarre fascination with it, too. As if the syllables themselves are tugging at the strings of my heart.

The girl, Bird, watches me, pulls her fingers through her hair, worrying at a thick, ink-black knot. "The uglies will get you, if you're not careful," she breathes out, tugging hard at the knot. "They always get you."

I stare at her as she pulls on her hair, pulls and pulls until the knot comes out in her hand, her face slick with pain. She throws the hair into the garbage pile, sinking back on her heels, head in her hands. "It's not working like it should…" she whispers, rocking back on her heels. "It wasn't supposed to be like this."

"Like what? What wasn't supposed to be like this?" I ask her, frustration sharpening my words, but she's standing, shaking her head, as she takes my wrist, plucking it.

And then she's dragging me toward the door. The night. The Snatchers.

"What are you *doing*?" I cry as she yanks the door open, the misshapen thing groaning beneath her hand as it swings to the side. Out we go. I dig my heels, but she's too strong for me. She's just a wisp herself… How can she possibly have so much strength?

And then we're standing at the foot of the stone steps, the light from the jars of the Wisps inside the church illuminating the ground around us, but not that much. Bird holds my wrist tightly, watching me, eyes wide, and then she looks out to the woods.

I follow her gaze, my heart pounding. Are there Snatchers there?

But no. There's…light.

As we watch, tiny glowing spheres begin to peek out from the trunks of trees, beneath fallen twigs, descending from clawing branches overhead. The forest floor begins to pulse with tiny embers of light, glowing orange and golden in the darkness.

"When the relations aren't around, they come out," whispers Bird. "Do you remember now?"

I stare at the glowing orbs, and back to Bird, shaking my head.

She lets go of my wrist, dropping it softly, quietly, so that it falls against my thigh. Then she steps forward, crouching, like a predator searching for prey. She straightens after a heartbeat, an orb floating closer to her.

Bird reaches out with a long first finger and touches it gently.

There's a flare of light.

Now, against her finger, a butterfly opens and closes its wings, thrumming with light, with life. I gasp, suddenly so weak, I can't breathe, can't see. I sink to my knees in the snow as this dizzying crescendo of light pulses around us.

Bird drops her hand, and—as suddenly as it came—the light disappears. The butterfly is gone. Lazy and slow, the Wisp bumbles over a fallen branch and disappears behind a crowd of trees.

"What just happened?" I whisper, clutching Bird's wrist. She crouches beside me, searching my face.

"You don't remember," she murmurs then, eyes downcast after a long moment. I want to shake her, I'm so frustrated. What just happened? A butterfly? She takes my hand, uncurls my fingers and presses her palm to mine. There's a slight tingle, and she holds up our hands, her right and my left together. Our hands look the same in the darkness, and she stares at me, breathing out, eyes wide, hopeful.

"I'm sorry... I can't..." I begin, but she shakes her head, rising, pointing to the horizon that's brightening as I watch it.

Daylight. Already. I stand, too, rubbing at my shoulders, skin pricking, strangeness sliding over my bones.

I turn, looking through the brightening woods. There is a shadow beyond the trees.

The *bad house*.

Bird's eyes look haunted as she watches me.

"You're going," she says, and it's not a question. How could she know? I take a step back as she scrabbles closer to me, closer and closer still until her nose is against mine, and she's closing her eyes, pressing her forehead to mine.

"Why won't you remember?" she breathes out, and when she steps back, there are tears in her eyes. She wraps her arms around her middle, rocking back on her heels. "*You were supposed to remember*."

"Why can't you tell me..." I begin, but she shakes her head, looks over my shoulder at the door, eyes wide.

"If they find out, everything we did, everything we *went* through is for *nothing*," she whispers to me, breathing out. "You'll do what you'll do," she says then, voice soft. "I just hope it's the right thing." She kisses my cheek, her lips chapped and worn and warm against my skin. "I'll see you," she says, and ascends the steps, shutting the church door behind her.

The woods, the quiet, silent woods, draw away from me like a map. As I step past the church, I look to the left, and I can see the house through the trees, its dark shadow. It's beckoning me on. I should resist that beckon...

The Snatchers wanted me to come here. They wanted me to find Bird. Bird acted as if she knew me.

What does any of it mean?

Frustration mounting within me, I turn back, look at the door of the church, rub at my wrist, in the place where Bird pinched.

It slides over me, warm and strange as it coats my insides: that spellbound feeling, as if I wandered through a wall of spider webs and they're dangling in sticky grey tendrils from my fingers. I brush my hands together but feel nothing but skin.

I know I must return to Abeo City. Charlie will be worried. And Violet and Edgar...my new friends. There's warmth in my stomach when I think of them. More warmth, in a different space in my heart, when I think of Charlie.

I don't want her—them—to worry about me.

But…

I look up at the shadow.

I need answers.

I won't be long. I'll be back in Abeo before sunset.

I set off through the forest, through this new day and daylight, angling toward the shadow ahead. As I walk, the church fades behind me, and the house begins to take shape between the trees. There's a moment, a half-time and half-place, when I turn to look back at the church and can only make out its shadow, and ahead—there is a house, I know, but I can only make out its shadow, too.

Right now, one step in either direction would bring the church or house into focus, no longer a shadow but something real.

It's a knowledge that's deep in me, now, turning:

I have a *choice*.

I stand very still in the quiet of the wood. But I pause for only a heartbeat.

Something tugs at my heart, pulling me along.

I take a step forward, and the house sharpens into view.

# Chapter Six: Sixers

I breathe in and out, stilled, as I stare at the house, its sprawling, piercing towers angling toward the sky; a misshapen, tangled nightmare of loose shingles and creaking shutters and windows boarded shut.

On the porch, as if they've been expecting me, two hooded forms sit on ramshackle chairs, as still and colorless as rubble, their hair tangled around the chair legs, tumbling over the ground.

I can't see their eyes, but I know they're watching me.

I have made my choice, and I will see it to its end. Fear stirs in my belly, clawing at my sides as I step forward, and then forward again, closing the distance between us until I'm at the porch steps, fingers on the worn wood of the banister.

"I'm Lottie," I whisper into the stillness. "I was wondering…if you could help me…"

As one, the two Sixers—for that's what they are, the unmistakable cloaked figures from the Wanting Market—cock their heads, but in opposite directions, like mirror reflections of each other.

"Help *you*," they whisper, a slithering *shush* of sound that crawls over the broken floorboards of the porch towards me.

The battered door opens slowly, and there is the

woman from the Need Shop, Matilda, arms folded, watching me with a superior smirk on her face.

In the back of my heart, as my world falls away, I know now: it's begun.

The two Sixers on the porch seem to blur along their edges, their cloaks of misting black elongating, contorting, and then there are not two Sixers but *four*. Four cloaked figures that watch me like hooded birds from the porch, staring down at me behind faceless voids.

My heart hammers against my bones, but I still stand strong, feet apart, hands curled into fists. I am afraid of them, so afraid, *so afraid*, the fear licking along my skin with a long, cold tongue.

But there is anger within me, too, tangled with my fear. Anger so hot that it burns away the terror, replacing it with a fire that fills my belly, burns me up.

"Two," I say then, say the word loudly, with a strength I wasn't sure I had. "Two turns into four. But where's your third?"

As one, the four stand, melt back into two so suddenly, as if they're pulled into one another, slippery, gliding like feet over ice. As one, the two Sixers take off their hoods, peeling them back from their skulls with fingers that bear claws—ugly, curving, sharpened things... And beneath their hoods, I see no faces: there is only more hair, tumbling down, black and endless.

I breathe out, take a step back.

Falter.

My entire world shatters as they stare down at me with eyes I cannot see, the Sixers.

The Sixers…

As one, they shriek, claws extended, descending off the porch, snaking their hands around me, fingers pinching my arms, a maelstrom of black hair and dark cloaks and clicking claws that seize me, take me.

The *Sixers.*

My sisters.

The black lines in my palms pulse, pulse, everything shifting, changing, as the memories flood back, the gate, at last, creaking open—wide.

*You'll do what you'll do*, Bird said. *I just hope it's the right thing.*

Darkness.

I crawl in a vast red land with my sisters.

There are the three of us—three with ugly, tattered wings, with sharp claws, our faces shaped like ill-formed masks, and we are crawling over the scorched rocks in search of something.

There, ahead of us. A pulse of light. We descend, screeching, and snatch it up. I am the youngest. The eldest always gets the first one. She takes the sphere of light and pulls it and twists it this way and that in her hands, until it's a string of light, a thread of light, that she loops over and over her sharp fingers. She gobbles it up, swallowing the light down, licking her lips and claws with a rotting tongue.

In one bite, she devoured a soul.

The red land, red as blood, stretches away from us. We aren't alone here. There are many more monsters like us: crawling beasts that roam over the shapeless hills and valleys, searching for the pulses of light that appear and disappear, wink in and out.

We are, all of us, hunting the light.

We scrape claws over the red ground, red like blood, like fire, an engorged, bloody sky dripping overhead to hang low, close to us, smothering. I watch the souls appear—and then disappear, as they're eaten… Flickering, moving orbs of light that roam slowly over the rocky ground. They are the tormented souls, and this is the in-between place for tormented souls, those not yet decided between the above or the below.

The new souls usually come all at once, and once a day, and we wait for them, hungry, *starved.* Their arrival prompts a frenzy of scrabbling and devouring…

But since we—my sisters and I—are not the strongest or the fastest, we pick at the remains, the leftovers, like buzzards.

The eldest is in a rare mood today as we begin to hunt a second soul for my second sister.

"The mortals call it Purgatory here," she hisses, gesturing with a clawed hand to the dry landscape ahead, devoid of light, of souls. "And it is a purgatory to *us.* Just because we know better, call it Twixt, doesn't change what it is. We are trapped here, as surely as the souls we eat."

I want to whisper, want to tell her, "But it wasn't always this way." I close my cracking eyes now, remember for a heartbeat what we used to be, what we *gave up.* What we sacrificed.

We were beautiful once, radiant…with streaming white wings and glowing countenance.

Once. Long ago.

I open my eyes, stare at my sisters, and I bark out a snare of bitter laughter, and the eldest raises a misshapen brow; I duck my head, silenced, and I follow behind as we prowl over the landscape.

We are hideous, deformed externally to reflect our thoughts and actions. We hunt mortal souls and devour them because they satiate our hunger for something…better.

"There! Ahead of us!" hisses the eldest, and we crouch, peering over a craggy grouping of blood-red rocks. There is a soul, the dancing orb of light, out ahead in a little crimson valley. I glance at the sky, foreboding dragging over my skin, but the eldest snatches at my wrist, pulls me down and into the valley, the three of us tumbling after the soul that now floats still, as if it is waiting for us.

We race toward it, crawling and running over the ground in turns, but I hear the sound of the sky tearing before we're there, before we reach the soul.

"No!" screeches the eldest, staring upward.

*This*, I think, raising my gaze to the shape descending through the red toward us. *This is what we once were.* I gape—we all gape—as one of our relations, with her gleaming wings and luminous shape, descends into Twixt, diving toward us.

"Grab it! Must I do everything myself?" the eldest snarls, leaping on top of the soul, taking it up in her claws, positioning it to enter her great maw. But our relation is too fast for my sister, extending her wings, crashing against her and rolling end over end.

Our relation stands, the orb in her hands, but I don't look at the orb. I look at her…

She is more beautiful than I can understand, her white wings sweeping against the ground, her skin glowing like a hundred thousand stars, her eyes bright and blue and all-seeing. Her right wing is a bit ragged, and I remember her now… I have seen this relation before. I don't know when. Perhaps when we three were not yet fallen, or perhaps after. Time is meaningless in Twixt, and memories are slippery, hard to grasp and keep.

All I know for certain is that she is so lovely, she makes my heart ache (despite everything, I think I still have a heart), and I fall to my knees before her as she gazes on us three, beatific face expressionless as she holds the orb of the soul against her body.

The eldest launches to her feet, begins to barrel across the ground, and with one dramatic upsurge, the relation takes to the sky, pumping her glorious wings with effortless power until the redness swallows her whole, and she and the soul are gone, above. I know that she takes the soul now to someplace better, that soul that was snatched out of the eldest's hands, even as she was about to devour it into nothingness.

Angered, my sister screams, a bellow that echoes, and claws at the sky.

“I will destroy her,” she hisses, curling her claws into fists, gouging out her palms until they bleed, the blood dripping into the red ground, disappearing entirely. “They can hurt us *still*, even here. This must change,” she says, lowering her face to our level.

I am afraid when I look into her eyes.

She plans something.

*The memory changes, lengthens, contorts…*

I gather with my two sisters around a green roaring fire built in a red-washed cave, far in the back where we are hidden from our relations, and my eldest sister paces back and forth, back and forth, in front of the flames.

“We need the souls for energy, for sustenance,” she says through cracked lips, pausing in front of the fire, pointing her claws to it. She speaks shrewdly, biting off the words as she watches us. “But what if we took a bit of that power and *spun* it into something more than a meal for a belly?”

I shrink away from her as the second sister asks, “What can you mean?”

The eldest watches me, eyes narrowed, as she

steps closer, into the green fire that hisses, burning up her broken and then rehealed legs, sizzling up and over her body as she snarls out, letting the fire scald her, scorch her, and doing nothing to stop it. Enjoying it. She shows us that she is the strongest, that we must listen to her, and I cower back in fear as she moves out of the fire now, stalking toward us.

"You do not seem interested, sister," she says to me, head to the side, staring down into my eyes. I do my best to hold her gaze, but I waver, and she sees this. She takes me up, her claws around my neck, suspending me high in the darkness.

"We Sixers must remain together," she hisses. "Always together, of one mind. Do not forget this."

I fall, crumpling, as she dashes me to the ground, upon the rocks, and she turns back to our second sister, the simpering sister who paws at the eldest's elbow, cooing quietly.

I rise to my knees, press my hand against the curve of shoulder and neck, loathing rising within me with such intensity, it devours me whole, as surely as we devour souls. For too long, the eldest has bullied me and broken me and told me over and over again how she is powerful and I am dust.

I am not *dust*.

"Here…" says the eldest, hissing, as she waves her hands over the green fire in sharp, bright patterns. Suddenly, there is a construct in the flames, an image that flickers with the heart of the fire. It's small and simple, hard to make out, but then I peer closer, and I see it: the construct is a city surrounded by a wall, surrounded by a forest, the trees badly sketched into the image before us, like half-formed, malformed twigs.

"The souls would appear here every day," she hisses, pointing to the center of the city. "The city would house them, and we could leech their souls from them slowly, store the ones we didn't want to devour for later. We need not even hunt them! We milk them for every bit of life they have, bleed them of their energy, use them up. With such time and leisure, we might invent *new* ways to devour them. We could make them *beg* us to take their souls. I have thought of ways..." She curls her fingers together with a snarl. "And our relations, the ones with white wings..." Her misshapen mouth scowls. "We could *twist* their countenances. Make them *hideous* to these souls. Make the souls run *from* them, as if for their very salvation!" She laughs so hard, spittle bubbles up from her lips.

And, inside of me, something shifts and pinches and hurts.

*No,* I think, but do not say.

No.

I do not want to do this thing. I do not want to build this illusion city. I do not want to torture the souls that come to this halfway place, already lost, already tortured.

It is new and strange, this want, but it's born here: I remember the time before I fell. I remember love and kindness, those curse words that my sisters now spit out of their mouths, marking them ugly, foul.

Though I cannot ever have it again, still...*I want it back.*

And, suddenly, I find my voice.

"I do not want to do this thing," I whisper, the words coming out as rough and ugly as I am. I shiver and shake under my sisters' baleful eyes as they watch me, unmoving, unspeaking.

I have spoken my truth.

Now will come my punishment.

They stare at me as if I've told them something absurd, as if I've told them we are not truly devils, after all. Of course we're devils. We made our choices.

The eldest hobbles toward me, and I raise my arms, my claws against her, waiting for the blow…but it does not come.

"*You* are our *sister*," says the eldest, pinching my elbow, dragging me to her, staring at me with her flashing red gaze. "And you *will* do this."

I shudder.

Many of our kind possess oddities of body or ability. We three sisters are the Sixers, for we three can become six. And, as I watch, cowering, my elder sisters now become four. And they gather about me. Me. Only me. One against three or two against six, I will lose this battle.

I am afraid of them. I have always been afraid of them. As the eldest twists my elbow, twisting it tighter and tighter beneath her curving, clawed fingers, I cry out in pain, but she doesn't stop twisting. She loves pain, relishes it, eating it up as she devours part of my spirit.

And my second sister simply watches while the eldest towers over me, eating up a part of my soul that I will never get back.

She drops me to the floor with my broken arm, and I cower beneath her as she turns, licking her long fingers thoughtfully.

My sister is not powerful enough to do what she wishes alone. She needs the energy of souls in order to build this city, what she will call, she tells us, Abeo City. She laughs as she speaks these words, as she snatches up the orbs of souls, lengthening them into glowing threads and spinning a city out of their somethingness.

How many souls does she use to build the city? I don't dare count. She sends us, our second sister and me, out gathering, soul after soul, and if we do not find them—and often, we don't—she breaks new bones in our bodies thoughtfully, very slowly.

I don't want to do this, but I do it still. I find her souls. I snatch them up in my monstrous hands, and I take them to her, too many, so many… Because I am no better than her. I do not stop her.

She spins the city, woven from spirited light, for seven days and seven nights. In the end, at last, she stands before her construct, this bubble of a city and forest that looks misplaced, comical in the red barren lands of Twixt.

"Come," the eldest says.

And we three step inside.

“Look at us,” she breathes, turning and twirling. Now the eldest has long black hair, wears a black dress and cloak, and she looks—more or less—like a human. Or the suggestion of a human. I glance down at my human hands (that are still claw-like), feel back for my hood and draw it over my head, dropping my eyes.

The illusion is well formed. There is the forest that slopes away from us, and ahead a wall that I know surrounds the city, as the eldest imagined it.

Darkness begins to fall, and red lines stretch away in the illusion: bits of Twixt showing through.

“What’s happening, sister?” asks the second sister, gripping the eldest’s black-sleeved arm. “Why is it becoming dark now?”

The eldest purses her lips, staring up at the counterfeit sky. “I…do not know. Perhaps I misjudged time and—”

Darkness falls instantly, absolutely, like a black cloak cast off, covering the forest and the city with its shadows.

There is a great tearing sound in the air. We three look up, and through the night descends a monster. It’s an atrocity built of bone and beak and wing, a truly ugly beast that frightens me, even though I know what it is, its true nature. Even though I know it is we who have made it appear this way.

It descends, flapping its wings, confused, turning its bone claws over and over again. It falls against the earth, rising, pushing off again. It crouches near us, watching us with deep black hollows for eyes.

"Do you *see* yourself, you ugly *perversion*?" The eldest whispers, advancing on our relation. "You are *hideous*, and every soul that comes to this place will run from you, *screaming*." She grabs its clavicle, heaving it up, though this thing is three times her size. "You will be run from. You will be cursed. People will fear you as they have feared *us*. Now *you* will know exile. The tables have turned," she says, smiling, and then she breaks off the bone she's holding. The creature howls, tilting its head back, but she is too quick. She clamps a hand around the creature's neck, and she *squeezes*.

It screams and screams as she devours its soul, and it crumbles to dust in her hands that she licks off her fingers, turning to stare at us, eyes red and glowing beneath her black hair, triumphant.

"Come, queens," she whispers, holding out her dusty hands to us. "Come see our city. Our *kingdom.*"

As we pass through the walls of the city together, we see shadows up ahead. A boy and a girl who wander toward us, eyes wide, clothing as ragged and dirty as the dismal city sprawling before us.

"Please…" the girl whispers. She has long brown hair and has been weeping. The boy grips her hand, won't speak, eyes wide and dark in the stillness. "We can't remember anything. Please help us…"

The eldest steps forward, a hungry look flitting over her face for a heartbeat before she lifts her chin, swallowing. She reaches into her pocket then, drawing out something dark that shifts in the small breezes here. She holds it up, and I stare at it as the boy and girl stare at it, too.

It is one of the feathers from our relations, blackened to fit their illusion in this place now. It is hideous in comparison to what the feathers look like truly: glowing, lovely things that shine with their own light.

You can place an illusion upon an object, but it retains, at its heart, its true essence. Even as she holds it, the feather is luminous in the dark.

"I will give this to you. It will give you a single memory back…" says the eldest, leaning toward the boy and girl with bright eyes, "but you must give me something in return…"

"What?" they whisper, staring at the feather, hands clasped together. They salivate as they stare at it, and my heart pinches again as the eldest leans toward them.

"I'll take a snip of your hair," she whispers, threading a hand through the girl's long mane. The girl shudders, leaning away from her, but she nods, and, quick as death, the eldest curls her fingers in the girl's hair, yanking down so hard, the girl drops to her knees, screams.

The eldest holds up the hank of hair, turning it over and over in her hands with shining eyes. "Here…" she whispers, letting the feather drop to the ground. And then slowly, almost reverently, she feeds the hair into her mouth, long tongue licking it up.

She swallows it down in a single gulp.

The boy and girl stare up at her, eyes wide, shaking. She stares down at them, holding up a single sharp claw.

"Let me show you how to use it…" she whispers, licking her lips again with a smile.

*Again, the memory shifts.*

I am pacing in my own small room in the house outside of the city.

The plan has followed as the eldest hoped it would: flawlessly, perfectly. Our relations have appeared to save the souls, and because the illusion paints them as hideous, monstrous, the souls run and hide from them. Though there have been a few souls that were not fast enough, were Snatched, as we are now calling it, for the most part, we retain the souls with no work at all.

And we devour these souls slowly, savoring the flavor of their spirits, and their pain.

And I grow sicker, angrier, wearier.

And the eldest knows.

I become two again, merging back to one as I nervously pace. Over and over, I become two and then one, two and then one. When I am two, we pace together. We do not look alike, but we are the same creature, she and I.

The eldest is at the door of my room, glancing at me. There is suspicion in her red eyes.

I stop pacing, sit, but I have already given myself away.

That night, when we return from the city and I enter my room, I pause, hand on the knob, still, the metallic scent of blood all around me. I glance up and up, up at the bodies of birds nailed to the wall, their drying blood too bright, their smell too sickening.

Eight clawed hands at the small of my back push me into the room, and the door is shut fast behind me. A key turns in the lock, and I know now that I am caught. That it is all over for me.

My favorite pastime is restricted: I can take only three steps across the room before I must turn now—because of the birds. I become two for comfort, for company, and we pace back and forth, moving like clockwork over the creaking boards.

The night is long and still and full of terror. At first light, my other glances at me, and we pause in the center of the floor. She holds up her hand, brow up, questioning, and I press my palm against her palm.

*They are coming for us.*

My eyes widen as I stare at her, at this knowledge she's given me that I did not possess. She cocks her head, shakes it softly, slowly.

*Too late.*

The door opens.

The eldest stands there, cloak tied about her chin. They have grown as grotesque as the Snatchers now, my sisters, with hair too long, dragging behind them, always tangled with trash and twigs. Because I have not devoured as many souls as they, my hair is more manageable, but still long enough to graze the ground.

I have not eaten a soul in days, days and days and days. I don't know how many days.

And now, finally, my sisters will reprimand me for it.

"Let us go for a walk," whispers the eldest, holding out her hand. I shake my head, *we* shake our heads, take a step back, but the eldest is in the doorway, becoming two, and they advance on us, hands out, smiling beneath the endless, shining hair.

"Come," she hisses to us, and then I am one again, and her hands are around my shoulders. The second sister is in the doorway, and she will not look at me, will only stare down at the floor.

"No," I whisper, clawing at the edge of the bed.

At the front of the house, there is a knock at the door.

The eldest drops me, and I bruise against the

ground. She snarls, turns, and slams the door shut behind her, turning the key in the lock.

Matilda is here, come to give the Sixers their morning report: how much Nox was consumed, how much more is required, even though we Sixers *know* this already, know *everything*. Matilda wants to be important. Here, now, I crawl over the floor, beneath the bed, clawing…

The memory jerks me to the side, and it's over. I don't know what happened between then and now, but I am beside the stream, and the eldest grips my hair with her hand, arching my head back, staring down at me with a too-wide smile.

Can you kill an immortal?

*Of course you can.*

Just like flying, you can fall.

Just like living, you can die.

She reaches down to me, tracing a hand over my throat almost lovingly before her claws are back, and in one smooth, slight motion, she slits my throat.

Somewhere outside of myself, I see her throw my body into the ice. It breaks the ice, forming a hole, tumbling beneath the water.

The second sister takes the eldest's arm as they walk away from the stream. They don't look back once.

But a Sixer was not meant to be murdered. Not in her own construct, the city she helped create.

So it didn't work.

But something…changed.

And when I awoke, my two halves were scattered, separated into two different bodies, and the lines of the illusion shifted to accommodate this mistake.

As the Sixers bore the illusion of youth, of humanity in their own city, the illusion stuck to me, as well, clung to me, but began to shape something different. I was the youngest, so I was a young woman still. But now there were two of me, the two halves to me, divided and apart.

Lottie.

And Bird.

As the memory begins to fade away, I see the girl appear at the edge of the hole in the ice. She's on her back, wearing a tattered black lace dress. Beside her, laying in the opposite direction, is a girl covered all over in furs. They both have black hair, these girls. They both have shocking blue eyes, which they open at the very same moment.

And as the first girl sits up, the second one bolts towards the valley.

And everything begins again.

My back arches beneath me, and I choke on air, trying to breathe, scrabbling as my bones contort, no longer my own.

I breathe in, and I breathe out.

The memory races beneath my skin, and it remains, though the rushing has subsided, though the raging pulse in my wrists has stilled. I hold up my hands, stare at my palms, at the black lines there.

*I contain multitudes.*

I close my eyes, press my fingers against my face, rub them over my skin that I know is not my skin, not really. I open my eyes again, stare at my fingers as if they'll change before my eyes, but of course they can't. They won't. The eldest has woven the construct too soundly for me to unmake it simply by thought, by remembering my hands as the claws they truly are.

I am nothing more than a monster. Less. I am *less* than a monster. Only half…

And now it all makes sense.

I woke up in the wrong place because everything was wrong from the beginning. I was not supposed to die here, was not supposed to *die,* and because I did, my soul bounced back in a strange, complicated way. I am separated from my other half, not whole. The Snatchers—our relations—did not want me because I am not a *real* soul or spirit, a human spirit, in need of saving. I am a monster, and a helpless one at that.

I breathe in and out, everything I hold inside of me breaking, like ice. I wanted out of this; I wanted to destroy Abeo City, our false, fatal playground. And my sisters murdered me because I was no longer theirs to control, and I—we, Bird and I—returned, because everything, all of this…was a *mistake*.

I stare at my hands as if seeing them for the first time: pale skin, blackened lines across their palms. They are soft and fair, like a young woman's hands...

All I am is a *lie*.

A sob escapes my throat, and I turn over onto my side. I'm on a bed. It crinkles beneath me, and I lift my gaze, knowing what I will see, dreading the sight.

There are small bodies nailed to the walls.

I sit up quickly, my heart hammering against my ribs.

Hundreds of birds are nailed to the walls, and even covering the door, in a tidy pattern—like wallpaper. A single rusty nail sticks out of the center of each of their feathered chests. Along the top of the wall, there is a border of crows, and everywhere else, there are songbirds, their beaks open, tiny tongues shriveled, their eyes dull in death.

Every inch of the walls is covered in small,

broken bodies. I cower in the center of the bed. They did this before they murdered me so that I would not go through the walls. I cannot walk through death, will not. It holds me here, trapped. My sisters know this.

Rage pulses through me like blood, like the blood dripped down the walls, solidified and staining.

I draw up my knees and hug them to me, pressing my forehead against them.

I breathe in and out.

And I listen.

"She has been separated."

I open my eyes. I can hear them through the door. Do they know I listen? Maybe they think I'm still Memming—a delayed reaction triggered, I think, by the nearness of my sisters, to the Nox I took at Black House...

I keep breathing evenly, still my racing heart.

"It won't be hard. Where in Abeo could she be hiding? We'll ransack all of the Safe Houses, no stone unturned. We will *kill* this one *again*, and then the other. Easy."

"I don't like it. It didn't work before."

"Perhaps we should kill them together?" ponders the eldest. I know her voice. It makes my whole being recoil.

"Yes, yes. Perhaps. Matilda, you will remain here. You will watch. You will see that she does not leave. And if she does, you will make her Mem so that you can contain her."

"Yes, ma'ams," comes her sniveling, groveling voice.

And then they are all gone.

Bird.

They're after *Bird*.

I know her now. Know why I recognized her, why I felt her so close to me, why she made sense.

Because she is part of me, as I am of her. We are divided, but we are the same, she and I, but so different. I chew at my thumbnail, feeling the tears squeeze at the corners of my eyes again, but I won't let them fall. I won't.

I have to get out. I take a deep breath, stilling my heart.

I have to.

I close my eyes.

It's a compulsion, the strongest one I've felt yet, stronger than when the Snatchers chased me.

Wait.

The Snatchers.

Our relations.

They wanted me to find Bird…led me to her.

I rake my fingers into my hair, tug. What does it all *mean*? I've remembered everything now, but I don't know how to put it together yet, and I must. Does Bird remember? Is that why she couldn't tell me, because the Sixers built this city, and they might hear her speak of it aloud?

I breathe in and out, shaking.

And the Sleepers.

Charlie and Violet and Edgar, all of them…

They're not Asleep. They'll never Wake.

They're *dead*.

I press the heels of my hands to my eyes until all I see are rich, changing colors. All I am inside is empty, is aching, is pain. Charlie thinks she's going to wake up. That she can try again, make her life better. But she's dead. Violet's dead. Edgar's dead.

And the Sixers are *sucking them dry* until there's nothing left. Until they Fade.

They won't exist, not a hair of them, once the Sixers finish with them.

I sit up again so quickly that my head whirls and

spins. No. They won't have them. They *won't.* I think of Charlie's kindness to me. Of her soft smile, the way she threads her fingers through mine. She doesn't know what I am, and now that *I* know... I swallow, the tears falling from my eyes.

What was happening between us is over. I'm a monster, only a monster. But I can still tell Charlie the truth.

Perhaps, I…I…

I gulp down air, gulp down a sob.

Could I help them escape? Could I guide them out of Abeo City, beyond the Gray Line, into Twixt? And then the Snatchers—not *Snatchers* at all, not really—could save them, carry them away from here.

Outside of the Gray Line, the illusion fades away. The Sixers only constructed the illusion up to the Gray Line, and after that, the truth is as plain as sight.

I rise from the bed, stand in the center of the macabre room, dead bird eyes staring at me.

My hands curl into fists.

The Sixers are powerful. They killed me before. They'll do it again, and this time…probably for good. Fragmented as I am now, I won't come back, not a second time. My sisters will take my half-soul, freshly vacated from its body, and they'll eat it up. And I will become nothingness.

*…everything we did is for* nothing.

That can't be. I have to find Bird. I have to find Charlie and Edgar and Violet. I have to tell them, tell them the truth. I close my eyes, bite my lip, swallowing tears as I imagine what Charlie will say, the look on her face, the betrayal in her eyes as she finds out that she is not sleeping, as she finds out that I am a monster. Hideous. Ugly beyond understanding.

My friends are so afraid of the Sixers, and *I* am a Sixer. I frightened them all, before…

But it doesn't matter, none of it, not if they can be saved. If they can get past the Gray Line.

Whatever happens to me, I will get them past the Gray Line.

I remember the Snatchers refusing me, herding me to Bird. Do they know?

Were they…trying to help me?

Too many questions. Too many missing answers. I pace the tight confines of the room, turning well before I reach the walls of birds. Three steps. All I'm allowed is three steps.

As I stare up at the walls, at the stiff wings and the open beaks, I pause for a moment, for a heartbeat. I stare harder at the flock of bodies, unfocus my eyes.

I still my breathing, still my thundering heart. This was my room. They kept me in here before they decided to murder me. I remember pacing; I remember that I could take only three steps. I remember what it felt like to contain myself and how my two halves were not really so separate, merging and unmerging at will.

I remember something else…

There are loose boards beneath the bed.

I gasp, turn, drop to my knees without a sound, crawling beneath the rickety bed frame—a bed I never slept upon, never needed.

Is this how I got out before, before they killed me? Didn't they know? Didn't they board it up? But even if they boarded it up, I could move *through* the boards, through the floor itself, as I've moved through doors, through walls…

Careless of them, not to nail dead birds to the floor, as well.

There's a basement. I remember a basement.

I'm too panicked to slip through the floor now, to concentrate, to calm. I pry at the boards until my fingertips begin to bleed. But there—one pops up, and I push it aside, reaching under to take up the other two.

Footsteps.

I still my breathing, peer out under the edge of the door, see Matilda's pointy-toed boots there, pausing before the locked door. But she pauses for only a heartbeat before she turns, begins to pace back in the small hall outside the room.

I edge back the third board, and there's enough space for my body. A trail of musty air wafts up from below, and I shove my feet and legs through, and I drop into the darkness.

It takes a moment for my eyes to adjust. Overhead, light filters down on me, but here, below, everything else is black as ink.

Now that I know what I am, my memories are coming back in small, uncontrolled glimpses. I knew about the boards, triggered by the birds' bodies, and I knew about the basement, triggered by the boards.

And now that I'm in the basement, I remember what we Sixers used it for.

A shifting sound, feet against dirt. A grinding sort of *hiss*. And then they stagger into view, into the light.

They are Sleepers. I repeat this to myself over and over, to displace the rising fear: *They are only Sleepers*. Their bodies are decayed, and some are almost transparent, these Sleepers gaunt and gray, their skin like thick dead flesh. But they are not dead, not physically alive *or* dead, because they are only spirits—as we all are, trapped in a perfect illusion that makes us appear a certain way, a way we are not.

In truth, these souls are not grotesque and emaciated. Beyond Abeo City, they are spheres of light, golden, glowing.

I am the one who's hideous through and through.

These Sleepers are on the verge of vanishing... They look unwell, failing, because they are almost all used up.

The girl standing before me has no hair. She reminds me of Florence: the brittle way she moves, stepping forward, hobbling because she doesn't have the strength to walk in a straight line. Her tattered dress hangs off of her like ribbons, and when she gazes at me, she has only one eye.

I can feel all that she is, the very essence of her—her energy—leeching away into the earth beneath her feet.

Feeding the Sixers, my sisters, Bird and me.

She will become nothingness before nightfall. I know that the moment I look upon her, and I know other things, too. I know that she lived in Black House. I know that she sold her hair for Nox until she had none left; she Memmed every memory of her life... And then she Faded away.

But she didn't, not really. Like the Harming Tree, Fading is a myth.

When everything she was had been sold, exhausted, she became the property of the Sixers. And the Sleepers saw her Fade, but only because she disappeared to reappear here, to be used and devoured completely.

She is so afraid. She trembles, as the others crawl up or stand up or kneel beside her, watching me in the darkness, their eyes dimly shining.

I gulp down my tears, curl my hands into fists.

"You are one of them," says the Sleeper before me, the girl who is almost gone. I can't deny it, so I don't. I stand very still, and then I nod stiffly.

"Yes," I whisper.

"You are the youngest," says an older man, skeletal and wilting like a dead plant, his eyes milky.

"The youngest Sixer."

"Yes," I whisper again. The truth is a blade, slicing open my heart. I can't deny what I am, now that I know.

The girl holds out a hand to me, lips trembling. "You were kind to me."

"W—what?" I stare at her.

"Don't you remember?" she whispers. "When you escaped? You opened the door for us, to the outside. Before they killed you," she says, voice soft. "We know they killed you. They laughed about it when they came back home… We heard their voices through the floorboards."

I shake my head. "If I opened the door, then why—"

"We are too weak, not fast enough, you see. We couldn't even climb the stairs. But it was a kind gesture, all the same."

I don't know what to say. I breathe out, press my fingernails into my palms.

"Will you save us now?" the girl whispers.

I stare at her, at her decayed body, at the illusion that looks so real.

She can't be saved. She will become nothingness too soon; I can't stop that. But there is such faith and trust in her face, in her voice.

"I'm one of them…" I say, voice cracking, but she steps forward, head shaking so hard, I can hear the *creak* of the bones in her neck.

"Don't talk to her, Estella," croaks one of the older women, curving away from me. "She's right. She's one of them. You're wasting your breath."

"I'm not," says the girl, her fingers curled toward me. "She's different."

"Do you know how many people have come through here?" asks the old woman, leering at me. The others watch me with glinting eyes, unseeing or seeing, it's impossible to tell. "Do you know how many souls you've eaten? How many your sisters have?"

I run my fingers through my hair, press my fingers against my face.

"And yet..." says the girl, inching forward again, "you tried to help us. Will you try again?"

I watch her carefully, my hands shaking. I curl my fingers into fists again so that I don't betray my fear.

"I'll try," I tell them, then, forcing strength into my voice. "I'm so sorry. Please... You can't forgive me. You can't possibly. But I'm going to try."

The girl breathes out, closes her eye, sags a little. "Through there..." She points.

There's a door above a staircase, cut into the earthen wall.

"The Sixers can go through the doors," whispers the girl. "We cannot. Not anymore."

"I'll come back for you." I gulp down air, spread my hands. "I'll be back, I promise. I'll get you out of this."

I follow the rough stone staircase and push through the door with my hands, step through the splintered wood as if it's made of air.

I find myself in a long, dark corridor illuminated with jars of Wisps along the bottom edges of the walls. I crouch down beside a jar for a moment, reach my hand out to touch it. The Wisps are souls, too, but they're worthless souls to the Sixers, animal souls, I remember. Hardly a morsel, a bite.

I touch the glass with a long finger, feel the Wisps bump up lazily against it, sharing their warmth.

I think of Bird's butterfly, and I rise, shaking.

At the other end of the room, there's a sharp scraping, a rustle of metal against metal. Chains?

I walk forward, breathing in and out, almost

panting.

There are cages. Cages three times my size, scuffing the ceiling of the hallway. And there are boxes. Wooden boxes and crates, filled to bursting with feathered darkness.

At the end of a row of empty cages, I pause, gaping in horror.

The last cage is occupied.

There are chains looped around its skeleton legs and around its skeleton wrists. There is a chain about its neck, and an iron band that's clamped around its beak. And its wings, once monstrously huge and shimmering black, are only bones now, for the Snatcher—the Snatcher trapped in the iron cage—has been plucked clean, its feathers filling the crates and boxes that surround it.

It watches me out of skull hollows, pinioned to the bottom of the cage, plucked and trapped and imprisoned.

I crouch beside the cage, can barely breathe as I kneel next to this being that *looks* like a monster, but isn't. It is my perfect opposite.

It watches me, and I feel such pity for it, such sadness. I press a hand to the floor, feel the earth below siphoning off energy, and I know then that my sisters are feeding off of our relation, this not-Snatcher. They will feed off of it until it is nothingness, like the poor souls in the basement.

It watches me, unable even to crack its beak. Might it speak, if it could open its mouth? Edgar said he encountered a Snatcher once that seemed as if it were trying to speak to him…

I remember them, the not-Snatchers, gliding across the sky, so beautiful that sight of them stole your breath. Their broad white wings streamed with light, their glowing faces so lovely, they looked like gods.

"Once," I whisper to the soul in the cage, "I was beautiful, too."

Tears seep from my closed eyes. Nothing I say can make up for this creature's pain, for its torture. For the great blasphemy its imprisonment has been. I tap the place over my heart, and I hold out my hand, through the bars.

The Snatcher gently, so gently, touches a sickle-claw to my outstretched palm.

I'm weeping.

There's no time for weeping.

I stand, wipe my tears away, touch the bars again, shaking my head.

Beyond the cage are steep, creaking steps. I run up them without looking back, pressing my shoulder against the doors at the end, pushing through them.

I burst through a back door out into the forest, awash in light from the setting sun.

I don't look back. I *don't look back* at the house that I built, that I was imprisoned within, that has imprisoned countless others. I don't look back when the bloody sunset slips away, when the gray lines and jagged edges of the trees become shadows that house a multitude of Snatchers.

I don't look back when I hear beaks click open, when I hear the shrieks and screams, when the air is filled with the slicing rush of black-feathered wings.

I know that they will not touch me. Though my skin crawls, though the ghost of fear moves beneath my bones, I *am not afraid* as I run through the darkness of this manufactured night. Of course time moves wrongly here. How does a devil measure time? It *doesn't*. The artificial sun, the artificial sunset and sunrise and night and day. All of it, *lies*.

Somewhere, the Sixers stalk through this night. They are looking for Bird, and so to Bird I run, to her church beneath the trees. There are lights on in the church, lights from the Wisps that Bird has gathered. And the door is open, when I reach it, when I vault up the steps.

But Bird is not there.

I gulp down air, lean against the solidity of the church walls. Have the Sixers taken her? Did she know they were coming? She must have known. She must have left, must have run.

*Please, I hope you ran.*

If they have her, if they kill her, will I feel it? Will I die, too?

I press my fingers against my wrist, in the place where Bird gripped me. Though it isn't, my skin feels solid, real. I'm still here, now. I still have time.

Bird is quick and clever. They might be chasing her, hunting her. But she could hide from them, as she's hidden all this time.

I stare back into the deep darkness of the forest. Up above me, the Snatchers are roosting in the trees.

They are watching me.

And they watch me run to Abeo, their bones ghost-white lanterns in the dark.

# Chapter Seven: Meant

The streets of Abeo lie as dark as my thoughts as I run, boots beating against the rocks and rubble. I fly through the wall, angling towards Mad House.

On the porch, I stop, pause, picking twigs and leaves out of my hair, before I step forward and pass through the door.

The jars of Wisps are smaller here than at the Sixers' house. It's a strange thing to notice as I make my way along the hall, headed toward the great room where the Sleepers gather.

But there's Charlie, sitting on the stairs, still as stone, staring at me with her eyes red and round and her mouth open.

And Charlie runs down the last steps, and she puts her arms around my neck, and her shoulders move in a single, wracking sob. "I thought you were *gone*," she whispers, holding me so tightly that I don't know where she ends and I begin. "I thought they'd taken you, Snatched you. I *thought you were gone…*"

My head is against her shoulder, and I can feel the sob that moves through her body, can feel her warmth against me, her hands at my waist now, pulling me close, holding me tightly, as if they'll never let go again. And a breath escapes me, and a single tear slides down my cheek, hot as scorched earth, because she thought I was gone forever, *Snatched,* and she'd mourned for me.

The truth is far worse.

She steps back, then, holds me out at arm's length; our eyes lock, both of us breathing hard, both of us crying.

Can she see the change in me? Can she see the *monster* in me?

But her gaze is soft, soft and brown. Affectionate. Warm.

She doesn't know what I am. She doesn't know what I've done, the pain I've caused or the souls I've ended. I have brought souls to nothingness. I have destroyed—for the sake of satiating my selfish hunger.

I should tell her now. I should pull away, cut these threads between us…

But when she curls her fingers around my hips, when she draws me forward, I put my arms about her neck as if I've done it a thousand times before. It's Charlie who dips her head down to meet mine, pressing her lips against my lips.

It's Charlie who kisses me.

And I kiss her back, because she is beautiful and good and kind and the best soul that I've ever known, that I could ever know. In all of my life. In all of my existence. I take this kiss because she gives it freely. And what comes after will be pain, all of it sharp, deep pain…

But I will keep this loveliness: the taste of her lips, how soft they are, how gentle but hungry; we are, the two of us, melded, connected, for these stolen heartbeats.

I will keep this memory for as long as my forever lasts.

She takes a step back, mouth closed, her eyes

searching mine, her face radiant, joyful. “Oh, Lottie,” she says, and her words crack, and there are tears in her eyes, and I can’t bear that joy, the *love* in her face, her smile—no, it's *wrong*—and I falter, move away, eyes downcast.

“Lottie?” she asks, voice trembling, but I take another step back, and then Violet is on the stairs, coming down, but Charlie doesn’t care. She comes forward, clasps her hands with mine. “Lottie, what is it? What’s the matter?” she whispers, lips parted with so many words left unsaid.

“I have something to tell you,” I whisper, looking up at Violet, avoiding Charlie’s searching gaze. “Can we go somewhere quiet?”

Violet glances meaningfully at the empty hall, but Charlie angles her chin toward the stairs, squeezing my fingers, and we walk up them and toward the room they gave me my first night here.

How long ago and far away that night seems.

My limbs are heavy, weighted by the burden of truth. I swallow down my tears, my regret, my deep ache, and I climb the steps with Charlie holding my hand, my fingers limp in hers. We reach the top of the stairs, and Abigail scuttles down the hall below, holding a lantern of Wisps aloft.

“Charlie, the Sixers are here,” she says, voice soft, low. “They came in through the kitchen entrance. They’re looking for..." Her eyes flick to me. "For Lottie.”

Charlie’s gaze is sharp, eyes wide, mouth open, but she whispers down to Abigail, “They can’t find her. Tell them she’s not here.”

“They’re saying they must search the Safe House, Charlie,” says Abigail, eyes dark and haunted. She shakes her head woefully. “They’ll find her.”

“Why are they after you? What did you *do*?”

Violet hisses at me, but I'm shaking my head, fear crawling up my spine with clicking claws. It can't be over before it's begun. *It can't be.* How did they find out so *quickly*?

"There's a balcony, off of my room," says Charlie, voice soft, putting her finger over her lips and motioning to Abigail to return to the Sixers. "Stall them," she hisses after her, and then places her hand at the small of my back, pushing. "You can climb out, down a drainpipe to the ground."

"Charlie, the Snatchers—" begins Violet, but I shake my head.

"They won't bother with me," I whisper. Violet's eyes are wide, and she stares at me as Charlie and I run past her, through Charlie's door and into her room.

Florence is in the corner, squatting there, rocking back and forth, back and forth; she looks up when we enter. "Florence, honey, you've got to be quiet, okay?" Charlie breathes, putting her finger over her lips again. "Can you be quiet for me, honey?"

Florence's head is cocked, watching us. She makes no indication that she heard Charlie's question, that she even understood it. She's more gaunt than she was before, if that's even possible. She looks as bad off as the girl in the basement, the last scrap of hair on her head sticking up at a wilting angle, the tatters of her dress doing little to cover the bones that stick out from under her skin.

I know now that Charlie was right; the Harming Tree is only a superstition, after all. An invention of the Sleepers, a desperate scrabbling for hope, and for some measure of control over their sad existences.

"Stay here," Charlie whispers, pointing to the floor where Florence crouches. "Stay here." Then Charlie takes my hand, pulling me through the room and to the window draped in black.

"If the Snatchers come," she whispers, peeling back the dark curtains, peering into the night, "run as fast as you can toward Black House and—"

"They won't take me, Charlie," I say, my words catching, folding in upon themselves. I swallow, steel myself. "Charlie, I have to tell you—"

I can hear the stairs creaking, bodies moving over them as quietly as they can. My eyes widen; Charlie opens and shuts her mouth, then shakes her head.

"They won't take you," she murmurs, as if to comfort herself, and opens the window soundlessly. "Here…" she breathes, taking my hand, and I crawl over the windowsill, out onto the balcony beneath.

The night air is still, quiet. Above me, on the arch of the roof, a Snatcher watches my progression, wings arched, claws hooked into the roof tiles. Waiting.

Charlie crawls out after me.

"What are you *doing*?" I hiss, but she shakes her head, moves past me, peering down at the ground.

"The drainpipe's here. Come *on*, Lottie," she whispers, ushering me over. "We've got to move quickly."

She hooks her hands around the drainpipe, easing her body off of the roof. The pipe creaks dangerously but holds as she begins to creep down its length. I wait until she's on the ground, peering over my shoulder at the window every thunderous heartbeat, but when she touches the rubble with her shoes, I'm out on the drainpipe after her, climbing hand under hand.

Halfway down the pipe, I hear the window creak again. I can't see it from my angle, and I wait, heart in my throat, until I see a skull peer over the edge of the balcony, eyes searching out Charlie and me.

Florence has crawled out after us.

I scrabble down to the ground.

"Florence, *get back inside*," Charlie's whisper roars around us, but Florence does not listen, instead peers at the drainpipe, as if she's trying to figure out how to climb over the balcony railing to get to it.

And then, as if the Snatcher had been waiting for this moment, this Sleeper, Florence…it opens its wings, unfurling them like black flags, unhooking its claws from the roof.

Charlie gazes up and up, face stricken, mouth open. "Florence, *get back inside*," she repeats, voice breaking, but Florence only gazes up at the Snatcher stalking over the roof toward her.

She doesn't move.

Charlie races past me, begins to climb the drainpipe again, but she's not fast enough, and the Snatcher is too quick. It glides off the roof, onto the balcony, and smoothly, with practiced skill, it hooks its claws around Florence's waist, takes one leap, and flies into the night. Disappears, black against black.

The world falls hideously still.

Charlie drops down, hitting the ground and falling against it, rolling as she lands on her knees, pressing her head against the earth and sucking in a fractured sob. I stare back up toward the balcony, at the shadows moving in Charlie's room. The Sixers? I can't tell, don't even want to know…

I take Charlie's arm, help her up, squeeze her hand, and together—Charlie crying, me trembling—we run across the street, hiding in the shadows of a tired building as the Sixers finally peer out of Charlie's window at the empty balcony…and move back inside the room.

"Florence," Charlie whispers over and over and over again, unable to breathe, her body wracked with quiet sobs. I hold her, lean her head against my shoulder, and feel her pain piercing me through.

"Charlie, please listen," I try to tell her, but she shakes her head, rocks back and forth.

"She trusted me to help her. She trusted me to save her..." She says it over and over again, a litany, a prayer.

"You did," I say, but she doesn't hear me, or doesn't understand, so I whisper it again, into the night, into her ear, "Charlie, you *did* save her. Please believe me. You *did.*"

"I *saved* her?" she spits out, laughing a little through her tears, rubbing at her face, pressing her mouth against her hand. "She was just *Snatched*, Lottie."

I gulp down air, breathe out. "Charlie, I know this sounds wrong. I know it does. But Florence will be okay now. It's...good that this happened, that she was...Snatched."

She stills, quiet as she watches me in the darkness, brown eyes wide with horror. "*What* did you just say?" The words cut deep, are too sharp coming from her mouth, but I shake my head, keep going.

"It's...it's good to be Snatched." I falter as she stares. "I... There's too much to explain. I have to go. You should—" My voice breaks, and I wonder if this will be the last time I'll ever see Charlie's face. If the Sixers find me... But I can't pity myself; I *chose* to become a monster, and I must accept the consequences of that choice.

"You should go back into Mad House," I say hoarsely, pushing her forward a little. "It's not safe out here for you."

"And it is for *you*? Lottie, why are the Sixers after you? Do you know?"

Yes, I know.

We stare at one another helplessly in the

darkness. She takes my hands, a soothing, familiar gesture, and threads her fingers through mine.

"Don't," I whisper, taking my hands from hers, the warmth torn from my palms too quickly. I shiver, stare down at the rubble beneath us, scrub away the tears from my cheeks.

"Why?" she asks, breathes out. She sounds so lost, so broken. "Do you regret the kiss—"

"No. *No*," I repeat, wracked with sorrow. Still, I don't tell her. How can I tell her? I can't bear the thought of the look on her face, the change that will come over her when she knows, when she knows everything. I can't. Not yet. Not now.

"You have to go—"

"I'm not leaving you, Lottie."

"You have to—"

"No." Tears shine on her face, but her expression is set, stubborn, and she wraps her arm around my waist, standing so near to me, so warm, so soft....

I move my eyes away, trembling with every breath. "We have to get somewhere safe," I manage, too weak to insist again that she leave me, too ashamed to look in her eyes. "Where can we go that's safe? That the…the Sixers can't find us?"

"Black House," she says, doesn't even pause, doesn't even think. "Edgar will keep us safe."

"Please, let's go." I move, tug at her fingers, and risk a glance at her, then: she's watching me carefully, eyes hooded and dark.

"Lottie," she begins, but I shake my head, swallow.

"Not yet. Let's get to Black House, to safety, first."

She nods, twice, and then we're running down the street, running away from Mad House, through Abeo

City.

Fetchers are fast, and Charlie's the fastest, but I keep up well enough as our feet skid over the rubble of the broken streets, as our bodies blur past the houses, past the garbage piles, where Wisps move quietly, softly, illuminating the night.

There are no sounds above us or behind us—no voices, no footsteps, no wings. I chance a glance at Charlie beside me, at her hair streaked back in the wind, at her red-rimmed eyes so fixed on what's ahead of her.

I swallow, look forward again.

Sooner or later, I have to tell her. Sooner or later, she'll know what I am. But for this moment, this heartbeat, she doesn't. Still, she bears pain, because she thinks that what's happened to Florence is terrible. Unthinkable. Unimaginable. In that, at least, I can offer her some comfort... Once she knows the truth about the Snatchers, her grief over Florence might ease.

We dash around the side of Black House, panting as we stand near the back door. Charlie jerks her thumb up to the window on the right, picks up a bit of broken brick and throws it at the window. "He'll not like that," she mutters, and it's true: when the curtain is inched back, when Edgar's wide eyes peer out into the air, and then down at us, his expression transforms from worry to anger in an instant.

He opens the window, glances up at the sky again, then at us. "What are you *doing* out there?"

"The Sixers are after Lottie," says Charlie, words quick.

Edgar's face changes again, softening. "Come up, come up," he says, gesturing, and tosses out a rope ladder.

"You kept it. I knew you'd keep it," says Charlie, when she reaches the top, when she embraces him. They help me in, then shut the window and draw the curtains back into place.

"They're after you?" says Edgar, brows up, smile making his moustache arch. He's impressed. I shake my head.

"It's not like that…" I mutter.

"Like what?" he asks, cocking his head. But Charlie's seated herself on the edge of the bed, is staring down at her hands. "What's wrong?" he asks, glancing from me to her. "What happened?"

"Florence," says Charlie, voice heavy. "Snatched."

"Oh," he whispers, paling. "Charlie…" He crosses over to her, sits down on the bed beside her, puts an arm around her shoulders. She takes a staggering breath, leans against him.

I chew on a fingernail, glance at the doorway as someone moves through the hall beyond it quietly. "Are we safe here?" I whisper, voice so soft I mouth the words more than speak them. Edgar nods, staring up at me.

"What did you do?" he asks mildly. I shake my head, begin to pace the room.

"I… It's not what you think," I repeat, but Charlie rubs her hand under her nose, sniffling, and glances up at me.

"Then what should we think, Lottie?" she asks.

I reach up, touch my lips with cold fingers. I remember what she tasted like, her softness, her nearness. I close my eyes, lean away from the both of them. It'll shatter, all of it, if I speak the truth.

"Did the Sixers come here, before Mad House?" I ask Edgar, and he nods, mouth drawn in a small line.

"They searched it. For you," he adds helpfully. "I was more or less expecting the both of you here after that, Snatchers or not. They said they were going to search all of the Safe Houses. There's a reward for you, by the way. So you know," he mutters, grimacing. "An entire crate of Nox."

"A reward…" I breathe out, stare down at the blackened lines in my palms. They've made me into a fugitive. No one must see me now. "Look…" I glance up, bite my lip. "Thank you so much for helping me. Both of you. But I have to go. I have to…" I don't know, honestly, what I have to do. I haven't figured it out yet. I have to find Bird. I have to get the Sleepers past the Gray Line, but how? I lean against the wall, slide down it until I clasp my knees with my arms, breathe out in a shudder.

I don't know what to do.

"Lottie." Charlie crosses the space between us, kneels down beside me. "No matter what's happened, we're still here for you. I still…" she breathes out, breathes in. "I still love you. No matter what."

I stare at her, eyes wide, tears filling them quickly. "No. You…" I swallow, shake my head. "You *can't* love me, Charlie."

"What?" There's anger, now, in her voice, as she sinks back on her heels. "I can't? What does that even *mean?*"

I sag, spent and numb. "You can't, because…"

"Because why?" Edgar prompts.

"Okay," I breathe, resolved. "I'll tell you." The words spill out softly, slowly. "I'm…*I'm* a Sixer."

I open my eyes, watch Charlie, watch Edgar. They stare at me for a long moment before they, as one, shake their heads. Edgar is actually smiling, but I draw in a deep breath, lean forward. "It's the *truth,*" I tell them, dragging out the words. "I am one of the three. The *third.* I am a Sixer."

"How can you be…" Charlie splutters, spreads her hands. "You look nothing like them—"

"Looks can be deceiving." I grit my teeth. "I

know how bizarre this must sound to you, but I am the youngest Sixer. My sisters…they killed me—"

"*What*?" Edgar gasps. "*What* did you say?"

"They killed me," I repeat, biting my lip. "But I came back. Listen… That's…that's not even the most important part." I clench and unclench my fists. "Twixt is… It's what your kind call Purgatory," I tell them quickly. "It's where souls go when they pass on, the…tortured souls."

They stare at me, lips parted, uncomprehending.

"Dead souls," I breathe out, holding back tears. "Charlie, Edgar," I say softly, quietly. "You're both dead."

Charlie sits back on the floorboards, elbows on her knees, watching me with unblinking eyes, swallowing. Edgar stands, then sits down again, then stands once more, taking a step forward.

"Say the word," he whispers, eyes wide, bright. "Say it again."

"Dead," I repeat, and when he opens his mouth, tries to say it, nothing comes out but a hiss of air. "It's part of the illusion," I tell him, trying to keep my voice calm, steady. "Sleepers can't talk about anything related to death. It's…to keep them calm," I spit out, pressing my fingernails into my palms. "To keep them from discovering the truth."

"I don't understand," says Charlie then, voice small, and I risk a glance at her, and my heart breaks into slivers, each piece stabbing a little deeper. She's watching me with guarded eyes, hurting eyes.

Fearful eyes.

"The Sixers built…" I exhale heavily. "*We* built Abeo City, in Twixt," I say, cradling my head, "to trap souls, so that we could devour them. Because that's what Sixers do." I look up at them, trembling. "Eat souls. Your souls. You sell bits of hair to the Sixers for

Nox, and the more hair you sell, the more of your soul you give over to them, until you Fade away. And then you belong solely to the Sixers, as if by contract, and they devour the last of you, and you become nothingness."

"Nothingness," Edgar repeats, his face pale.

I nod, breathing in. "It's a finely made trap. An illusion. Nothing more. All of this is," I say, holding up my hands, not my hands, palms up. "And I… I wanted to stop. I didn't want to be part of it anymore. Sixers…" I swallow. "We're demons. But we weren't always demons," I whisper.

Charlie shifts, drawing her legs up to her chin.

I go on, because silence now would be worse than anything I might say. "The Snatchers? They're made to look ugly, monstrous, but they're not really, not at all. They're lovely. They're rescuers. Snatchers save you, take you away from here. They're good…" I finish, faltering, as Charlie's eyes fill with tears.

"Florence…" whispers Charlie, and I nod.

"Florence being taken was a good thing," I tell her, breathing the words. "If she hadn't been taken, she would have Faded, and then…"

Charlie rests her head against her knees.

"I know it's hard to believe. Everything in Abeo City was constructed to make you fear the Snatchers. But it's all a lie. *Everything* here is a lie," I say hoarsely, with a sort of wild finality, falling back against the wall, closing my eyes.

"Lottie," says Edgar slowly, carefully. "I know there have been strange things about you. And it's true—I haven't seen the third Sixer in a long time. But…" He trails off, searching for the words. "How long have you known this?"

"I remembered only today," I tell him, gazing up at him, unwavering. "I didn't know until today."

“Why should we believe you?” he asks then.

I stare at him, open my mouth, whisper, "I don't know." Why *should* they believe me? All I have is the truth, no evidence. Only words. I don’t know what else to say, or do, but Charlie gets up, breathes out, glances at Edgar.

“I believe her,” she says, words soft.

Edgar licks his lips, sits back down on the edge of the bed.

"Lottie," Charlie says, and her voice sends a shiver through me—of fear, of hope, of want…

I look up at her.

Charlie offers me a hand, but she won’t look at me as I take it, and the hope that had swelled in my heart deflates as I stand, as we both stand there awkwardly, leaning away from one another, together and apart.

“Look,” says Edgar, voice tired, “I have a lot to think about right now. You two need some privacy, I’m sure… After Florence, I mean.” He unfolds himself and stands, edging toward the door.

Charlie watches him go. “Edgar—”

“It’s a lot to think about.” He pauses before the door, considering me. Doubt darkens his gaze. “See you in the morning,” he says brusquely, and then he’s gone.

We're alone, Charlie and me.

Perhaps Edgar has gone to fetch the Sixers. I wonder if I should follow him, beg him not to tell, not before I can convince the Sleepers to go to the Gray Line…

“He won't tell," Charlie says then, heavily, reading my thoughts. "I think…I think he was just afraid of you,” she finishes, sighing. Still, she won’t look at me; she's staring at her hands.

I curl my own hands into weak fists as a blunt ache presses between my ribs. “Charlie,” I start, but I don't know what else to say. I just needed to whisper her name while it's still mine to whisper, while she's still here with me.

"I believe you," she says, staring down at the floor. "I just lost Florence. I know what you said… I know you said the Snatchers were…good. But as a Fetcher, I'm wired to run from Snatchers, to keep people safe *from* them. And now you're telling me that they're the safety. It's just…just overwhelming, you know? Like everything you've ever known, changing. And not all for the better." She glances up, then, and she stares at me with wet, brown eyes. She looks at me, truly looks at me, searching deeply, and I feel so naked beneath her gaze, as if she can see into my marrow, see under my skin to the monster that lies beneath.

I take a step back. I can't stand for her to look at me like this: detached, considering. It's not the disgusted look I expected, the revulsion. I thought she would run. I thought—

"Lottie…"

I hold my breath, brace myself. The moment hovers: I don't know what her next words will be.

I close my eyes, breathe out. Wait.

"Lottie."

I open my eyes.

She steps forward slowly, as if she's not really moving at all. Charlie reaches up her hand, and then the warmth of her palm is against my arm, my shoulder as she traces it up and over the skin of my neck, cupping my cheek with her hand. I stay very still, breathing in and out as I feel the warmth of her against me, her black-lined palm against my face.

It's all too much, the stillness, the warmth, her softness. "What are you doing?" I whisper, closing my eyes, biting back tears, swallowing raggedly. "I told you—"

“I remember,” she says, breathing out, “the first time I saw the third Sixer. She walked behind the others on their way to the Need Shop. I was in the Wanting Market, with Edgar. He’s the one who Fetched me, you know. He was telling me that the Sixers couldn’t be trusted, and she looked up at us, then, across the Market. That third one, the youngest. She saw us. I guess she heard us. Her hood fell back, and she didn’t look like the other Sixers, not exactly. Her eyes were red, and there were tears… Lottie, she was weeping.”

I feel as if all the air has gone from me. I sag, crouch down, sit on the cold, wooden boards of the floor. I feel horrified that Charlie saw me like that; I don't remember it, don't want to remember anything more from that part of my existence. I bow my head, flushed and sad.

Charlie squats down in front of me, tilts up my chin, and searches my eyes.

“The thing about Twixt,” she says, voice cracking. She swallows, continues, “Is that everyone is obsessed with the past, right? Everyone. But in Twixt, we can’t touch the past anymore. All we can do is *watch* it. And we have no future. Everything in Twixt points to this moment. Right here. Right now. Because it’s *all we have*.”

She’s holding my hand. I don’t remember her reaching across the space between us; I don’t remember her threading her fingers through mine. Cold tears falls down my face, and all I am is empty, is pain. “Charlie…”

“No,” she whispers, shaking her head. “We’ve come to this place. We’re together. You, me. How do you explain that?”

I breathe out. “Sometimes things just happen—”

“This?” She looks down at our hands, presses

her other hand to her heart. “This didn’t just happen.”

I can’t stand to see her hand with my hand, try to disentangle them. “I’m a *monster*,” I breathe. “I’m not what you *see*. It’s an *illusion*, Charlie. I told you. I’m *hideous*—don’t you understand? Worse than what you've seen of the Snatchers, far worse. I’m a fallen creature. I’ve devoured souls; I’ve *lived* to devour souls—”

“They killed you,” she says softly, leaning forward, “because you stopped.”

“Oh, Charlie.” I press my face against her shoulder, feel her warmth as she wraps her arms around me, holding me close. I am so ashamed, disgrace slick on my skin, eating through to my insides.

“I don’t know what’s going to happen tomorrow," Charlie says, smoothing her hand over my hair. "I have nothing left, except for you. And you are the most lovely—”

“Don't.” I’m shaking my head, trying to push away from her, but she stills me, arms firm, hands along my arms, eyes locked on mine.

“Whatever you are, Lottie, I love you,” she whispers.

“I don’t deserve it,” I’m telling her, but she’s shaking her head, tracing her fingers up my arm to my cheek, pressing a long finger against my lips.

“It’s not about deserving. None of us has a past here, Lottie. And now…" She gazes at me, a faint smile curving her lips. "Now is *ours*. Let's not let it slip away."

My heart aches—with pain and love, twined together, inseparable.

"I love you, Lottie.”

I reach across the space between us, curve my fingers through her hair, draw her to me, my lips against her lips, kissing her like she contains the air I need to breathe, like *she* is my air, my sky, the only thing that's real inside an artificial world.

I kiss her, and I don't know what's going to happen now. I am so *afraid*, and I am so tired of being afraid. The Sixers, my sisters... They're not afraid of anything, have never been afraid. They are, after all, monsters, and what does a monster need to fear?

Charlie is warm and soft and lovely. She tastes of cinnamon, of fire, and when she drifts her fingers down my neck and shoulders again, taking the collar of my dress with them, her skin against mine is like cinnamon, too, a dusting of spice, of warmth, as she shrugs out of her coat and shirt, as I shrug out of my dress, the cloth crumpling against the floor like a textured shadow.

In the darkness of the room, with the gentle, constant *plinking* of the Wisps against their glass jars, there's just enough light to make out features, just enough light to be ashamed beneath her gaze. I feel the heat rising in me, and I cover myself, trying to hide even as I gaze up at her, at her strength as she stands before me, beautiful, perfect, her curves swelling with her shadows in the soft yellow light.

"Stop," she says, and she takes my hands. "Stop," she murmurs, her mouth against my skin. "You're *beautiful*," she says, and she whispers it over and over as my tears come, as we lay down on Edgar's bed, as I move beneath her fingers, her lips, all I am a heartbeat.

She presses her palms against my palms, our black lines merging together as I close my eyes, feeling her length over mine, like stars over earth. I remember stars as she captures my mouth with hers.

I've never loved. There was nothing to pin that feeling to, that intensity of growing heart, that rush of blood through veins. Love was the luxury of beings who could die, because then life was precious, not a commodity. Not something to be devoured.

But I died, didn't I? I was killed, and I know what things are precious, and maybe I knew before, when I was sickened by our gluttony, by our greed. As she touches me, her fingers moving over my skin like light, like shadow, I know a new hunger. I know what things are precious. And they can merge together, these two concepts...

They have.

I love her, I know. And with the acknowledgment of that, I am no longer afraid as she tastes me, touches me, as I taste and touch her. The fear falls away like a husk, like a metamorphosis, as she tears away the layers of ugliness to what I am beneath.

In her eyes, something lovely.

She whispers my name in the dark. The name she gave me.

"Lottie…"

And her love devours me whole, shaping me. Changing me. Making me over, new.

I am not afraid.

# Chapter Eight: Hunt

"Well."

I sit up, breath coming fast, Charlie opening an eye beside me blearily, not making a single motion to cover up. We're both sprawled on the bed, limbs tangled together like string that you'll never unravel.

"It's not like I haven't caught you in the act a thousand times," is what Charlie tells Edgar, who stands at the foot of the bed, arms crossed, smug smile curving his lips up beneath his mustache.

"True, true. But it *is* my bed."

"Oh. Yeah." Charlie sits up then, runs her fingers through her hair, grinning at me. Edgar picks up her pants gingerly, tossing them to her from the floor, and she swings her legs over the side of the bed, sliding the pants on one leg at a time. I watch her distractedly, thinking over last night…and yesterday.

"The Sixers are moving up the Bone Feast," says Edgar then, smile falling away from his face. "I just heard the news. I think they're using it to try to flush Lottie out of hiding. They're doing it *tomorrow*."

"Shit," Charlie murmurs, glancing at me.

"They won't find me. I know what I have to do," I tell both of them. "It's just…" I trail off, pick at a thread disentangling itself from the blanket, wrap it around my fingers. “It just seems impossible.”

“I love impossible things,” says Edgar, folding his arms. “For example: a Sleeper and a Sixer falling in love! Nothing is as impossible as it seems, ever.” He seems so resolute when he says that, and tips his hat cheerfully.

So he believes me now. And…I don't think he's afraid of me anymore.

I take a deep breath, glance to Charlie. She's still grinning at me. I smile back.

“Well,” I say slowly, carefully, sobering. “It *seems* impossible, because I need to convince the Sleepers to give in to their worst fear—to get Snatched.”

Edgar and Charlie, Fetchers who have been trained to avoid the Snatchers at all costs, lean forward, though I can't help noticing how their faces pale, how Charlie's grin vanishes.

I stare at the floor, swallow, but Charlie moves against me and covers my hands with hers.

“We’re listening,” she promises, bending down to brush her lips over my fingers.

I remain in Edgar’s room, because I can’t be seen. If I’m seen, the Sixers will hear about it, fast. Anyone besides Charlie, besides Edgar and Violet, would rather have the reward of Nox than protect me and risk the Sixers' wrath. And I can't blame them.

Charlie’s left, and Edgar, too. I watched them walk away from Black House without looking back as I peeked around the edge of the curtains, wishing I were with them. This place, being trapped in this place, with no way out, makes my heart race. But at nightfall, I'll be free again, and tomorrow, everything will begin.

I pace the room quietly, counting my footsteps. I lean against the wall, think about last night, my body aching for her, for Charlie. It feels so much, this body. I stare down at my hands, touch my fingers to my palms. When she left today, right in front of Edgar, she put her arms around my waist, drew me forward and kissed me deeply. It made my heart leap up against my ribs, that kiss, and when she stepped back, she was grinning, eyes downcast, hair feathered and floating around her head like light. I loved her so much in that moment, it was this fierceness of knowing that flooded through me, so warm it made me breathe out, breathless.

I promised Charlie that I would to try to stay in the present. Now, here. In the only moment I have. But it's impossible, really… I have to think about tomorrow. I have to think about all of the people who need to know the truth—about Twixt, about themselves. The people I hope to save. The people I might fail utterly.

This, all of this, could crumble at any moment for any number of reasons. If the Sixers find me—if they kill me again, devour my soul… I'd be lying to say that I don't fear it. Of course I do. I can't imagine nothingness, though I've brought it about myself so many times.

But I fear more what will happen to these people if I don't act, if I don't try to shift things. And now Charlie and Edgar know. If the Sixers find me, eat me up, Charlie and Edgar could lead the Sleepers. They could start a revolution. I know they would. They would change things, and that's enough. That has to be enough for me.

But still, I pace.

Edgar and Charlie went to find Violet, and though I'm no judge of daylight, I think it's halfway through the day when I hear footsteps outside Edgar's door. Though I've been peeking out of the curtains at intervals, I might have missed their return.

A creak of boards, feet against wood. And the door does not open.

There's a knock against it.

Not Charlie, then. Not Edgar. I stare at the door, heart pounding. I glance at the bed that's so far away, that's too close to the ground, anyway, to hide me, and then I look to the curtains.

When the door opens, when Isabel steps in, I have my body pressed as close to the wall as I can, breathing in and out softly. The curtain is likely still gusting from my movements, when I twitched them aside and inserted my body into a natural fold. I can see Isabel only peripherally; she steps into the room, casting her eyes about, hands on her hips.

She pauses for far too long, and then she turns, angling her body towards the curtains.

She locks eyes with me, peering through the curtain's crack against the wall.

"Isabel?" calls Miss Black from the hall. "Anything?"

"No, Miss Black," she says sweetly, stepping forward, kicking the door shut behind her. "I see you," she whispers then, in a chilling, singsong voice.

I push the heavy curtains aside, watching her, panting. I consider the window, leaping from it, but it's daylight outside, and this close to the Wanting Market, there are Sleepers out there. They'll see me. And if I injure myself, I won't be able to run fast enough to escape, hide…

I could run past Isabel, out the door, down into Black House. But are there Sixers in here? Did they demand another search? Is that why Isabel's here, looking in Edgar's room?

We stare at one another for a long moment, Isabel and I.

I lick my lips. I open my mouth. "Isabel—"

"I'll scream," she whispers.

We stay still, standing, staring at one another.

"What do you want?" I ask then, heavily.

She watches me for a long moment, nose up, lips in a sneer. But it falters—for a heartbeat, the bitter curve slips from her mouth, and in its place, there's something…pain-filled. Longing.

"Is Charlie going to get into trouble because of you?" she hisses then, startling me.

I blink, silent for so long that she gets angry, takes a step forward, hands balled into fists.

"Why would you care?" The words whip from my tongue, shocking her motionless.

She opens and shuts her mouth. There are tears in her eyes, and she dashes them away with the backs of her wrists, turns, puts her hand on the doorknob.

"I don't know," I answer her, then. "I don't know if she will suffer because of me. It's all… All of this is wrong, Isabel. If you'd just let me tell you the truth—"

"I won't say I found you," she whispers and, pasting a smile on her face, lets herself out into the hall, shutting the door with a *click* behind her.

I stare at the door, slumping, kneeling down upon the floorboards, my whole body shaking.

I don't know if she'll keep her word; she might trot off to Miss Black right now, or to the Sixers themselves. But there was something in the way she spoke…

I think I believe her.

Charlie did love her once, after all.

I itch at my skin, lean against the wall, close my eyes, try not to think too much about Charlie embracing

Isabel, kissing her, whispering into her ear, tracing her fingers over her pale skin.

I scrub at my eyes, stare down at my palms, my hands.

All that time, Isabel was using Charlie…wasn't she?

*Is Charlie going to get into trouble because of you?*

I don't know how much time passes, but the next time the door opens, Edgar and Violet are there. And Charlie… Oh, Charlie. I rise stiffly from the floor, race across the space between us and put my arms around her shoulders. I kiss her once, then back up, breathing out as she smiles at me worriedly, squeezing my hands with her reassuring fingers.

"Hi," says Violet, shoving her hands into her pockets, mouth sideways, pushing past us to get into the room. "Are you…okay?"

"Yeah," I manage, glancing to Edgar, who leans against the now-shut door. I don't want to talk about Isabel, not with Charlie—and, after all, Isabel promised not to say anything.

And the Sixers haven't come for me yet.

"What's going on outside?" I ask.

"They're preparing for the Bone Feast and ripping Abeo apart looking for you," says Edgar softly, studying his nails again. "But it seems they've stopped searching the Safe Houses. And I really do think they're assuming you'll come out of hiding for the Bone Feast. Or that you'll be much easier to find then. Who can guess how a Sixer thinks?"

There's a moment of tension, as I draw my mouth closed and stare intently at the wall. No one speaks, the answer to Edgar's question quivering in the air.

Who can guess how a Sixer thinks…but a Sixer

herself?

I run my hands through my hair, separate from Charlie, go back to pacing the small room. "The Sixers built Abeo. They can find anyone or anything, but I don't think they can find themselves. *Me*. I think I'm hidden from them. I must be, or they would have found me already, wouldn't they have?" I bite my lip.

"We've a night. Tomorrow morning, the Bone Feast begins, and that's when we've got to start moving." Edgar smoothes his mustache, sighs, pausing. "You know, I've been giving this a lot of thought, and I must say, Lottie—it would be so much easier to sell this story to the Sleeping mob if it wasn't all leading up to getting *Snatched*."

"The Sixers set it up that way on purpose." My voice is so small. "The Snatchers needed to be as terrifying as possible so that no one would figure out that they were the way to escape Abeo City."

"It's just hard to swallow, is all," says Violet, then, leaning against the wall. She hasn't smiled at me, hasn't really looked at me since coming in. "All of this."

"Violet," says Charlie, watching her, but she shakes her head, pushes off and crosses her arms.

"I know you both explained it to me. I got it all. It's just…" Violet shrugs her shoulders, eyes on the floor.

I glance to Edgar, who raises his eyebrows. "We can't say the 'd' word, but we can sure as hell say 'not living,' apparently." He winks at me.

"But, Lottie…" Violet lets her arms fall and gazes at me now. There's fear in her eyes, a trembling in the blue. "A Sixer?"

"I'm sorry," I say, and bow my head.

I am sorry. I'm responsible, in part, for all of this. Perhaps I'm even worse than my sisters, because I always felt it was wrong, and I let it happen, anyway. My hands knot together, and I stand before the window, the curtains drawn tight.

"No," mutters Charlie, then, standing a little straighter. "We are what we are, Vi. You *know* that. And we do what we can with what we are and what we've been given. We can't *help* where we come from, but we can sure as Snatchers help where we're going."

I turn from the window, look to Violet. She watches Charlie for a long moment, shifts her gaze back to me. My feet are planted firmly beneath my hips, and I stand there, fingernails dug into my palms but locking eyes with her.

"It's just hard," Violet begins, and falters when she sees my face.

"Tell me about it," I say quietly, simply.

We stare at one another, and she relents, stepping forward, putting her arms around me. "Lottie, I'm afraid."

"Of me?" I close my eyes, returning the embrace, my arms loose around her shoulders.

"No," she says, then, shaking her head against my shoulder, and I believe her. "Of all of this. Of the other Sixers. Of the Snatchers. Of Abeo. Of Twixt. To imagine that there could be an ending to this…not a *terrible* ending, like I always thought I'd get, but something all right… And it *is* all right, what comes after. Right, Lottie?"

I squeeze her tightly, work my jaw. "Yes. That I remember, for the people flown away from Twixt, it was…all right."

"To imagine that…" she huffs out, pressing her nose to my shoulder. "It's *hard* to imagine that, because all I've been doing is running from everything since I got here, just like everyone else. But to imagine something better is… It's hard to find a word for it."

She falters, presses away from me, searching my face.

I breathe out, nodding.

I can't find the word, either.

Night. Darkness drags along the ground as Charlie and I move from shadow to shadow in the street, making our way through Abeo City. I've got to get back to Mad House, because Mad House is closest to the wall, and outside the wall is the Sixers' house, and that's where I need to be tomorrow.

Tomorrow, during the Bone Feast.

That's when it ends.

Charlie got me a coat with a hood, and I have it pulled tight about my face, though it's not as if there are many people traversing the streets at night in Abeo City, with the Snatchers watching, sentinel, perching along every rooftop, crouching on the skeletons of broken buildings. They make no move to stir, don't lift a wing as we race past them, but they watch us, pale skulls turning as we pass.

"It's bizarre," says Charlie, raking her fingers through her hair. Her hands are shaking. "I've never seen them act like this before."

"They know something's happening. Something's about to change. They know…" I whisper, glancing up. I nod, once, to the nearest Snatcher, the one on the ridgepole of a dilapidated building, more rubble than wall.

The Snatcher has a ragged right wing, and it tilts its skull toward me as it watches us pass.

We're almost to Mad House—just one more

corner—when the bulky shadow moves out from beneath the cover of a shredded awning. We stop, cold, as it shuffles forward, peeling back a hood, revealing the white face beneath.

And then I relax, almost collapsing with relief, as I take the final two steps and embrace Bird so tightly, I have to pull back, worried that she isn't able to breathe.

Charlie watches us for a moment, working her jaw.

"This is Bird, Charlie," I tell her, and understanding dawns on her face.

After Charlie and Edgar came back to Black House with Violet, I told them all about Bird, explaining as best as I could manage that Bird was part of me, that she and I had been the third Sixer together.

"It's you…" Charlie murmurs now, stepping forward, looking from me, to Bird, back to me again. "You don't… I was thinking you'd look alike."

"What's done is done. Wasn't meant to look pretty," says Bird, hands on her hips. She cocks her head, birdlike, as she watches me. "They're after you, lovely," she says, clucking her tongue.

I feel better with Bird here, near me. Stronger. I wonder…

"Bird, now that we're together—can we join up again? I don't think this separation is natural. We're not supposed to be…" I trail off as her gaze narrows, dark eyes flashing.

"What's done is done," she says, taking my hand, squeezing it. "We're apart for a *reason*. Tomorrow…"

"Tomorrow," I repeat, nodding. Somehow, she knows.

"I'll see you when the bodies need saving," she whispers, darting forward, pressing her chapped lips against my cheek. "Somehow, this will come to rights.

It must, mustn't it? How can the play end on a sour note?" She shakes her head, turns to go. "Best get inside. You don't want to see the hunt that's beginning." And, just like that, she's merged with the shadows, disappearing like ink into the ground.

"The hunt..." Charlie whispers. "Why does she talk like that?"

"I don't know," I tell her, the truth. I turn to her, reach out, touch her arm, realize my fingers are shaking, and shiver.

"We need to get to Mad House, is what she meant," Charlie growls, and then we're running down the street, and there's only one corner, really, between us and the house, but I pause—we both do—because there are voices ahead that seem to originate near Mad House.

Voices I recognize.

I stare at Charlie, eyes wide with fear.

"Sixers," I breathe out, and she takes my wrist, tugging me into the skeleton of a broken building, crouching behind a pile of rubble.

"Why have they come out *again*?" Charlie's voice hisses, and her eyes are angry, but her mouth is trembling. "They've searched the stupid house *three times* now..."

I press a finger to her lips and listen, breathing out quietly.

The Snatchers lining the rooftops flutter their wings, a *whoosh* like a sigh. I can hear the Sixers' boots on the rubble outside our hiding place, can hear them coo softly to one another, a sound that makes the hair on the back of my neck rise. I remember, half-remember, like a memory from a dream, them making that same cooing sound when they locked me into the room the first time, after the key slid into the lock of the bird-covered door.

"What are they doing?" Charlie mouths to me,

eyes wide in the dark. I shake my head, and we crouch, muscles straining, barely breathing, until we hear the scream.

It's a piercing shriek that the Snatcher makes, far different from the creatures' characteristic wails. This scream is extended, a scream of pain. There's a sound of meat against meat, a dull *thud*, and then silence.

And the Sixers laugh—their voices cold, drawn out and stabbing, like barbs. I risk a look, rising from my hiding place, peering over the mound of rubble out to the street.

There, my sisters hold up their hands, claws extended, and between them on the ground, curled up in a bony heap on top of and entangled in their hair, is a Snatcher.

I stare as the creature curls in upon itself, using its wings as a shield against my sisters, cowering beneath their gaze. I watch, breathing out, breath catching, as the hair seems to *move*, seems to crawl up and over the Snatcher, pinioning its bones to the rubble-strewn streets.

The Snatcher writhes, screams, tries to rise, but the hair is like a net, pinning it there.

One of the Sixers glances at the Snatchers upon the roof, hooks a curling finger in their direction, and the nearest Snatcher falls, as if it suddenly lost its balance, tumbling to the ground with a heavy thud. The Sixer that felled it stalks forward, hooking her fingers toward her slowly, her hair dragging behind her but also moving with her, like a shadow. The fallen Snatcher scrapes along the ground, rolling in front of her, toward her, pausing at her feet. And her hair, like a predator, spiderwebs over the rubble and over the Snatcher, tangling itself with the white bones.

I stare, heart racing, breath coming too fast—they'll *hear*! I try to calm down, hold my breath, gripping Charlie's arm and shutting my eyes.

The Snatchers are hideous, terrifying; they were *made* to appear that way, fear built into their feathers and bones like the spun nightmare Abeo is. But I know what they are now, truly, beneath their dreadfulness. And even if I didn't know... These are creatures wracked with pain, helpless, struggling, and ensnared by a pair of pitiless oppressors. My sisters.

The second Sixer laughs again, plucks something out from beneath her arm, unfurls it. A sack of shadow lowers over the Snatchers, growing to accommodate the creatures' scale, pooling across the ground. Then the sack opens, dark maw gaping, and swallows both of the Snatchers in a quick, silent moment.

The eldest Sixer ties the bag closed with one vicious movement, and then she and my other sister drag the sack down the street, away from Mad House. The contents within the sack of darkness squirm, a claw pressing against the cloth, reaching back toward us, almost pleading.

Even after they turn the corner, the Sixers' hair snakes over the ground. I stare at it in morbid fascination. It seems...alive. Could it see us, *snare* us, if we shot out into the road now?

I feel Charlie's gaze, turn to look at her. She stares at me with wide eyes, still seated beside me, leaning against the pile of rubble. "What just happened?" she asks, voice soft.

I stare up at the Snatchers whose heads are tilted toward us, every last one—waiting.

"I think the Bone Feast has begun," I whisper.

# Chapter Nine: Bone

The Bone Feast starts, in earnest, at first light.

I rest against Charlie's chest, her hand woven through my hair, as the darkness ebbs and light bleeds through the edges of the curtains in her room.

There's an outcry outside; the shouting seems to go on forever, and it's accompanied by voices, so many voices, outside of Mad House as the Sleepers stream into the streets, gathering together.

Charlie presses a kiss to the top of my head and rises, tugging at the sleeves of her coat, combing her fingers through her hair. "How do I look?" she laughs wryly, smiling at me, but her mouth twitches sideways, like it doesn't wish to hold a grin but a frown.

"Beautiful," I tell her, putting my arms about her neck, pulling her down to meet my mouth. My insides squeeze, tighten, as her lips touch mine, because it's the beginning of the end, and I'm doing my best to hold myself together. I'm not afraid, not for myself. But as I feel Charlie's warmth against me, her body a perfect fit for my mine, feel the gentleness of her hands at my waist, holding me, I'm afraid for what we've become. And what we're going to lose.

"Lottie?" asks Charlie, then, breathing my name into my ear. I sigh, look up at her, force a smile. As if she knows what I'm thinking, she shakes her head. "Lottie, it's worth it, all of this. We can free them all."

*We*, she said. Not *you*.

I'm not alone. She said *we*.

I nod, swallow the melancholy, put my hands at the small of her back. "I'll watch from the window," I tell her, and she nods, too, reaching back and squeezing my hand, and then diving in for one last kiss.

I feel dizzy when we part; she leaves the room too quickly, and an ache unfurls in my heart.

Charlie has to go to the Bone Feast, has to represent Mad House with Abigail. If she doesn't go, the Sixers will be suspicious of her, and I can't let myself think of how they would hurt her, what they would do…

She had to go.

But I feel her absence like a hole within me.

Now I'm alone. I press my black-lined palm against my cheek, and I still feel Charlie's warmth against my skin, her lips...

Down below, in the streets, Violet and Edgar will already be moving amongst the other Sleepers. And Bird is probably all right, for now.

We are all still connected, even though we're apart: strands drawn taut from one heart to the next. The sharpest pair of scissors could not sever us.

I pace, and my skin itches. I want to be out there. I want to begin this. But I have to wait for tonight.

Just a few hours more.

I step to the curtain, draw it back a sliver, and peek at the street below.

There are strings of jars and lanterns laced across the tops of the buildings, along the ridge of the piles of rubble. Inside the glass confines, Wisps dance, adding a warm glow to the already brightening streets. There are so many Sleepers, I lose my breath. So many… I hadn't seen, hadn't known there were so many.

And it's strange: watching them, I almost remember…

I remain still for a long moment, curtain pinched between my fingers, thinking back, trying to dislodge a memory teasing at my thoughts. Ever since the Sixers spoke to me, small memories return, unbidden, often catching me unawares.

I don't remember the Sleepers gathering *here* for the Bone Feast before, in front of Mad House. I stare down at the throngs of people, unseeing. Yes. They used to gather in the Wanting Market, would move the tents aside so that the center of the square was open enough to contain all of the Sleepers in Abeo. It's rare, for the Sleepers to linger outdoors for hours together. Normally, they stay within the Safe Houses, where they're protected from Snatchers. Sleepers never gather like this, only during the Bone Feast. The Wanting Market is the only space large enough to hold all of them.

So why are they having *this* Bone Feast in the street before Mad House? It makes no sense, but even as I think the question, I already know the answer, and my heart sinks.

*They know.*

Down below, the Sixers stride between the Sleepers, two hooded figures that the crowd parts for, the Sleepers edging back from their black cloaks and writhing black hair. As one, the Sixers glance up at Charlie's window, my window, their hoods hiding their faces, and I let the curtain fall.

I step back, heart thundering against my ribs, then press my eye to a tiny pinprick hole in the fabric. They still watch the window, the two of them as unmoving as the broken fountain statue in the square.

The hair on the back of my neck rises, and I hold my breath, and my heart hardly dares to beat... But after a long, pointed moment, they glide along, walking slowly down the street, seeming to flow over the ground like spilled black water.

My eyes drift to faces I recognize in the crowd: Violet and Edgar, standing close together, near Mad House. And, as I watch, Edgar moves his hand slowly until it's following the bow of Violet's side. She doesn't move away from him; she leans *into* him, glancing up at him, the corners of her mouth, so often pulled down, curving up. He cocks his hat, grins back, and they stroll through the crowd, away from my window, linked together.

A bright starburst flares in my belly—for Edgar, who wanted this; for Violet, who finally let it happen, after holding Edgar off for so long...because she was afraid to care that much about someone else.

I think of Charlie and something crumples inside of me. I clutch a handful of curtain and rake in a deep breath.

Time is drawing close. Everyone feels it. I step back from the window, sitting down on the edge of Charlie's bed for a long moment, pressing my hand against my thrumming heart, the other gripping the soft covers. I can feel time moving all around me, like air, like breath, a breeze of minutes tugging at the encroaching night.

And then, like a sigh, the murmur of voices fades to nothingness outside.

I get up, cross to the curtain once more, peer through the tiny hole. All of the people are facing one direction. I move to the edge of the curtain, twitch it aside to gain a better view of the street.

Below, the lanterns and jars burn bright. The amassed Sleepers turn, as one, toward the edge of the street, where the two Sixers stand on a pile of rubble, still and silent as shadows, their hair dripping away from them like a bizarre, blackened waterfall. The eldest Sixer raises her hand, crooking a long, bony claw of a finger.

A cage is drawn into view from around the edge of the dilapidated building. And then the purity of silence crumbles as the Sleepers shout, moving, jostling to see, to witness.

A huge and rusty iron cage turns, suspended upon nothing, though it swings as if on an invisible chain over the pile of rubble. And crumpled upon the floor of the cage are the two Snatchers from last night, the ones the Sixers caught while Charlie and I hid in the darkness. They crouch, monstrously huge—though, in the daylight, they seem diminished. Misplaced and, somehow, *less*.

The people begin to laugh, because the Snatchers' great wings are plucked clean, now only sharp dull bone, like the rest of their bodies. They curve these bone wings around their shoulders, trying to shield themselves from the people pointing, jeering, but the smaller one stands, staring at the crowd, hollow eyes unseeing but seeing all the same.

"Look!" say the Sixers together, as one. My throat scratches as they do this, and I lean against the wall for support. "Look at the monsters now! The great Snatchers, fallen to us! You will feast upon their Nox, but look at what hunts you. *Pathetic*," they hiss, the word rising into the sky, burrowing into every ear, snakelike and writhing.

*Pathetic.*

The Snatchers cower in the center of the cage, their great bulk of bones pressing up against one another, entwining, as the Sleepers surge forward on a wave of anger. One Sleeper, a man, hefts a rock from the rubble and throws it at the cage. It glances harmlessly off the bars, the metallic ring of the iron echoing, but then others follow his example, grasp rocks, rubble, bricks, and begin to pelt the Snatchers with them. Their fear of being Snatched has been transformed into fury, fury directed at these two featherless Snatchers. A rock cracks against bone, and a brick smashes a dome of ribs, but the Snatchers don't shriek, don't plead, hardly even move. They only watch the crowd with beaks bent low.

I remember what they are. I remember *who* they are, who's held captive within the illusion that warps them, and I claw at the wall and swallow my tears. I am weak with revulsion, so sickened that I sink to my knees. Our relations, pelted with rocks, broken apart into sharp white pieces.

With wet eyes, I kneel forward, peer through the bottom of the window, search out the crowd for Charlie, for Edgar, for Violet, for some comfort and restraint in the violent scene that rages outside, amidst the screams of anger, of hatred and derision, spotting the air like a spray of blood.

And there…

Below, gazing up at my window, is Charlie. Her eyes are bright and brown and tear-filled, and she sees me, dares the flicker of a sad, sad smile. She glances meaningfully toward the lengthening shadows, at the darkness that begins to creep—too soon, far too soon—along the street, pointing black fingers toward her.

The night is descending.

I press my fingers to my lips and then to the glass, and Charlie bows her head.

I rub at my eyes, stand, let the curtain shift back into place, hiding the hideous scene from view.

It's almost over.

At the thought, I'm half afraid, half relieved.

It's almost *over*.

Charlie meets me at the foot of the stairs, Mad House empty now, the only sound my echoing footsteps on the landing below, and then Charlie's footsteps as she leans forward, as she embraces me, drawing her arms around my form so tightly, it seems like she'll never let go.

And I don't want her to. When she lets me go, it's over.

Why can't we stay here? Why can't we stay in this house, together—always?

"Are you ready?" she whispers into my ear. I pause for a heartbeat, feel her warmth and nearness and strength and love all around me and within me.

*No.*

"Yes." My voice breaks on the word, and she hugs me harder, but I step away from her, squeezing her hands, brushing my lips over her cheek, against her sweet mouth. She kisses me deeply. Cinnamon. No matter what happens, I'll remember the taste of her: warmth and cinnamon. I'll remember that until I stop remembering. Until there is no memory, no...me.

"Lottie, I…" She steps back from me, watching me with luminous eyes, wide in the darkness, in the soft light of the Wisps. "Whatever happens tonight…" She falters, shaking her head, raking a hand through her hair, head ducked, before she looks up at me again, fingers holding my hips, a gravity and force so strong and gentle, it makes my breath catch.

"Whatever happens tonight," she repeats, licking her lips, leaning close, everything she is a warmth, a pulse, a mirror to my heartbeat, "I have loved you fiercely."

I breathe out, heart surging within me. And then I put my arms around her neck and kiss her once more. Once more. Only once more. And I step away from her, my fingers still entwined with hers, and I bend my head, touching my lips to her palm, to her black lines, feel the heat of my breath unfurl in her hand.

"And I, you," I whisper to the Nox beneath her skin, to the artificial pulse there, to all that is Charlie, and ever was.

And then, moving together, we run to the back of Mad House, past the countless jars of Wisps, past the Great Room that's silent, vacant, like a haunted place, back into the hidden closet where this all began, that first night, the walls leaning far away from us, dark and unknowable.

We erupt through the walls into the forest.

It's night, the shadows and darkness absolute, stretching away from us in sharp, black contours. The glow from the Bone Feast can still be seen over the imposing wall as I glance back, the voices of the Sleepers loud, even here.

"Come on," Charlie whispers, taking up my hand, and we begin to run in the woods.

As we make our way through the darkness, past the bony trees, the hair on the back of my neck stands on end, and I glance over my shoulder. I can feel eyes on me. Or…perhaps not eyes but hollows where eyes should be—and *are*, beneath the Sixers' illusion. The Snatchers are here, even if I can't see them. They're watching us, still waiting to find out what the rebel Sixer will do to set things right.

We run, angling through the forest, stretching always to our left.

There, up ahead of us, is a shadow darker than the smudges of dead trees, reaching upward, pointing to the sky: Bird's church. Tonight, the windows are lightless, and as we reach the front steps, I glance inside the open maw of doors. The jars of Wisps are empty.

Bird set the Wisps free.

I stumble again, foot caught in one of the holes

dug into the ground of the churchyard. Charlie catches me, and we leap over another hole together, and then I pause for a moment, snared in an abrupt memory.

I recognize them now—those holes. The Sixers built the illusion of Abeo City, shaping it to resemble, in all ways, a city, but a broken city, because that's the only image a broken being can conjure. But they sewed together the illusion too well. In front of the weathered church, gravestones appeared of their own accord, the ultimate reminder of death to dead things. So they plucked out the gravestones and obliterated them, smashed them to bits in their clawed hands, but the silent holes the stones once filled remain, dark wounds in the earth that never healed.

I squeeze Charlie's hand tighter, move quickly past the church, running fast as breath, as blood, as we move together beneath the clawing trees.

The shadow looms near, the hulking darkness of the Sixers' house. We reach the half-place: the church behind us blurring, the house ahead almost sharp enough to see. I do not hesitate this time. I know where my future lies, and I know what I must do.

And the house comes into focus, a hulking shadow of boarded-up windows and doors, a ragged porch that seems to fall forward toward us, as if drawn by our awaited presence.

Like the church, the house is dark, too, an unnatural darkness that seems to *breathe* as we race toward it. I try not to raise my eyes, try not to examine this house that we Sixers, we sisters, built together, this house that imprisoned me. I shudder as we draw close.

"The basement," I tell Charlie, though I don't need to. She knows the plan; we've gone through it at least a dozen times. We run around the side of the house, and we're at the basement door, a different door than the one I escaped from when I last left the Sixers' house. This door is made of cobbled-together boards, bound with a length of rusting iron chain. A chain that could keep no one out, and nothing in—save for the sapped Sleepers below, who lack the energy to walk up the steps and through the walls.

Without a thought, I curl my fingers beneath the links and yank at the metal. In my hands, because the chain was built by Sixers, because it is one of our illusions, it obeys me, snapping in two. I thread the length of it through the handles as the iron chain *clinks* to rest upon the earth.

Beside me, Charlie nods once, panting, eyes hooded in the dark. I throw open the doors, the grim creak of them loud in the stillness, and hand in hand, we descend.

Though it was dark in the woods, that darkness can't compare to the creeping black of the basement. We stumble down the rough-hewn steps, and it takes a heartbeat or two for my eyes to adjust, even though there is a single jar of Wisps in the center of the earthen room. After a moment, I can see pale mounds clustered around the jar. The emaciated, shimmering forms of the almost-gone Sleepers take shape as they raise their heads slowly, as they glance up at us in surprise. Charlie stares with wide eyes at them as they stare back at us.

"Arthur?" Charlie whispers, after a long moment, moving forward. She approaches an old man huddled on the far side of the space, his mustache drooping, his face caving in slowly. He raises milky eyes to her, and they're suddenly tear-filled as he totters forward on rotting legs, gripping the earthen wall with a curving hand of bone.

"Charlie," he whispers, and she gingerly gathers him up into an embrace. The others Sleepers begin to hobble forward, pressing gently up against one another to get nearer to the two of us, expectant, breathless and silent.

"We're *leaving*," I whisper, leaning forward, pressing a finger against my lips. "But you must be quiet, or the Sixers will sense you. We're going to go to Abeo City together, because the other Sleepers, when they see you, when they see what the *Sixers* have done to you... They'll believe me when I tell them the truth about the Sixers and the Snatchers, and that we must all get Snatched in order to escape Abeo City. And then..." I swallow. "Then we're all going to get Snatched..." I trail off as the Sleepers watch me, as my own plan passes over my lips again, unspoken except to Charlie and Edgar and Violet, now voiced to Sleepers that the Sixers have tortured, Sleepers so weak they could fade into nothingness at any moment, Sleepers taught for far longer than most of the Sleepers in Abeo City that you must avoid the Snatchers, the *monsters*, at all costs.

To expect them to make the journey to Abeo City, even though it's not so very far, when they can hardly move, have hardly moved in who knows how long, seems an impossible request. As I stand there, as I watch them, curled up around the edges of the floor, hardly standing, leaning against the wooden beams in the basement, I wonder if the Sleepers would take my word alone as proof enough. If I ran back, leaving Charlie here with them, so that she could help them out of the basement, have them all wait for me here, maybe I could—

"I'll come with you," says the old man that Charlie called Arthur. He steps forward, wobbling, as Charlie hooks his bony arm around her shoulder.

"Well, we can't stay *here*," says another Sleeper, a shriveled woman who glances up at me with brightly flashing eyes, though the rest of her has nearly worn away to nothingness. "We'll come with you." She frowns. "As best as we can."

The others chorus agreement, though some eye me with trepidation, some with fear. I am a Sixer, after all. To follow me, to put *faith* in me, is a tremendous show of bravery on their part. I flush, feeling a rush of shame.

But I shake it off, rub my hands together, my cool palms pressing against one another, creating a spark. "Thank you," I murmur, backing away. Charlie gives me a meaningful glance, then helps Arthur toward the steps leading to the forest. I leave the Sleepers and Charlie for a moment, edging back toward the other door at the end of the earthen room. I venture through it, holding my breath. I don't know what I'll see on the other side, in the hall that used to contain the Nox and the Snatcher.

I didn't realize how large the room was before, probably because it was filled floor to ceiling with crates of Nox. The crates are gone now, taken to the Bone Feast, most likely. But there, in the far corner of the room, like before, is the cage, and lying broken at the bottom of it is the Snatcher.

It watches me with hollow eyes, resting on its side, curled up like a dead body, but I know its heart beats still. It shifts its bones, reaches a claw toward me, but then, as if its strength is gone, its arm falls limp. I cross the wide, echoing space between us, and the Snatcher shudders as I near it, quaking in a tremor and then resuming its stillness. I know, standing beyond the iron bars, touching their cold, rough metal with my fingers, why the Sixers captured two new Snatchers to parade around at the Bone Feast, and why they left this one behind. He looks pathetic, sad, so broken, and the Sixers need to keep up the illusion that the Snatchers are fearsome beasts to be terrified of, that they vanquished *monsters* in order to bring Nox to the Sleepers, that the Sixers should be revered and feared because of this favor.

If they'd brought this Snatcher before the assembled Sleepers at the Bone Feast, I wonder if they would have thrown stones, still. I wonder if the Sleepers would have laughed and jeered, or if they would have paused for a moment, looking over its broken, misshapen form, crumpled in the center of the cage like a shattered doll, and dropped the stones and bricks at their feet, pity putting out the fire of their fury.

I don't know, can't guess.

But pity moves through my own heart now. I try to swallow it down. I don't want to *pity* this Snatcher, this relation. It wouldn't *want* my pity. Especially not *mine.* I feel the solidity of the iron beneath my black-lined palms, and I curl my fingers around the bars and pull with all my might.

Like the chain outside, this cage was built by Sixers, and it bends beneath my hands. The metal groans, and the door swings open, creaking like a half-choked scream.

The Snatcher raises its head, half of its upper beak broken off, the hollows sunken into its skull, and it angles its empty gaze toward me.

"You... You're free." My voice sounds dull, flat. I swallow. "It's happening tonight," I breathe, but then I step forward, because I wonder if it can even *move*, and I kneel down beside its white, clattering bulk. Even broken apart as it is, the Snatcher, like all Snatchers, is monstrously huge, bone wings devoid of feathers taking up the entire span of the large cage, coiling around me as it twitches them, trying to shift before falling back against the bottom bars of the floor.

I know I can't lift the weight of this Snatcher, but I try to, anyway, moving one of its wickedly sharp-edged arms around my neck, its claws dragging on the ground as I help it to its feet, heaving with all of my might, pushing off from the ground.

The Snatcher tries to push off the ground, too, but after a tortured collection of heartbeats, it sags again, slumping down like a marionette with cut strings. I sprawl beside it, swallow, panting, running my fingers through my hair, heart aching.

"Please get up," I beg it, reaching my hands out to it, propping up its broken skull. I drag it into my lap, and it lets me as I run a palm over its smooth bone head, warm to the touch, not cold like I'd imagined. This close, it's not so very monstrous. As I watch it, as I watch its head trembling against me, I feel a surge of pain move through me, a great aching sadness.

"Please…" I whisper again, stroking its head. "You need to *escape*. You can get out of here, and then you can pass the Gray Line, and the other Snatchers—they'll help you, I'm sure of it."

It watches me, silent, and after a long, weighted pause, it shakes its great head against me, almost imperceptibly. Weakly.

*No*.

"Please," I try again, but a knock sounds from the other side of the wooden door, startling me.

"Lottie, we have to go. There's not enough time." Charlie's voice is muffled as she speaks through the door. I know she's right—the unpredictable span of night might not be long enough, *anyway*, and we need the Snatchers, and the Snatchers only come out at night. I glance over my shoulder at the door and kneel once more, try once more.

"Please," I repeat, but the Snatcher lets its skull roll to the side, against the iron bars, and it won't look at me.

Before my eyes, it seems to grow smaller, spindlier. The iron of the bars seems to grow darker, and I feel the energy shifting beneath me, feel the Sixers drawing upon its energy from elsewhere, though I could never say how I feel it. It's like water over the skin, or under it, that sensation. But then the Snatcher fades away to nothingness before my eyes: there one moment, and then absolutely not the next.

Devoured. Lost.

Somewhere, I feel the Sixers grow stronger. Here and now, the breath is knocked out of me as I fall against the bars, staring at the spot the Snatcher used to fill.

And yet, even as I stare, a cold little voice asks me, *Why are you so shocked, Lottie? You have seen this countless times before, participated in the destruction of souls* countless *times—willingly, hungrily.*

The bitter taste in my mouth makes me spit out, and I rub at my eyes with the heels of my hands.

I am no better than my sisters.

Despair begins to click slowly up my spine, bone by bone, aiming for my heart.

"Lottie, *please*," murmurs Charlie through the door again, and I shudder, shake myself, push off from the iron bars. And I rise, for the Sleepers and the Snatchers.

This—*all* of this—stops *tonight.*

"Coming," I whisper, pacing down the hall quickly. I pause only once, hand on the door, glancing back at the empty iron cage, the room taking my panting breath away and echoing through the space until it's gone.

I move back through the door soundlessly and descend the steps into the room of Sleepers, heart aching, hands pressed against a wall at my back, as if it can hold me up.

"Come on," says Charlie quietly, taking up one of my hands, threading her fingers through mine. She squeezes once, eyes searching my face, but I can't look at her, won't be able to look at her for a while yet.

I cross to the center of the room with Charlie, pluck up the jar of Wisps with my other hand.

I clear my throat, raise my head. “Follow me, if you choose,” I tell the Sleepers quietly, and together, we begin to move out of the basement. Charlie and I must carry most of the Sleepers up the stone stairs, and our progress is achingly slow. But finally, everyone stands together upon the forest floor, in the shadow of the house of the Sixers, the house that imprisoned Sleepers and a Snatcher and a Sixer and a hundred thousand secrets.

The gathering of thin faces watches me, eyes bright and milky or hollow in the darkness.

I open the jar of Wisps, twisting off the creaking lid with shaking fingers. I drop the lid to the forest floor, hold up the jar.

The Wisps bump against the glass for a moment, for a heartbeat. But then, suddenly, triumphantly, they rise, floating out of the jar, their prison, upwards and upwards, up into the sky, bright orbs that burn in the coal black night like stars.

I drop the jar, breathe out. The Sleepers still watch me, but they breathe deeper now, more evenly. Some tilt their heads back to gaze at the Wisps so high. Free.

“We have to move quickly,” I tell the Sleepers, voice soft, “if we’re going to get to Abeo City and back out here, to the woods, before morning comes. And we *must* get to the woods before morning comes, because we might have to run all the way to the Gray Line to escape. There are so many Sleepers, and only so many Snatchers,” I whisper. “And if the Snatchers don’t get us, the Sixers will. And then…it’ll all be for nothing.”

All for nothing. I breathe out, glance around us, at Charlie beside me, at the Sleepers looking uncertain and wide-eyed.

Still no sign of Bird.

My stomach twists. Has something happened to her? I try not to think about it as we turn and begin moving through the woods, everyone shuffling along as quickly as they're able, Charlie and I helping some of the weaker ones step over fallen trees and the jagged underbrush.

My skin pricks as we move closer to the long, low wall of Abeo City.

# Chapter Ten: Truth

As we move through the trees, limping, half-running, Charlie and I helping the Sleepers along, I keep glancing up at the broken branches over our heads, clawing at the sky. There are still no Snatchers in the trees, and it drives a bolt of fear through my heart. Without Snatchers, this plan falls to dust.

The Sixers promise that, during the Bone Feast, no Snatcher will come to Abeo City—and after witnessing the torture of the Snatchers in the cage, it's obvious why that happens. The Sixers make it “safe” for the Sleepers to stay out after dark: hence, the atmosphere of revelry.

But the forest is a different matter. The Sixers never promised that there would be no Snatchers in the *woods* on Bone Feast night.

I think something’s wrong, but I can’t quite put my finger on it. Something is off; something feels strange, making my skin crawl as we angle closer and closer to the wall of Abeo City, its monstrous shadow, and the light drifting over it, a yellow glow.

Charlie leads the way, keeps glancing up at the buildings and wall as we edge closer and closer. She changes direction only once, and then, only a little. When we reach the wall, we pause. Even through the stone, or over it, we can hear voices and laughter still, the Bone Feast in full swing. I glance at Charlie, who nods once, Arthur's arm looped around her shoulder. I look over the faces of the Sleepers around me.

"Are you up for this?" I ask them. "I know you're weak, but there's no other way…"

One by one, they nod their heads.

"Okay. Together," I whisper, and turn back to the wall. I press my hand against it, weakening the illusion for a moment, so that the thin, shimmering Sleepers can pass through the stone (not stone at all, not *anything*) more easily.

We move into Abeo City.

Charlie placed us perfectly. We are at the end of the street that runs past Mad House, and before us spreads the Bone Feast. The lanterns and jars, dangling in long lines, dazzle, brightening the night. The Sleepers beneath them move as if dancing, but I know they're not dancing. Nox flutters from hand to hand, the black feathers trembling beneath Wisp light. A Sleeper drops, even as we watch, little scissors flashing, as more people place Nox along the palms of their hands.

There are Sleepers Memming everywhere—it's hard to walk without stepping on someone. The people who are *not* Memming seem to shift as we watch. They move restlessly amongst themselves, and gradually, one after the other, they turn to gaze down toward the end of the street, sensing something amiss.

And when they look, they see us, and they stop.

I walk forward, Charlie beside me, the Sleepers behind, straggling along, breathing hard, limping, but standing strong as I stop, watching the Sleepers watching us.

"They've been lying to you," I say, but my voice isn't loud enough; it shakes. I clear my throat and repeat, growling the words into the night, "*The Sixers have been lying to you.*"

They turn from me, the Sleepers, glance up to the top of the rubble heap, and there next to the cage of Snatchers the Sixers loom. Their hoods are back, and through the thick manes of black, I know they're staring down at me, scowling at me as if I'm a troublesome insect they wish to grind into dust under their palms.

"The Sixers are not who you think they are," I say then, stepping forward, pulling my gaze from my sisters' shadows. "They built Abeo City so that they could devour souls. You. Your souls. They built this city to devour *you.* You're not Sleepers. You're not *sleeping.*" I glance to Charlie, and she squeezes my hand. With a deep breath, I say, "You're dead."

The words echo around me, whirled away, moving through the Sleepers, from one pair of ears to the next, their eyes widening, looking from me to the Sixers, back to me again. My hands are curled into fists, my fingernails pressing along my black lines, and I can feel them pulsing, surging, those lines that hold within them the feathers of my relations.

There's no going back now.

"Behind me," I say, gesturing back to include all of the broken Sleepers, "are some Sleepers who Faded. But they didn't Fade, really. Fading's a myth. When you Fade, you appear in the Sixers' house, and then the Sixers bleed you dry. These are the only ones who remain of *all* of the people who have Faded since Abeo City was created. All of the others' souls were devoured." I curl my hands into fists. "*They no longer exist.* They are nothingness. Gone."

There is a quiet murmur beginning to build, whispers that sound like wind between stones, a hush, but a hush with great power behind it. I stand firm, feet apart, watching the Sixers carefully out of the corner of my eye. They have not moved.

"These Sleepers are my proof that all the Sixers have done is lie. They sell you Nox for hair, but every bit of hair you give them is a part of yourself, your *soul*, that you sell." I lick my lips. "You're selling your souls to the Sixers," I say, breathing out, raising up my hand as the murmuring reaches a crescendo pitch. "But there's a way to get out of this, all of this," I tell them, taking one step forward. "The Snatchers have been—"

But when I say the word *Snatcher*, the murmur builds to a roar, an angry hiss of sound, and my words are swallowed whole.

And then the eldest Sixer, my sister, laughs. She tilts back her head, and she breathes a wickedly sharp, clawed sound into being, and the crowd grows quiet again, intimidated to silence.

"Why don't you tell them, *Lottie*, how you know all of this? Why don't you tell them what you *are*?" she asks, voice stabbing through my ears like a threaded needle. I breathe out, feel my heart beating, knocking against my ribs, begging to be released from its cage of bones. But I breathe in and out again, cherishing Charlie's steady warmth beside me.

"I know this," I tell the crowd, the deathly silent crowd who watches only me now, "because *I* am the third Sixer."

"She is one of us!" crows the eldest, throwing back her head again. "She is not *innocent*..." She draws out the word, picking at its syllables with her angry tongue. "How can you *believe* her if she's *exactly* what she cries out against?" She takes one step over the rubble, and then another, back arched like an angry animal, claws curving as she advances slowly toward me.

"You murdered me!" I scream at her, taking another step forward. The Sleepers fall silent, standing still as stone as they watch my two sisters and me. "You murdered me because I would no longer do what you did. Because I threatened to tell everyone the truth!"

"Our youngest is addled in the head," says the eldest, hissing out the words as she covers the rubble, moving faster now, her hair dragged out behind her like a last dying breath. "You are ruining our beloved Bone Feast, my dear," she says, voice wheedling.

"To get out of Abeo City, you must be *Snatched*," I shout to the Sleepers, voice wavering but still strong. "If you want to be free, follow us into the forest! You'll see!" Charlie and I turn to go, Edgar and Violet detaching from the crowd, moving along the edge of the buildings like shadows, following us. They approach quickly, hand in hand.

I see Isabel at the edge of the crowd then. She stands unmoving, watching, her hands curled into fists at the sides of her too-clean dress. As I walk past her, I see her eyes fill with tears as Charlie takes my hand, threading her fingers through mine, squeezing tightly.

*Please come with us*, I think, but I'm moving too fast to speak, already past her, though I turn and glance over my shoulder, my eyes catching Isabel's. I can't stop; the Sixers are almost to the bottom of the rubble pile, picking up speed as they follow us, hissing, drawing out air in a slicing, severed sound.

We are nearly before the wall when I look over my shoulder again. The crowd has drawn apart as if it were cut down the middle—sliced by a shining pair of shears. Half of the assembled Sleepers have begun to follow us down the street, toward the wall and the woods and what comes after that. They move slowly, cautiously, still watching the Sixers out of the corners of their eyes, the Sixers who have stopped at the edge of the rubble, watching the Sleepers move without a single sound.

But half of the Sleepers remain behind, clustered

around the people Memming, the people that I can't reach, no matter how much I shout, not until they come out of their trance. The other lagging Sleepers hold Nox in their hands, hold the shears over their hearts, as if considering. But then, one by one, they slice their palms; they lay in the Nox, their heads bowed, turning away.

*Too many,* I think. *Too many left behind. Half!* Mourning, I hit the wall running and move through it into darkness. My last sight of the streets of Abeo City is of the people whispering amongst each other, Sleepers Memming in the streets, and Isabel: in a fleeting glimpse, I see her slit her palm open, dropping a black feather into the open wound with a grimace.

I pause on the other side of the wall, watching the Sleepers come through, Charlie beside me, and Edgar and Violet hovering nearby. We begin to run, trotting as slowly as we can, glancing over our shoulders as more and more Sleepers appear through the stone, as Abeo City looms behind us, glowing dimly.

The Sixers are nowhere in sight. Fear drags at my belly as Arthur's arm pulls at my neck. I try to help him over the frozen, rutted ground. All around me, the Sleepers are working together, the Sleepers from Abeo helping the ones from the Sixers' house, carrying the ones who can't walk any farther.

But we're not moving fast enough. I know this deeply, and the knowledge cuts me, burning, souring my stomach. "They'll be after us," I whisper, my voice rising in the dark, but the Sleepers don't need me to urge them on.

They know fear intimately.

It's at that exact moment that I glance back again, toward Abeo City, and I see movement at the wall. Through the stone, the blackened shadows of the Sixers crawl on all fours like spiders, dragging their hair behind them, but even as I watch, they dissolve into the darkness of the woods, like a stolen breath. I knew them on sight like I know my own shadow, knew how they moved, crawling after us. Hunting us.

They've merged with the black of the woods, and I can no longer see them, but I *feel* them there, following, and fear is slick on my tongue as I help Arthur over a tree trunk, look over my shoulder at the straggling Sleepers behind us.

Charlie looks to me, glancing up, biting her lip. Her hands are shaking.

Above us, there is not a Snatcher in the sky.

"We'll...we'll just have to get past the Gray Line," I whisper to Charlie. If we get past the Gray Line, we're beyond the power of the Sixers, and though they can still hunt and devour us, surely the Snatchers will be there, past the Gray Line, will swoop and save as many of us as they can. Surely we will be Snatched *there*.

Charlie nods at me, agreeing as she helps a waif of a girl over a rut. She's so small in Charlie's hands, small as Florence was.

Florence, who was Snatched.

Where *are* the Snatchers?

We run through the woods, the Sleepers straggling out behind us in a wavering line of desperation. They're moving as quickly as they can, hobbling and hurrying along.

I feel eyes on me, then, and I glance up at the trees, heart surging with hope. If it's the Snatchers, we are safe and saved, and, *yes,* I see movement, and for one single heartbeat, though the shadows are wrong, all wrong, I still wonder and hope that it's the Snatchers descending through the dark toward us.

But it's not. And the constant, sickening *fear* roars up, a devouring of terror that swells over me, swallowing me whole as I watch the Sixers darkening the trees. They blur in my sight as they leap from one trunk to the other, clinging to the bark with claw hands and moving on to the next so quickly, I can hardly follow their movements with my eyes. They are as fast as thought, as breath, their hair streaming out behind them, and they're angling closer to us, descending down toward us, claws aimed at us with such fury. And I know, then, they are so angry that I will not live to tell tales again.

There is so much hopelessness in me as I pause, gaping up at the trees, up at the stalking Sixers who descend, their prey scented and sighted, who will reach us and devour us, *all* of us, plucking us up from the forest floor as easily as acorns. I think of what they'll do to me, their sister who betrayed them, their sister that they killed once before. They'll make certain I stay dead this time.

Soon, I'll be gone.

I won't exist.

I think of the Sleepers we've left behind, who didn't believe me or didn't want to believe me or didn't want to take the chance. I think of all the broken Sleepers around us who went all the way to Abeo City, and then pushed themselves to venture toward the Gray Line. I think of all the Sleepers who *believed* me, despite everything, who came with us. I think of Edgar and Violet, who I can barely see out of the corner of my eye, running through the woods with us, arms linked. I think of Isabel, Memming back in Abeo because she did love Charlie, truly did, no matter what she'd said or done.

And I think of Charlie beside me, who glances over at me with wide, fearless eyes. She's afraid, I know—must be afraid—but she's swallowed it down; she's determined to be strong for me, so that I can feel that strength in her, even when I cannot feel it in myself, as it leeches into the earth beneath me, flowing away and almost gone, as my hopelessness takes root.

Charlie squeezes my hand again, swallowing, nose toward the Gray Line as she continues to run.

And I move with her.

As if the night has parted, a door opening in the darkness, there is another shadow that moves through the darkness then, beside me. Bird. She smiles at me, mouth tipping up at the corners, eyes shining, and she says nothing, but points ahead of us.

I know how close we are, then. I can taste it, freedom, possibility, an end to Twixt and Abeo and all the lies and darkness. I don't know what will happen to me once I'm past the Gray Line. I don't know if the Sixers will take me as the other Sleepers get Snatched. If they'll kill me again. But as I race quietly, quickly, through the last stretch of Abeo's forest, Charlie's hand in mine, I breathe in and out, and I feel strong, and I feel courageous, and I glance sideways at Charlie, whose eyes glitter in the darkness.

And I am not afraid.

We move past the Gray Line, the Sleepers, the Sixers who screech, who dive for me and Charlie and Bird and all the Sleepers, claws extended. But as we race past the Gray Line, there's a flare of light, and light and light and light everywhere.

Charlie presses her lips to my hand, and there is light and white wings and the powerful wind beneath wingbeats as I see the Snatchers, not the Snatchers, but our relations, beautiful and glowing as they angle through a red sky, descending toward us.

The Sleepers ascend, borne on white wings. Charlie is lifted, floating, flying... With a choking sob, I watch her go, grateful and mournful all at once, my hands reaching up.

I feel a swelling as Bird soars above my head, laughing, waving down at me.

And I turn and watch my sisters scream, claws outstretched as they reach me, hooking into the front of a dress that was bought for me with a bit of soul.

But then I—*I*—am lifted, too, by a relation with a beautiful ragged right wing.

Everything is light is ascending is magnificent as Twixt falls away beneath me, devoured by the darkness at my feet and the endlessness of light overhead.

*And I am not afraid.*

I open my eyes.

*Fin*

**The following is an excerpt from S.E. Diemer's novel**

# *The Dark Wife*

**The YA, lesbian retelling of the Persephone myth. *The Dark Wife* is available wherever you purchase your eBooks, and in print format.**

It was not sudden, how the room behind me grew dark, throwing long shadows from the torchlight upon the balcony floor. It was a gradual thing, and I almost failed to notice it, but for the silence. No one laughed or spoke; there was no clink of goblet or twang of lyre. Everything, everything fell to a silence that crawled into my ears and roared.

I shook my head, straightened, peered again around the column at the great room. All throughout the palace, a deep quiet crept, cold as a chill. I saw the gods and goddesses shudder, and then the darkness fell like a curtain, became complete. The stars themselves were blotted out for three terrible heartbeats.

There was the sound of footsteps upon the marble, and the light returned.

"Hades has come." I heard the whisper—Athena's whisper—and I started. Hades? I stood on the tips of my toes, trying to catch a glimpse.

All of us there had been touched by Zeus' cruelty, in some form or another. We were meaningless to him, toys to be played with and tossed. But the story of Zeus's ultimate betrayal was well known.

Zeus and Poseidon and Hades were created from the earth in the time before time—the time of the Titans.

They cast lots to determine which of them would rule the kingdom of the sea, the kingdom of the dead, and the kingdom of the sky. Poseidon and Zeus chose the longest straws, so Hades was left with no choice but to reign over the kingdom of the dead, the Underworld.

It did not come to light until later that Zeus had fixed the proceedings to make certain he would get his way—to become ruler of the greatest kingdom, as well as all of the gods. He would never have risked a fair game of chance. Could never have hidden away his splendor in that world of endless darkness.

I shivered, wrapping my arms about my middle. Hades rarely appeared at Olympus, choosing to spend his time, instead, sequestered away in that place of shadows, alone.

My eyes searched the murmuring crowd. Though I was uncertain as to Hades' appearance, I assumed I would recognize the god of the Underworld when I saw him.

But where was he? Over there were Poseidon and Athena, whispering behind their hands. I saw Artemis and Apollo break apart as Zeus moved between them, climbed several high steps and staggered into his towering throne, hefting his goblet of ambrosia aloft.

"Persephone." I jumped, heart racing, and Hermes grinned down at me, his face a handbreadth from my own.

"You have a habit of startling me," I whispered to him, but he shook his head, pressed a finger to his lips. My brow furrowed as he took my hand and led me out onto the floor of the great room, to linger again amidst the gods. I felt naked, misplaced, but Hermes stood behind me and elbowed me forward. I yielded and stumbled a step, two steps. Finally, my frustration rising, I turned to admonish him but paused mid-motion because—I had run into someone.

Life slowed, slowed, slowed. I muttered, "Excuse me," looked up at the woman I did not recognize, had never before seen, my heart slack until it thundered in one gigantic leap against my bones.

Everything stopped.

Her eyes were black, every part of them, her skin pale, like milk. Her hair dropped to the small of her back, night-colored curls that shone, smooth and liquid, as she cocked her head, as she gazed down at me without a change of expression. She wasn't beautiful—the lines of her jaw, her nose, were too proud, too sharp and straight. But she was mesmerizing, like a whirlpool of dark water, where secrets lurked.

I looked up at her, and I was lost in the black of her eyes, and I did not see her take my hand, but I felt her hold it, as if it were meant to be in the cage of her fingers, gently cradled.

"Hello," she said, her voice softer than a whisper. I blinked once, twice, trying to shake the feeling I had heard her speak before—perhaps in a dream.

And then, "I am Hades," she said.

My world fell away.

Hades…Hades, the lord of the underworld…was a woman.

"But, but…" I spluttered, and she watched me with catlike curiosity, head tilted to the sound of my voice as I attempted to regain my senses. "They call you the lord of the Underworld. I thought—"

"It is a slur," she breathed. I had to lean forward to hear her words. Her face remained still, placid, as if she were wearing a mask.

I didn't know what to say—that I was sheltered? Should I apologize that I hadn't known? She still held my hand, fingers curled into my palm like a vine. "I'm sorry," I managed. There was nothing else within me, and the moment stretched on into an eternity as my heart beat against the door of my chest.

I'd forgotten Hermes was there, and he cleared his throat now, stepping alongside us, staring down at our hands, together.

"Hades," he murmured, chin inclined, smile twisting up and up. "It's begun, now that you've met her."

"What?" My head spun; everything was happening too fast. Her eyes had never once left mine, two dark stars pulling me in. My blood pounded fast and hot, and I didn't understand what was happening, but my body did. No, she was not beautiful, but she didn't need to be. I was drawn to her, bewitched by her, a plant angling up to drink in her sun. Still, still, she had not let go of my hand.

"Hermes, may I have a moment with her?" she asked, turning toward him. When her eyes moved away, I felt an emptiness, a hollow, a great, dark ache.

Hermes frowned, shook his head once, twice, and shimmered into nothingness.

She raised my hand, then, so slowly that I held my breath until her lips pressed against my skin, warmer than I'd imagined, and soft. Something within me shattered as she swallowed me up again with her dark eyes, said: "You are lovely, Persephone."

I stared down at her bent head, spellbound.

"Thank you," I whispered. She rose.

Where Zeus's lips had been wet, rough, pushing hard enough against my hand to leave a bruise…she was the opposite—gentle. Yet I felt her everywhere. I shivered, closed my eyes. She did not let go of my hand but turned it over, tracing the line of my palm with her thumb.

"It has been a deep honor, meeting you, seeing you. You defy my imaginings." A small smile played over her mouth as she shook her head, traced her fingers against the hollow of my hand. "I hope to see you again."

She looked as if she might say more—she looked hopeful—but something changed, and her eyes flickered. She sighed, pressed her lips together, squeezed my hand. Hades turned and disappeared into the crowd of Olympians.

"No—" I put my hand over my heart, breathed in and out.

"In front of all the others." Hermes was shimmering beside me, leaning close; he shook his head. "She's either stupid or very brave."

I felt as if I were waking from a very long sleep. I stared at the floor, wondering what was real, what was a dream. "I don't understand. That…she was Hades?"

"In the death," he snickered, and he held up his goblet of ambrosia to me, as if in a toast. "It has begun."

# Acknowledgements

I am deeply and unconditionally grateful to everyone who has ever purchased my work, told someone they loved about it and spread the word. I am *shockingly* able to do what I love for a living because people believe in these stories enough. Without my wonderful, humbling and amazing fans, these stories are meaningless. What I write is, always and forever, for you. Thank you, from the bottom of my heart, for being, for wanting these stories.

Jennifer Adam loved *Twixt* from the very beginning and was endlessly and constantly supportive of its journey. Without her, it would never have been—she brought it into the world through her unwavering support, good humor and friendship, and I am deeply grateful to her for never giving up on it—or me. Rachel Melcher is one of the staunchest and best friends I could ever have wished on a star for—when I have felt truly defeated, she's brought me back. Thank you for being. Rhiannon Matich is a pillar of my life—her sweetness, laughter and love are unending inspirations for me. Katelyn Verrill has unwaveringly believed in this story, and me, and her friendship is a priceless support in my life. Valerie Reho is one of the best things marrying into a family has ever accomplished in this world. Her unwavering support and cheerleading and kindness have meant so much to me. Gemma Dubaldo is a light in my life, and a constant, beautiful support. Rachel Gogan and Katie Raynes remind me, ceaselessly, that life is beautiful, and I am deeply indebted to their friendship and adore them both fiercely. My friendship with James Femmer is one of the best things that ever happened because of *The Dark Wife*. I love you so much, sir, and am so grateful for your humor, mischief and the type of support that skyscrapers can only dream of.

The good fairy is one of the dearest people in my life. If "'tis nothing good or bad / But thinking makes it so," / I must confess, dear friend, / This truth to me you've shown, / For your friendship is one of the / Most treasured things I've known.

Bree Zimmerman deserves heaps of roses and barrels of gem-encrusted skulls for the amount of times she's read this book, in its eight million incarnations, and for her invaluable feedback and belief in this story. So much of this book's existence is because she believed in it so wholeheartedly. My unending gratitude to you, Miss Hallow's Eve.

Tara Taylor is an essential aspect of my entire writing process. Her editor's eye is flawless, and I trust her with my life, and my words. My deep, abiding gratitude to you, Miss Pithia.

This book is dedicated to Madeline Claire Franklin, who has been one of the best friends that anyone in this world could ever ask for. She is one of the most brilliant writers I've ever had the pleasure to meet, and her wholehearted love of *Twixt* is why it exists in the first place—she would never let me give up on it. I love you, Miss Maddie.

Without the support of the congregation at Pullman Memorial Universalist Church, I would never be able to do what I do. In a harsh, cruel world, they give Jenn and I a beautiful, safe space to be who we are. It is a sanctuary, and our home.

My wife, Jennifer Diemer, is my world. Without her editing prowess, her attention to detail and fine eye, this novel would be a mere husk of what it has become. Any errors left are mine alone. I have the supreme pleasure of walking through this life with my beloved other half at my side. You make of my days something shining and lovely, baby. Knowing you is the only memory I'd sell my hair for.

There are many more beautiful people than I have space to list who I appreciate immensely, who make my writing life (and life, in general) a joy. You know who you are. I love you. Thank you for reminding me that magic exists outside of fairy tales.

# About the Author

S.E. Diemer is an award-winning author of lesbian young adult (YA), speculative fiction. She lives in a purple-doored cottage in Western New York with her beloved wife, several furred creatures and a few mischievous pixies. She enjoys covering things in glitter (and putting them on Etsy), and is a professional fairy. She is addicted to tea.

Her debut novel, The Dark Wife, the YA, lesbian retelling of the Persephone myth won the 2012 Golden Crown Literary Award for Speculative Fiction, and was nominated for a Parsec Award (first two chapters of the audiobook).

She co-writes Project Unicorn, a Lesbian YA Extravaganza with her wife, author Jennifer Diemer, a year long fiction project that aims to add two short stories a week, featuring lesbian heroines, to Muse Rising, making them available for free.

She shares that blog with Jenn at MuseisRising.Wordpress.com, where she talks about being gay, queer books and other sparkly things. Twitter (@SEDiemer) and Tumblr (AuthorSEDiemer.Tumblr.com) are some of her favorite places.

She believes, wholeheartedly, in happily ever afters.

Made in the USA
Monee, IL
19 November 2019

17022387R00139